SHIFT OF HEART

SHIFTER LORDS

S.E. BABIN

OLIVERHEBERBOOKS

CHAPTER

One

Business at Little Shop of Florals was bustling this morning. Too bad I was a little too hungover to enjoy it. The instigator, my friend Moira, hummed happily as she sorted through the newest batch of baby's breath, carefully choosing the best specimens and setting them off to one side. We had a large order due this afternoon for one of our best customers, a rich woman named Hattie, who had a standing weekly order for fresh, seasonally appropriate flowers. Since she paid extra to secure the freshest blooms, we did our best to ensure we never disappointed her.

I snipped spent heads from batches of roses and peonies, carefully adding the best to a purple vase filled with water and plant food.

Moira's lips twitched when she spotted me glaring at her every few seconds. "Oh, now," she said with a click of her tongue. "I told you to take it easy on that stuff."

"It takes a truckload of booze to get me wasted," I hissed. "What the hell was in that stuff?" I had an insane metabolism thanks to my muddled heritage, my DNA a mix of my mother, my father, and some from an event five years ago I still hadn't come

"

to terms with. Because of my messy DNA, I rarely even felt a buzz from alcohol, much less had a hangover twelve hours later.

Moira grinned, her too-sharp incisors gleaming in the warm lights. She was a ninety-year-old vampire who looked to be in her mid-twenties, and a terrible influence on my liver. Though this was the first time she'd ever succeeded in getting me white girl wasted, it was certainly not for lack of trying.

"That would be courtesy of our favorite witch, Hazel," Moira said. "I asked her for something with a little more kick, and she mailed me a bottle straight from Scotland." She sighed wistfully. "Home of the best whiskey and the hottest men on the planet."

I grunted. While Moira wasn't wrong, I had very mixed feelings about Scotland. "Enchanted whiskey, then?"

Hazel and I had a strange relationship. The witch had saved my life some years ago, and we'd stayed in touch. In many ways, Hazel was responsible for my new life here in Joy Springs and for the friends I'd made, among other things. I cared about Hazel, and she cared about me, but we weren't exactly friends.

Moira shrugged. "No idea, but it certainly put some hair on my chest."

I tossed a spent bloom at her. "Next time, give a girl some warning, would you?"

"Mmm. Can't promise anything. Wasted Evie is the best Evie." She winked and pushed the baby's breath toward me. "Take those. I'll save the rest for the shop bouquets."

I slid them closer, giving them all an unnecessarily critical eye. Moira might be a vampire, but she had an eye and nose for the best blooms and could slap together a stunning bouquet in less than a minute flat.

Hattie was our oldest and most discerning customer. I wasn't sure I'd ever met a human older than that woman. Her wrinkles gave birth to more wrinkles, and I could barely see her eyes when I made her deliveries because of the lines and deep folds in her face. When I saw her, I couldn't help but think of a Shar Pei, which always made me feel guilty.

Hattie was rich and sharp as a tack, and even though her eyes seemed concealed under all that extra skin, she missed nothing.

Plus, I liked crabby old people, and she more than fit the bill.

Tess, our resident banshee and current store intern, stood behind the register, ringing up a customer who'd purchased one of our spring bouquets. When she'd slid the change across the desk, the customer chirped a cheery goodbye. Tess stared at the customer until the woman's friendly smile slid from her face, and she took her purchase and hurried out the door.

"Tess," I said with a sigh. "When someone says goodbye, all you have to do is say something like 'Have a nice day,' or 'Take care!' Staring at them and staying silent makes it weird."

The banshee turned her strange, pale eyes to me. "But that would be a lie. We're all walking piles of bones anyway, so who cares if the day is nice or not?"

Moira snorted and reached for the peonies. "She's got you there."

I pegged the vampire in the head with a clipped stem. "We may all be walking piles of bones, but it doesn't mean we shouldn't be courteous."

I walked over to the register and tapped on the laminated cue sheet I'd made for Tess a few months ago. "Remember. Just look at this if you can't figure out what to do."

"Now that thing makes it weird," Moira murmured under her breath.

I sighed. "It's not weird. Some people need more guidance. Especially if they haven't worked in customer service before."

I skimmed the sheet and found where I'd written, "customer says goodbye" under the Action column and tapped. "See, Tess?"

Then I moved my finger over to the Reaction column next to it, where it said, "Say goodbye or have a nice day." And the banshee's favorite, "Offer a smile."

Tess did that weird banshee moan that sounded like that magic academy toilet ghost from those popular books. "I'll try."

"Try really hard, okay?" I encouraged.

Tess moaned again.

Moira coughed to cover up her laugh. Shaking my head, I returned to my table and finished putting together Hattie's flowers.

Customers filtered in and out, most not buying anything. Those were usually the tourists who came in out of curiosity rather than intending to buy. When I first opened the shop, the tourists made me itchy, but after a while, they became one more quirky thing about this place.

Joy Springs is a cute little town tucked between Fredericksburg and Luckenbach, Texas, smack in the middle of wine country and wide-open nothingness. It isn't a large place, but it has more than enough charm to make up for its lack of size. Coming from Seattle, adjusting to this slower pace of life took some doing, but now I found myself more relaxed and able to go with the flow.

It helped that the residents were just as weird as Seattleites, so even with my strange new bloodline and eating habits, I fit right in.

My shop hummed with life—human, magical, and flora—and that was my dirty little secret. Or clean little secret, depending on how you looked at it. The dirt under my nails, the surrounding blooms, and greenery soothed my senses more than anything else could. I might be a freak of magic, but my Floromancy still hummed brightly in my veins, each flower vibrating energy, all links in the extraordinary chain of life.

I was powerful in this place, the home I made when circumstances had forced me from the other one. Every flower had a story, every plant an opportunity to learn about the world. I reached out to stroke the glossy leaf of one of my many pothoses, and the vine stretched for my fingers, entwining itself around my wrist. I gave the leaf a stroke and gently extricated myself to return my attention to Hattie's bouquet.

It was almost closing time, the sun beginning to dip behind a canopy of rolling hills. Early May was the time when the days grew warm but not too hot, and the evening temps dipped into the fifties. Still cool enough for a sweater. Moira slid some more baby's breath over, along with several sprigs of eucalyptus for decor and scent. The plants reacted to my proximity, moving closer and trying to curl around my fingers as I picked them up, one by one.

Once I added the final touches to Hattie's weekly flowers, I straightened, stretching a tweak out of my spine from hours of being hunched over, and glanced at the time.

"Tess, mind locking up for me?"

The banshee didn't respond but got up from her seat and did a double check of the store to ensure all our customers were gone. I never performed magic in the front unless we were locked down, but I didn't want to move this bouquet too much before we got it to Hattie's house. It was absolutely perfect. The less jostling, the better.

Once I heard the front door lock click several times, and the weight of the shop's warding spell settled over my shoulders, I let out a slow breath and smiled. The spell was a hum of comfort against my skin, silently whispering I was safe behind these walls.

Ever since the attack, my magic acted out in odd and varying ways, but the build-up was the most annoying part. I had to siphon power out during the day constantly. If I didn't, I was a walking storm of magic and grumpiness.

The positive side effect of this was how much healthier all the plants and flowers in the shop looked now. Granted, they always looked amazing, and our online reviews proved it, but now, there wasn't a shop in the entire United States that could compete with the quality of our product.

Every few minutes, I had to reach out and touch a plant or a bloom or go outside and refresh the blooming flowers in the urns, and sometimes it got so bad, I walked down the stretch of shops and perked their blooms up, too—though I tried to take more care with this as a few people had mentioned something about it in passing, marveling at how well their plants were doing when it wasn't quite the right season for it. While this grounded me and stabilized my magic, I realized it was fast becoming somewhat of a compulsion, this urge to purge and boost growth anywhere around me. But it was also a need. When the power built up inside me and I was without an outlet, I wasn't quite myself.

This was one of the main reasons my house had a powerful glamour over it, and I trusted only a few people inside. My place looked like one of the world's wonders, no matter if we were in the dead of winter. Life was my magic, and the world responded to my power like a cat arching against questing fingers.

Moira and Tess gathered around, and a shuffling from the back revealed Ash, yawning and stretching as he walked over. He was a dryad who lived in the shop and one of my best friends. Ash was tall and lean, with golden brown skin and tawny hair streaked in gold and light brown. His eyes were a strange moss color and changed to a stunning emerald when he performed magic. If anyone were closer to the earth than me, it was Ash. Every few months, he had to return to his tree to refresh his magic, but for the most part, he was here helping out during the busier parts of the year. It always felt odd when he wanted to watch me perform magic, but when I asked him, he'd given me an odd look and merely said, "You are the heartbeat of the earth, Evie. No greater life magic exists. I am merely the power of a single Heart Tree. You are the world."

I had no idea what he meant by that, but it made me feel weird, so I didn't ask him to explain.

Moira, Tess, and Ash gathered chairs and put them around me in a semicircle. Shaking my head, I closed my eyes and steadied my breath.

Every week, I added some kind of blessing to Hattie's flowers. She had no idea, nor was I sure she'd welcome it if she did. But it kept her coming back to us, and it was something positive I could do when the rest of my magic was so dangerous. I liked building her bouquets because it was something small I had control over while the rest of my life spiraled.

"What shall we do this week?" I asked.

"Last time she was in, she mentioned her hips were hurting," Moira said.

A healing blessing. Always a good one and easy to perform, but my magic strained and pushed against me, so I wanted to do a little more.

"She mentioned she gets pretty lonely in that house," Ash said. "Maybe something to bring more visitors or opportunities to get out of the house?"

I nodded. "Both of those are good. Tess?"

The banshee's reaction made me smile. Even if she didn't mean to, the breeze from Tess's sigh rattled the wind chimes and made the plants sway.

"I suppose if I have to come up with something..." Tess paused as she thought. "She mentioned her favorite restaurant no longer delivered to her house."

There wasn't much I could do about that. "Anything else?"

Tess frowned. "She said she likes it when the peonies are in season, and she wishes she could grow them here."

A slow grin curved my lips. "Ah. Perfect. We can definitely help her with that."

A soft green light trickled from my fingertips, and I wrapped my hands around Hattie's vase, keeping my intentions firmly locked in my thoughts. A swirl of pink flowed over the green—a small spell for pain relief and ease of movement, followed by another swirl of orange, the color of warmth and nature, to open Hattie up to the possibility of more social gatherings. When the inevitable crimson sparks followed at the end of the spell, I pretended not to notice and filed the knowledge away in the deep recesses of my mind that liked living in the delusion that I was not a freak of nature.

Growing peonies was another matter, but I had that well in

hand. When the spell had soaked into the vase and the plants, I smiled and flicked my fingers, shaking the rest of the magic away.

My audience clapped and whistled, making me laugh. "Cute, guys." I waved my hands at them. "Let's hurry up and get the shop cleaned up so we can make this delivery."

"If I had a scorecard, it would be a ten out of ten! You could ruffle my blooms any day!" Moira called, as everyone scrambled out of their seats.

She went for a broom. Tess floated in the air and investigated every nook and cranny for any weaknesses in the wards and protection spells woven throughout the shop. Ash brushed his hands over the bottom of all the potted plants, checking all the roots and nutrition. Today, he winced only once when he touched one of my aloe plants. He picked up the small pot and hid it behind his back to take with him when he retreated to the back. I pretended not to notice. Ash would "unlove" it for me and return the plant to the front once he'd depleted some of the magic I'd added to its roots.

Normally all was well, but when I first started siphoning my magic into the flora, he had to move some plants away from the brunt of my attention with a gentle warning. "Sometimes you can love something a little too much, Evie."

As an apology, I had Ash double-checking all the plants a few times a week to ensure I wasn't going too overboard with my "love," as he put it. I was getting better, but sometimes I added a little too much oomph to one versus spreading it out to all my plants.

I counted out the registers and wiped down the area before picking up my glass mister and paying some extra attention to the orchids blooming in the window. Fredericksburg wasn't nearly as humid as Seattle was, so some of the plants I'd brought with me needed a little extra TLC while they acclimated. And some, like the tender orchids before me, never acclimated at all, and I was keeping them alive by sheer force of magic.

It was a small sacrifice considering how long it took them all to re-acclimate to me when I returned with the new magic boiling in my veins.

For a long while, I thought I'd never be able to use my Floromancy again, but all it took was time.

And even though my magic had eventually come back stronger than ever, time would never heal my wounds from that night or the changes the attack had wrought in my soul. But every day I woke up still myself, still *Evie*, I counted it as a blessing.

CHAPTER

Two

For everyone else, it was too late to plant peonies in the season, but the laws of nature, at least in this regard, did not apply to me. Next spring, Hattie would have peonies of all sizes and varieties popping out of the ground in a stunning riot of color. She asked me what I was doing, and I told her I was just adding some nutrients I'd brought over to her soil. Hattie hadn't questioned me, though her eyes had lingered on me for a moment too long.

Most people in Joy Springs thought I was a nutter, so it didn't bother me too much, but Hattie's gaze was a little too eagle-eyed for my comfort. Maybe magically boosting her soil and plant bulbs was a bad idea, but I hoped by spring she'd be so pleased by the display, she'd forget about the strange florist who'd done it for her.

The delivery and bulb planting didn't take more than an hour, so I had plenty of time to burn before the restaurants and shops closed. My stomach had been growling for a while now, another side effect of the magic burning through me, and my favorite place to eat was close by.

With a wave and a promise to deliver Hattie's next bouquet in a week, I hurried to my bicycle, stowing my empty canvas bag into the basket hooked to the handlebars. As transportation went, it wasn't much, but it kept me in good shape, and I didn't have to pay a car note. The basket did double duty as my foraging container and unhooked whenever I needed it.

The Thistle and Thread Cafe was an adorable tearoom and restaurant that doubled as a potion shop once all the tourists were tucked safely in their beds. I'd never made use of their offerings, but it never stopped them from offering.

When I first spotted the place, I thought it was adorable, but the name was a constant reminder of the thistle tattoo on my arm, hiding the secret of my blood. For a while, I avoided the cafe, even going so far as to cross the road to avoid inhaling the delicious scents coming from within.

That was until Marnie and Twila, the two Hedgewitch sisters who owned it, stopped by with a basket of still-warm blueberry scones drizzled with lemon icing and a pot of Lavender Fog tea, lightly sweetened with wildflower honey, and topped with a touch of blueberry creamer.

After the first bite of that damn scone, I was a goner.

Even after all this time, the scents coming from inside made all my stress lift from my shoulders and float away. I pushed open the door and smiled at Marnie.

She was the smaller, more boisterous of the sisters. Marnie smiled and waved, motioning me over to her. Behind her, two large, wicked-looking knitting needles clicked and clacked, quickly knitting a baby blue blanket with fuzzy yarn. I'd asked her once how she got away with it with the number of humans coming in and out of her cafe. She shrugged, her pale blue eyes twinkling, patted my hand, and said, "Darling, they want to see the magic, not believe it. Joy Springs is television magic to them, tricks of the lights, tricks of the camera. They believe the needles are mechanical, so that's what they become."

It made sense in a terrible way, I supposed. Humans let an awful lot of things slide, and when things got a little too real, the government always slid in with some slick explanation of things like EMP pulses or NASA balloons.

A small chalkboard resting by the register announced today's special, the swirling handwriting and drawings created with brightly colored chalk. Lavender and Earl Grey muffins, French onion soup, and Reuben sandwiches.

I rubbed my hands together in glee. "That soup and sandwich sound delicious. Are there any left over?"

Marnie's dimple peeked from her plump cheek. "Always for you, darling Evie."

She rang me up, and when I frowned at the price, Marnie waved it away. "It's always the same song and dance. We will never charge you full price, so stop insisting!"

I sighed and handed her less than half of the price listed on the board.

Marnie reached over and patted me gently on the cheek. "I'll bring you something special to drink. Now go on over and find a seat."

"Thanks, Marnie."

"Anytime, peach."

I grabbed silverware and napkins before finding a table by the windows overlooking the town square. A small pulse of distress caught my attention, and I turned to see what it was. My eyes trailed over the few humans enjoying their dinner before finding three pothos tangled together on the ledge close to the ceiling. I hadn't seen them before, but they were all rootbound and crying out for more light. Tucking my purse under my arm, I headed over and waved at Marnie.

"You mind?" I called.

Marnie's eyebrows furrowed before she realized I was pointing to the plants.

"Do your thing, honey."

I smiled and tossed my purse onto a table before climbing onto a wooden chair and reaching for a plant, only to realize the vines were hopelessly tangled. Frowning, I scooped up all three, wobbling as I tried to keep my balance.

Whoa. Those were much heavier than I expected.

Warm arms wrapped around my calves, calloused palms sliding over my skin.

"Steady," a deep, rumbly voice said.

My heart leapt into my throat. It had been so long since someone had touched me, and I froze into place, unable to move. The beginning of fangs pushed against my gums, and I squeezed my eyes shut as a warm, golden light shone against the opposite wall. Being surprised was terrible for my control, and it didn't help that whoever it was had a staggering amount of power.

The man's arms were strong and muscled and felt far warmer than normal. His heat pressed against my skin, comforting and terrifying at the same time.

"Need help?" that voice rumbled again.

"Err. No. No, I don't. Sorry." I jostled the plants until I got a better grip and slowly bent. The man released my legs but stayed close and reached for one of the plants.

I had to bite my tongue to keep from snapping at him. My reaction wasn't his fault. "They're tangled together. If I give you one, the roots will tear."

I still couldn't see who I spoke to, but power rippled over my skin, animalistic and savage. A shifter, for sure, but unlike any I'd ever been around.

"Then I'll move the table a little closer."

With one swift, smooth motion, he slid the table within inches of my hands. "Thank you," I breathed as I set the plants down.

"No problem. You got it under control now?"

Everything but my fangs still yearning to slide from my teeth. "I do. Thank you."

"Good." He sauntered off, and I sagged in relief as I climbed off the chair. I turned to get a good look at him, but he was at the front register now, and all I could see was his back.

And what a back it was.

Denim hugged the curves of his spectacular rear end, loosening around well-muscled thighs and calves before ending in a boot cut. His shoes were leather sneakers, scuffed and worn. My eyes dragged up to his back. He wore a forest green pullover that pulled slightly against muscled shoulders before tapering into a slim waist. The man's hair was dark and tousled, and my fingers itched to run through its waves.

"Get a grip, idiot," I hissed to myself.

The man's shoulders stiffened. I closed my eyes and turned away, cursing my pale features, now burning with embarrassment. Shifters had uncanny hearing. No doubt the guy could smell how hot I thought he was, and he definitely heard me telling myself to cool it.

I could not turn around until he was gone. He hadn't seen my face. We could remain faceless, and I could pretend I wasn't a giant horny moron.

Except...he was a shifter, and he could pick my unique scent out in a concert crowd. But maybe there were so many scents in here he'd have trouble identifying me later.

One could only dream.

Way to go, Evie. Making friends and influencing people, just like always. Maybe dating again wouldn't be so bad. As long as that person was blind or content to ignore all my proudly waving red flags. Maybe I could find a ghost as a soulmate.

A sigh escaped me as I pulled up a chair and sat down, my back facing the register. The least I could do was finish taking care of these plants since that guy would probably never come back here because of the weird girl, aka me, lusting after his cute butt.

A deep chuckle made my hands still. There was no way he heard that. I'd said it in my head, right?

Right?

If it wouldn't damage Marnie's restaurant, I'd cut a hole in the ground and bury myself alive.

I straightened my shoulders, took a deep breath, and pushed

all thoughts of the shifter out of my head. Out of sight, out of mind.

With that, I went to work on the plants.

Several minutes later, I'd gotten all three untangled, which lessened their distress, but they were all still suffering. I couldn't do magic with the humans still inside, so when Marnie brought over my food and the brew she'd specially made, I whispered to her that I'd either come back before opening time or I could wait until the restaurant closed.

"We're closing in twenty. Best do it tonight if they're doing that poorly." Marnie clicked her tongue. "Someone dropped those by today and asked if we wanted them. I hadn't even had the chance to look at them yet, but you heard their call, didn't you?"

I never spoke about my abilities, but Marnie and her sister knew I had a way with flowers. My answer was a shrug. She patted me on the shoulder. "Just let me know what you need, darling. I'll let you know when we officially close up."

Thirty minutes later, I left three happy plants in brand new spots and two grateful witches cleaning up for the night. When one table, full of humans who'd overstayed their welcome, stared at my work a little too hard, Marnie bustled over, winked, and said to them, "Evie is such a wizard with plants! I've never seen a greener thumb on anyone except her grandmother! If you think this is amazing, you should pop over to her shop…"

I left Marnie happily plugging my business, while the humans stared at her wide-eyed and overwhelmed.

The town square still bustled with people, though most had sparkling auras telling me they were all residents of Joy Springs and not tourists. Not everyone here had magic, but for the most part, this place attracted its fair share of witches and shifters. Moira was one of maybe half a dozen vampires who lived here, and Ash was the only dryad I knew of. Tess was the only banshee I'd ever met, though she hung out in the local cemetery, and I could only assume she had one or two banshee friends living there.

I waved at a few people I recognized from coming into my shop and kept walking until I found the local gelato food truck. My appetite always went haywire when I used a lot of magic, and today I'd burned more than normal. Hattie's peony planting tipped me over the edge, and even though Marnie had fed me enough food for an army, I still had a little room for gelato.

La Sirena Gelato had no set schedule. It appeared when the proprietor, Sirena, felt like showing up. Interestingly enough, it was always here when I hankered for one of her unique flavors. The line was surprisingly busy tonight, so I got behind a small woman to wait my turn.

The truck was hand-painted a soothing blue and decorated with swirls of sea foam and celestial doodles. A constantly changing menu was tacked to the side of the truck right next to the window where you ordered. Two new flavors were listed: Moonberry Mint, a mix of pistachio, berry, and wild mint that was supposed to clear any regrets you had for the day. Not a bad choice. The other was a lavender and citrus gelato that might cause lucid dreaming if you ate it too close to the witching hour. I glanced at my silver watch. Eleven p.m. I should be safe.

When it was my turn, Sirena leaned out the window and gave me a flirty wink. I grinned and tossed a dollar in her tip jar before ordering. Her name wasn't just pretty, it was a direct description of what she was.

Sirena had dark hair, sea foam green eyes, and a body that would stop traffic. I was always on my guard around her because Sirena was a siren. She could literally lure you into the back of her truck, seduce you, drain your bank account, and turn you back onto the street with a smile on your face. And Sirena wasn't choosy. If you were attractive, she was game.

"Hello, lovely girl," Sirena said, her low and husky voice brushing against my skin. Goosebumps rose on my arms. "What can I get you tonight?"

"You can turn it down some, first of all," I said dryly.

Sirena dripped magic even when she wasn't trying, but from

the way her eyes were sparkling, she was definitely trying tonight.

She pouted. "You're far too beautiful to be so lonely, Evangeline."

I stiffened. Evangeline was my full name, and only my mother called me that.

Sirena leaned a little farther out the window, her bosoms right at eye level. "You know, I'd give you a spin for free if you were interested."

I blinked. "Err. I appreciate that, but I'm just here for the gelato."

Sirena huffed and retreated back into the window. "I'd make it worth your while, darling. If you change your mind, I'll be here."

That's what I was afraid of. "Just the lavender for this evening, Sirena. Though I'm flattered by the offer, I'm not in the market and have no interest in dating."

Her seafoam eyes swirled with magic. "You will, little Evangeline. Sooner than you think."

I stilled. This was the second time she'd called me Evangeline. No one knew my real name, and no one called me by it. Sirena wasn't close enough to me for the familiarity she used. My nostrils flared, and I opened my mouth to give her a piece of my mind and remind her to keep her pert little nose out of my business when she handed me a wad of napkins, a spoon, and a larger cup of gelato than the one I ordered.

"On the house this time," she said with a rueful smile. "I'm rarely a pain in the ass, but there's something in the air tonight." Sirena rubbed her hands over her arms. "Dangerous things prowl this evening."

I took the gelato, unable to formulate a proper response.

"The lavender is a good choice. Soothing and grounding for all the magic you'll use tonight." Sirena winked. "I'll see you soon, Evie."

"See you soon," I echoed, shaking my head as I turned away. I had zero plans to use any magic tonight, so it was an odd thing to say.

What a strange evening. I snorted as I spooned some gelato into my mouth. Plus, her line about me dating?

Laughable.

But as I dug into my gelato, I happened to glance up, only to see a pair of golden eyes watching me. As soon as I blinked, they disappeared as if they'd never been there. A shiver rolled down my spine, and a chilly wind brushed against my skin.

Coincidence. That's all.

Three

The siren might be a pain in the ass, but her gelato was magical. Literally and figuratively. If not done correctly, using lavender in any food product could make it taste like soap. I knew this from unfortunate experience. Sirena's gelato had the perfect hint of floral with a burst of sunshiny citrus flavor. Combined with the smooth creaminess of high-quality cream and vanilla bean, I went to heaven while sitting on a park bench.

When I finished and was about to toss the container into the recycle bin, a gaggle of fae children rushed past, magic sparkling around them. To a human, the group would seem like adorable, borderline cherubic children with perfect curls and rosy cheeks, and laughter that sounded like bells. To someone with my abilities, all I sensed was danger.

I didn't like most fae, even though I was one of them. They were too tricky, too fickle, too violent, and too...eager. Fae children were better than adults, but they had zero restraint, and their magic was still unformed and wild. I pulled my legs in tight to my body and sat still on the bench while they passed me.

Just when I thought I was in the clear, one of them brushed a little too close and made skin-to-skin contact. Magic skittered over my arm, sparking in my blood. Normally, I'd be able to control my shift, but the moon hung heavy in the sky tonight, and the tight grip I kept on my dangerous magic had already slipped once tonight after the shifter had touched me. My already tenuous hold loosened. Fangs poked from my gums, and my eyes turned the strange crimson and gold of my mixed heritage. I lurched to my feet, turning away before I made a spectacle of myself, and fumbled over to my bike.

The fae children didn't turn back, giggling as they ran through the square, completely oblivious to what they'd done. But I had to get out of here before anyone started asking questions.

Shifters' eyes could be many colors, but never gold. Only the Shifter Lords' magic was gold, and no one could explain it because the color was normally reserved for divinity. If anyone spotted me losing control, especially a shifter, I'd be marked for death.

I hissed in pain when I banged my shin painfully against the bike pedals. A few people turned to stare when I muttered a too-loud curse, but by then, I was speeding away, headed straight for the woods.

The wonderful thing about Joy Springs was most of the town had easy access to a large, forested area, kept green by the numerous earth witches living in town. I didn't know much about how it operated, but the shifters needed space to roam and preferred green things, and the witches could easily provide it. They agreed on a barter, but no one knew what the shifters did for the witches. Since the agreement had been going on for at least a hundred years, it must be worth it.

I parked my bike about half a mile inside the woods, using the kickstand to keep it upright, next to a massive oak tree. Lying my hand against the rough, lichen-covered bark, I soaked in the tree's unforgiving but gentle strength, allowing it to calm me.

It took a few minutes, but eventually my eyes reverted to their normal azure blue and my fangs retreated back into my gums.

I blew out a slow breath and pressed my forehead against the tree. "Thank you," I whispered.

The tree's magic pulsed against my skin in welcome. With a smile, I pushed away and turned my attention to my bike, unsnapping the basket from the handlebars. I needed to forage anyway, and tonight's full moon was the perfect time.

Magic soaked into the forest, the moon's rays a soothing balm to my shaken countenance. I'd almost lost control twice tonight, something that hadn't happened since the first few months after my involuntary change. What was going on with me?

I headed deeper into the woods, the basket's heavy weight bumping against my thigh. Moonlight filtered through the thick tree canopy, casting the forest in a wash of dappled silver sparkles.

Full moons were my favorite time to gather things for the shop and for my own personal use. Unusual flowers bloomed during this time, and rare mushrooms burst from the ground, there and gone again in the space of a few hours. I inhaled the deep and loamy scent of fertile ground and rare blooms, smiling as a sense of rare peace settled into my soul.

For the next few hours, I busied myself with gathering and communing with the forest, ensuring I asked permission to take its bounty before using my amethyst-tipped silver athame to gather only what I needed, leaving the rest for other witches and spirits, and to ensure the continued health of the plant. As I explored, day blooming flowers opened, sensing my presence and welcoming me into their home.

I used a silver spoon I always kept in the bottom of the basket for gently extricating mushrooms from the ground, keeping them separate from the blooms and wild herbs. Ash was a whiz in the kitchen with any type of fungi. I was no slouch in the culinary arts, but he had a legitimate magical touch with anything I brought home after an evening spent in the forest.

When my neck and back ached from all the bending and crouching, I straightened with a deep sigh, and a wide smile stretched my lips.

A soft sound, not from animal or insect life, came from several feet ahead. I froze, body poised to run, when the noise came again.

Another groan of pain sounded before falling deathly silent. The forest went still. Against my better judgment, I crept forward on silent feet. One of my fatal flaws was being unable to stand anything in pain. Human, animal, or creepy crawly alike, it hurt something inside me to walk away when I could help.

The absence of further noise made it difficult to find where the sound had come from, but I stayed on the path, eyes sweeping back and forth for any disturbances in the soil and leaf cover. Eventually, I came to an open clearing. The scent of blood hit me first, and I stopped, eyes once again sweeping the area.

I closed my eyes and sent my senses out, searching for any heartbeats lingering behind. But there was only one, which was far too slow, coming from a prone figure lying a few feet away.

Swearing under my breath, I turned to run. I couldn't afford trouble in my life, not when I was barely holding things together five years later. But I couldn't do it. Whoever was lying there was a person.

I squeezed my eyes shut and blew out a breath. Knowing I'd regret it later, but unable to resist the tug drawing me to the prone figure, I set my basket down and hurried over.

The person was male and powerfully built. Something had ripped his clothes into shreds. What was once a pair of blue jeans lay in tatters against his golden skin. His t-shirt was ripped in half and lying in shreds around him, deep claw marks pulsing with poisonous magic.

A soft 'oh' of horror escaped me at his condition. I reached out and touched his skin, closing my eyes to get a read on his injuries, and almost jerked them away when I realized the male lying before me was no person at all.

He was a shifter. A powerful one.

Our magic stirred against each other, a sense of recognition I didn't understand. He felt familiar somehow, but I knew I'd never met him.

I could still run. No one would know. I'd go back to the shop and never mention this to anyone. My life would return to normal.

But …

But as my power seeped into his skin and I mentally catalogued the shifter's injuries, one thing became glaringly apparent.

If I didn't intervene, he would die.

And it would be my fault.

Not completely. I wasn't the one who attacked him. But leaving him to die when I was more than able to help felt akin to doing the same thing as his attackers had done, in a more passive way.

Foreign magic beat in the claw marks, a strange poison seeping through the shifter's body, overpowering his innate magic and preventing him from healing. I'd never sensed it before, but the feel of it made me want to snatch my hand away from him and run.

The rest would have been minor injuries if not for the poison. Several broken ribs, a broken leg, numerous abrasions, a concussion, a dislocated shoulder, and more. The more injuries that assailed my magic, the more empathy I felt for this stranger.

Someone or something wanted him dead and had damn near succeeded.

And that thought made me hesitate. One wasn't a daughter of the gods without believing in Fate and all its fickle tendencies. A demi-goddess did not believe in coincidence.

Had I been drawn here on this night and for this purpose?

If so, why?

Should I leave him to his inevitable death, or was there a reason I felt the urge to heal him?

The shifter's heartbeat trickled toward true death. I swore again, did a final sweep for prying eyes, and allowed my magic to rise in full force, something I hadn't done since the attack.

A gentle wind blew through the trees, sweeping my hair away from my face. Magical, night-blooming, rare flowers sprang from the ground, encasing the shifter and me in a glowing circle. The earth reached for me, yearning for the healing touch of my power. I sank to the ground beside the shifter and kicked off my shoes, ensuring the entire bottoms of my feet were in contact with the ground.

Magic rose from deep within the heart of the world, traveling through my feet and legs, my pelvis and waist, through my heart and head, and swept out through my fingers. I glowed a soft pink and green, the color of watermelon tourmaline mined straight from the heart of a mountain, then reached for the wounded creature.

Healing magic swept through his body, touching every single wound, old and new. Even so close to succumbing, he fought against death with a furious rage.

This power was the secret I guarded with my life, the one that would make me hunted if anyone ever knew. I was a Floromancer, but I was so much more.

My power could heal any wound, no matter what caused it. Divine weapons could not overpower my healing touch. I could reverse someone's age, taking them twenty, thirty, or more years in their past, reverting their body to their youth. This was a secret I'd never divulged because it could get me killed.

No one, not even my mother, knew this about my power. I hadn't even known about it until a few months after the Chimera attack.

But this gift had a couple of fatal flaws. I was completely vulnerable when using it and for at least an hour afterward, and if anyone knew about it, life as I knew it would end.

I'd discovered it by accident when Hazel, the witch who'd saved me after my attack, was mortally wounded. She'd stumbled into her small cabin in the woods and bled out on her wooden floor, and I'd reacted without hesitation.

When Hazel woke, she found me fused to her wooden floor, my body having grown roots to the earth below. She'd asked me a dozen questions, and I pretended not to have a clue what happened.

I hadn't used the power since.

But something drove me to save this man, and, though I might regret it, I poured magic into his veins, sweeping away his hurts, and forcing the magic out of his body and into the earth, where I destroyed it with barely a thought. And as I did, my thoughts floated, becoming one with the shifter. He had a prior hip injury from what looked like either an attack or fight, something so severe not even his shifter magic could heal completely. I blasted away the arthritis inside the joint and loosened the pins holding him together, forcing them out of his body and onto the ground.

He had a deep scar on his upper thigh, close to the femoral artery, another death blow he'd somehow managed to survive. I cleaned up the scar tissue and moved on.

After a ragged gasp of air and a final expulsion of foreign magic, old scar tissue, and bone fragments from his body made the earth shudder, I cut off the connection and tried to stand, hoping I could at least get back to my bike.

No dice. I managed to get to my feet but only made it a few steps away before I swayed and went to my knees, exhaustion overpowering me. Seconds later, I sank into the earth, the forest's cool embrace healing my body as my fingers and toes grew roots.

I sank into Mother Earth's power, the gentle touch of her womb soothing my exhaustion, forcing me into a deep slumber while my magic replenished.

Four

I jerked awake sometime later, a moan of pain slipping past my lips. Roots retracted from my body, reverting to fingers and toes. Unaware of how long I'd been out, I blinked my eyes open, relieved to see it was still dark.

Then I remembered what happened, and a sound of dismay came from me as I sat up. To my extreme relief, the shifter still lay face down. I hurried to my feet, brushing away the leaf litter and flowers that covered me while the earth restored me.

He still lay in a glowing circle of white flowers, the heady scent blowing from their swaying petals not of this world.

I crept over and peered down at his back, relieved to see the skin whole and blemish-free. On silent feet, I snatched up my shoes and basket and hurried back to my bike, but as I ran, I hesitated.

Leaving him here felt callous and uncaring. Should I stay until he woke up to ensure he knew where he was and didn't need any additional help?

No. I'd already gone against my instincts by getting involved. Waking up before him was a gift from the gods, and I'd be a fool to squander such a boon. I could leave and remain anonymous.

With one last glance at the sleeping shifter, I squashed my inner goodwill down and opted for safety.

Tonight, I'd sleep like the dead, and tomorrow I might be good for nothing, but I'd healed him, and that was good enough for me.

A FIGURE SAT on my porch when I rode up. My feet stalled on the bike pedals until I realized it was Moira. Relief filled me when I pulled into the driveway and hopped off, guiding my bike up the stairs. Every bit of movement ached. The vampire stood, her eyebrows rising when she spotted my disheveled condition.

"I hope you met a handsome stranger with even handsomer friends, and you had a wild orgy in the woods, but something tells me your story is much worse."

I snorted and winced when even that slight motion hurt. "Definitely worse," I croaked.

She held out her hands, and I fished through my pocket and dropped the keys into her palm. While Moira opened the door, I unlatched my basket. She took it from me and waited until I got inside and curled onto the couch before grilling me.

At her third question, I held my hand up. "Moira. I get you were worried, but I'm exhausted. Can we talk about this tomorrow?"

Her lips thinned. "At least tell me where you were and what happened. You're never this late, and we were all worried sick when you didn't answer your phone."

I frowned and patted my back pocket. No cell phone. Muttering a curse, I went to the basket and dug through it, but it wasn't there either.

I must have dropped it in the woods. Worry speared me. If the shifter found it, he might link me to his miraculous recovery. I'd have to go back out to retrieve it.

It'd be best if I did it tonight, but I couldn't muster up the energy. Even sitting here, sleep was dragging me down.

I explained what happened, leaving out a bunch of information. Basically, Moira got the extremely clean version as I left out losing control not once, but twice, and that I used my strange and disturbing magic to heal a stranger.

The story I told was quick. I went into the woods to forage for tomorrow and found an injured man. I whipped up a healing potion potent enough to get him to his feet and helped him back out to the town square.

Moira's eyebrows lifted. She knew I was full of shit, but her mojo powers didn't work on me. Nor could she smell the lies wafting from my body. Part of my new weird magic. Being fae helped. It always confused shifter senses, but the chimera's magic made me a blank page.

When the silence went on too long, I rose, hissing in pain as my back muscles twinged. I healed extremely fast, but the magic I used had drained me faster than my power could repair.

Moira's lips thinned. "You know I hate when you lie to me."

"That's why I almost never do."

"Except for tonight."

I remained silent.

She exhaled and rose. "At least tell me you're okay."

I smiled, trying to make it reassuring, but at her grimace, I knew I'd failed. "I'll be much better after a good night's sleep and some of your amazing coffee tomorrow."

"We'll open for you. Don't come in early."

I gave her a grateful smile. "Thanks, Moira."

She rolled her eyes and pointed to my bedroom. "March. I'll start the shower for you."

Dutifully, I turned and headed to the back. Within moments, the spray of water sounded in the master bath, and I had a handful of soft pajamas I couldn't wait to climb into.

I CAME in two hours later than normal, thankful I had good friends. Everything still hurt, but I had a few things at the shop to help me recover faster. When I came in from the back, three sets of eyes swung my way.

Ash's light eyebrows rose. His eyes glowed once before he slowly nodded. "I see," he murmured. "You've spent some time...communing."

That was the word he used when he spoke of earth magic. Ash did a lot of communing with the local trees.

"Something like that," I agreed.

Tess floated over. My eyes widened at her careless display of magic.

"Relax," she breathed, "we don't have any customers right now."

Moira sprawled across one of the chairs, braiding sweetgrass, and cursing occasionally when one of the stems would slip from the weave. She eyed me and jerked her head toward the coffee pot. "Made that special blend you like. There's half a pot left."

"And I left a vial of healing potion next to the pot," Ash added as he eyed me critically from head to toe. "Moira mentioned you might need it."

I smiled. "Thanks." Ash's healing potions were legendary. I made a mean one, but he always put an extra bit of oomph in his. When I mentioned selling them in the shop, he clammed up and refused, saying his gifts were reserved for those he cared about and not for sale to the general public. He was so solemn and serious about it, which was completely unlike Ash on a normal day, that I never mentioned it again.

Half an hour later, after coffee and a dropper of the dryad's potion, my pain was down to a solid three, and I felt worlds better. I dropped a kiss on top of Ash's head when I passed by on my way to the register, and he blustered a little before his cheeks turned bright pink.

"You're the best, Ash!"

He grumbled something under his breath and went back to training his bonsai maple into submission. We didn't have many of those to sell because it took Ash months to create them, but they went for a pretty penny when we did. I tried to give Ash all the money when we sold the first one, but he flat out refused and insisted on giving me a twenty percent commission.

As dryads went, he was the strangest one I'd ever met. He was also my favorite, so it evened out.

Moira and the others broke for lunch around noon, after I insisted on staying behind and making up the slack for my late arrival. It was a Tuesday, and customers were slow to come in, so I powered up my e-reader and caught up on my newest romantic fantasy obsession, a tale about pirates and the female serial killer who falls in love with the captain of a cursed ship.

AROUND ONE, Ash and Tess burst into the shop, back from their lunch break.

"Evie!" Ash breathed. "Have you heard?"

The shop was slow enough that I'd heard nothing except the imaginary, breathy moans of a killer as the handsome pirate captain plundered the main character's booty. "Nope," I called, regretfully putting my device down. Number one on the agenda once the shop closed was finishing that book.

Ash rounded the corner first and plowed into the register desk, eyes wide with glee. "The Shifter Lord was spotted coming out of the forest this morning wearing barely anything!"

Tess came up beside him, her normally expressionless face lit up with the thrill of hot gossip.

I'd never met the Texas Shifter Lord, nor did I ever want to, but Ash's words made my stomach sink like a stone.

Moira rounded up my friend group, her face somber, and her eyes filled with worry.

Shit. Shit. Shit!

I pasted a smile on my face. "Oh? He must have had some rendezvous out there!" Mustering a half-hearted chuckle, I reached for my e-reader and tucked it into my purse.

"But that's not the best part!" Tess breathed. "He's on the hunt for someone. A female."

I stilled. "How do you know that?"

Ash's jaw dropped. "How? The entire town is talking about it! He met a woman in the forest, and apparently, he's now obsessed. Caelan is offering a massive reward for whoever hunts her down."

I was going to hurl. Healing a random shifter was one thing. But healing the freaking Shifter Lord? That was an entire truckload of trouble about to land on my doorstep.

"I don't understand. He doesn't know who she is?" I busied my hands with closing out the register.

Moira had yet to utter a word. Judgment marred her pretty face, but she hadn't sold me out to the others. Something I'd thank her for later.

Ash waved his hand. "Semantics. What I want to know is who is this mystery woman? What did she do? And why is Caelan so insistent on uncovering her identity?"

Tess swooned. "It's like Cinderella."

"Except with sharper teeth and more danger," I said ruefully.

Ash's eyes narrowed. "You always like hot tea, Evie. What's crawled up your butt today?"

"Nothing good will come of the Shifter Lord's attention," I said quietly.

Ash snorted. "Hmm. He's rich, famous, mysterious, and one of the seven most powerful creatures in existence. Most women would throw themselves at his feet if he spared them even a single glance."

I grimaced. "No thanks."

He shook his head and sighed. "Hopeless, I tell you. This is why you'll be a spinster forever. Little Evie and her avoidant attachment syndrome."

Usually, I laughed when Ash psychoanalyzed me. Today, it felt like a knife in the heart. I closed the register drawer. "Moira, mind taking care of this? I'm going to head out a little early today."

The vampire nodded, sympathy flickering in her eyes. "Of course. I'll pop by later for dinner if you're up for it."

I offered a wan smile. "I'll text you later."

Grabbing my purse, I headed toward the back, only to hear Ash and Tess murmuring. Moira's sharp rebuke echoed behind me.

CHAPTER

Five

CAELAN

"I can't tell you anything other than she smelled like jasmine," I barked. "If I knew who she was, I would find her!" I held the mystery woman's cell phone, broken beyond repair but with a faint touch of her scent. Oddly, there was no trace of a magical scent on the device, only the slightest hint of flowers.

Simone, my quiet, reliable Omega, studied me. "The Joy Springs gossip lines are on fire today, Caelan. You shouldn't seem quite so eager to find her. It may attract...other things her way."

I ran a hand through my hair and bit out a quiet curse. "You don't understand. I should have died." And that was a real kick in the teeth. Very few things could kill me, and those things I shouldn't be able to come back from. What that woman had done defied both logic and magic.

I didn't like things I couldn't understand.

Ninety-nine percent of people would have left me to die. I deserved to die for all the things I'd done. Most of them would spit on my grave. This woman had brought me back from the brink of death, and not only that, she'd done more.

My skin looked like a newborn baby's. Not a mark marred my

skin. No aches, no pains, no tiredness. No...nothing. I felt like a goddamn teenager again.

All I could remember about her was a sweep of dark hair, glowing eyes, and staggering power. Something like her should not exist. She'd brought me back from the brink of death, and that was something I couldn't ignore.

Simone nodded. "I do understand. Something more powerful than you stumbled upon you during the most vulnerable moment you've ever had and showed mercy."

She sighed and crossed her leanly muscled arms, watching me with a look I didn't like. "Perhaps you should accept this as the gift it is and leave it alone. This woman did not have an ulterior motive. If she did, she would have stayed with you and demanded payment."

Simone was right, and I liked her logic even less. "Perhaps she's biding her time, hiding out like a spider until she needs a favor," I grumbled.

My Omega rolled her eyes, a gesture no one else would be brave enough to direct at me. "Healers are rarely terrible people, Caelan. She saw an injured man, and she healed him. You should take this as the gift it's meant to be and leave the poor woman alone."

"And if she shows up wanting money, or worse?"

Simone snorted. "Then you throw a fucking bank's worth of money at her and call it a day. Few problems cannot be solved with proper monetary compensation, and she saved your miserable life. As far as I'm concerned, she did you a favor you can't possibly repay."

I rubbed my jaw. Did the healer know who I was? Or was Simone right? Was she just a woman who'd been in the right place at the right time? "Maybe you're right," I conceded.

Simone laughed. "Maybe?"

A begrudging smile tipped my lips up. "Fine. But I would still like to find her and reward her. Handsomely."

Simone studied me for a long moment. "Liar." She untangled

her lanky form from my couch and stood. "I have a bad feeling about this. It feels like other forces are in play, and we both know how things go when you aren't in the driver's seat."

My Omega touched my hand, her comforting magic pulsing against my skin. "I also think you're worried about the wrong thing. You shouldn't concern yourself with the healer. You should concern yourself with the people who made you need her."

Rage pulsed in my veins. Few people ever got the drop on me. Terrible magic was involved. Magic I needed to find and destroy. Simone was right, but I knew I wouldn't back down when it came to the healer. This woman, whoever she was, I wanted to meet her, and look her in the eye. I wanted to ask her why.

There was something so familiar about that scent. Had I smelled it before? Maybe in town? I shook my head. Downtown Joy Springs was a nightmare for scent tracking. Too many types of magic and creatures made it impossible to differentiate. Plus, there were coffee shops and cafe's...I was nose blind any time I walked anywhere around there.

My wolf, normally a silent, wise partner, had been unusually vocal since we'd woken up in the forest, soaked in blood and with the tantalizing scent of jasmine swirling in the air. He stalked the corners of my mind, agitated and anxious for us to hunt. Not food. Her.

But there was more to it. More I buried deep inside.

A secret between my wolf and me.

I'd find this woman if it was the last thing I ever did.

She was the first to ever see me broken and had not taken advantage of my vulnerability. Finding her had become my top priority.

CHAPTER

Six

"Are you insane?" Moira hissed as she breezed into my house. The smell of garlic and basil followed her, and honestly, I was so hungry I was more focused on that than the barely suppressed rage in her voice.

"Can we eat first?" I begged.

Moira slammed the bags down on the kitchen counter. "Evie." She squeezed the space between her brows. "You healed the Shifter Lord?"

I took the bags from her and started digging out the to-go containers. "In my defense, I didn't know it was him."

"How could you not know?" Moira said through gritted teeth.

I pushed the Bolognese her way and took the Alfredo. "It was dark. I was tired. He was face down and covered in blood and wounds."

Moira stared. "Did you know he was a shifter?"

"Not until I touched him."

She opened her container and shook some Parmesan over the top. "You could have walked away. You should have."

I took the cheese from her and did the same to my dish. "You know how difficult it is for me to see things in pain."

Her eyes softened. "I do," she agreed.

She should. It was how we'd met. I reached over and squeezed her hand. "It will be fine. The thistle protects my identity. He won't be able to track me."

Hazel had done a hell of a job on the thistle tattoo. It kept me hidden from anyone searching—even the gods. Caelan could hire the best tracker in the world, and it wouldn't help.

As long as I stayed out of his direct path, I'd be safe.

"What about your scent?" Moira asked, diving right into the heart of my fear.

I shrugged. "Caelan was so close to death, I doubt he caught it."

Moira's lips thinned. "I know you're keeping secrets. I get why you have to, but you're treating me like an idiot. We both know how powerful a regular shifter's senses are, but you healed Caelan, the Shifter Lord. That guy could sniff a specific grain of pepper from a vat of the stuff."

She opened a bottle of wine with a flick of her wrist, a feat I was always jealous of. "The amount of magic you had to expend to heal him must have been tremendous."

I opened my mouth to speak, but Moira held up her hand to silence me. "Nope. I'm not finished."

She poured us both a huge glass and pushed mine over before she tilted hers up, drained it, and refilled her glass.

I winced.

"I can only assume the forest floor is saturated with your power. He might not be able to track you due to the spell on your arm, but if you ever use similar magic in his presence, he will be able to identify you."

"That will never happen," I assured her.

Moira grunted. "And you healing the Shifter Lord never should have happened, and yet here I am, close to having a nervous breakdown in your kitchen."

"I'm sorry," I whispered.

Moira snorted. "You never have to apologize to me, Evie. I'm worried about you. Not me."

She gathered up her food and headed into the living room. I trailed behind her, quickly losing my appetite. "None of us could bear it if anything happened to you." She ducked her head. "You gave us all a home. We owe everything to you."

I shook my head. "No. Never. You owe me nothing." Tears filled my eyes. "Family has no debts, Moira."

Pink tears appeared at the corners of Moira's eyes. "Don't die, okay?"

A startled laugh broke from me. "I'll do my best."

Her watery smile broke my heart. "He won't find me. But if he does, maybe it won't be so bad. I saved his life, after all, didn't I?"

I nudged her playfully. "Maybe he'll give us a gift card to that cool new bookstore down the road. We've been meaning to visit there, and free books are an excellent reward for a good deed."

Neither one of us believed there wouldn't be consequences if Caelan found me, but my words served as a natural way to end the conversation and focus on other things.

Like pasta from our favorite restaurant.

My DREAMS that night were strange and jarring.

I stood in a glowing forest of colorful blooms and watery moonlight. A massive man with moss and fungi-covered golden antlers atop his head sat cross-legged on a large tree stump, watching me.

My heart pounded in my chest, but I felt no urge to run. The man, or whatever he was, felt familiar, though I knew I'd never met him. I made no move to come any closer, nor did he move from his stump.

I couldn't make out all of his features. The night was too dark, and everything was thrown into shadow. He tilted his head, and I could see a proud nose and high cheekbones. His eyes glowed with fae magic.

My breath caught.

I knew who this was. And all of a sudden, I knew this was no dream.

"Cernunnos," I breathed.

"Evangeline." His voice vibrated with power, rolling over my skin with sparks of light. I shivered at the sheer magnitude of his magic, both in fear and awe.

"Is this a dream?" I had to make sure.

"A warning." His voice sounded like a savage, wild forest, deep and rumbling like a fall thunderstorm. He slid off the stump and came closer. I was a small woman, but I'd never felt quite so overwhelmed by a male presence. He towered over me, his physical height mind-boggling, antlers rising another several feet above his head.

Cernunnos' eyes glowed with ancient magic, the irises swirling with silver and golden sparks, unfathomable power simmering in their depths. Deep wisdom rested in his gaze, making my breath catch when his eyes rested on me.

His antlers were akin to a crown, marking his position as king of his land, ruler of the forest, and all its flora and fauna. Cernunnos' hair cascaded past his shoulders and swayed in a gentle fae wind, the strands the color of doe skin and twisted with moss and mushrooms, twigs, and stones. His nose was straight and proud, his cheekbones sharp, and his lips full.

He stood before me bare-chested and leanly muscled, his skin the color and texture of bark. He wore leather breeches crusted with moss and vines, tangling in intricate patterns around his powerful thighs.

I swallowed hard, my dry throat clicking. "I'm not sure what the fae king would need to warn me about."

His clothing melted as I watched, changing into a pair of joggers and a white t-shirt.

I blinked in surprise at the switch, almost laughing as he strode toward me. The new clothing made him look like a personal trainer at a 24-hour gym. His face lost that inhuman edge, but anyone would know Cernunnos wasn't quite human if they saw him. His eyes shone like burnished silver—dimmed but still unearthly.

"Your blood smells different."

It wasn't a question but a loaded observation.

My mouth fell open. When had Cernunnos ever smelled my blood? "I'm sorry?"

He waved a hand. A large stone with a flat top rumbled up from the ground. Cernunnos held his hand out to me. "Sit with me for a while."

This night had taken a decidedly weird turn, but I obliged, and Cernunnos, king of the fae, technically my king, hopped onto the rock next to me in one lithe move.

As we sat there like teenagers who snuck out of their house for an illicit meetup, Cernunnos sighed.

"What happened to you?"

I shrugged. Many things. Everything. One terrible thing. "Long story."

"I have time."

For a while, neither of us spoke.

"You have a long time before the Hunt comes. Why are you here?" The world was seven months away from the Winter Solstice, the time when Cernunnos rode through the world. For twelve days, Cernunnos brought the souls of the dead together before the wheel of the year turned once more.

His smile made the edges of his eyes crinkle. Cernunnos was beautiful, but I didn't feel any attraction toward him. I felt curiosity more than anything. Imagine all the things he'd seen or done, all the years he'd walked the worlds.

"You're right," he acknowledged. "I rarely return to this world, but I felt it necessary to visit. However, I'm not technically here on Earth right now. I'm only in your psyche."

"That isn't as comforting as you think it is."

His laugh warmed me from the inside. "Tell me, Evangeline. What happened?"

I crossed my arms over my chest.

"I don't like talking about it."

"Have you ever talked about it?"

I shot him a look. Cernunnos' expression was mild and non-judgmental.

"No," I said mulishly.

"Then how do you know you won't feel better when you unburden yourself?"

"The great Cernunnos acting as a therapist?" I grumbled. "I thought I'd never see the day."

"I'm not here to be your therapist. The balance of your blood is vastly different, Evangeline. You have not accepted those changes. Until you do, you will be…" His voice trailed off until he stretched his hands apart. "Split. Two pieces of one whole."

Cernunnos shook his head sadly. "You will not be complete until you come to terms with what happened to you and learn to embrace your new power as it emerges."

My heartbeat picked up at his words. I suspected something like that, but hearing it spoken aloud sent defeat rushing through me. I'd fought for so long and so hard to suppress the chimera's curse, and I knew I'd eventually lose. I just didn't expect it to happen this soon. "And if I don't want to?"

A heavy exhale escaped him.

"You already know what happened to me, don't you?" Sitting next to Cernunnos felt like sitting in front of a furnace. I always associated the fae with cool spring nights and early autumn evenings, but the king's power felt like a deeply hidden pool of lava.

"I know everything about you, Evangeline."

I stiffened. "Why?"

"That is a question I am not ready to answer."

His power might feel like a volcano, but he was just as cagey as the rest of the fae. "Why should I trust you?"

"Because you already know the truth. You feel the difference in your blood, the battle your body is fighting. Still fighting all these years later. Perhaps if you allow yourself to examine this, you may find some interesting surprises."

My thoughts briefly flicked to Caelan and how I felt like I couldn't physically walk away from him. But something about Cernunnos' words bothered me. I didn't want any interesting surprises.

Surprises were for people who didn't have to hide themselves. I'd done a deep dive on the chimera race after my attack, studying every piece of literature I could get my hands on. I knew what they were capable of. Why would Cernunnos imply I'd find a surprise if I fully embraced the chimera's magic?

Whatever the answer might be, I wanted no reminder of that night, and I'd devoted myself to searching for a way to purge its magic from my body. Without much luck, granted, but I still had a few irons in the fire.

Something about sitting out here with the king of the fae in my dreamscape during a cool, stunning summer evening made me try raw honesty.

"I don't want to give up who I am." My voice sounded meek. Small. "I like my life." A tear slipped down my face. Even though I knew things weren't perfect, they were good enough. Weren't they?

Cernunnos said nothing for a long moment. A mixture of emotions played over the planes of his face. "Do you think a child knows who it is, Evie?"

I frowned. "Of course not."

"A child's growth and personality depend on many factors. Physical and emotional environment, life experiences, education. A child who knows nothing but love feels free to give love, but one who knows rejection hides their pain and refuses to believe love is real when it's offered. They learn to survive."

His words plucked at all the raw pieces inside me, all the places that had never healed when I was a little girl who only wanted to be loved.

"And so they grow up," he continued, "and they get jobs, fall in love, maybe have kids. Then maybe they get divorced, or have a miscarriage, or become paralyzed in an accident. Or worse."

He lifted a powerful shoulder in a shrug. "Or better. There's no way to tell. But as the child grows, their minds and personalities are shaped with everything happening around them and to them. For most people, the same cycle continues until they either give up or they die."

His words struck something inside me. My magic churned like acid in my gut. "Are you saying I don't know who I am?"

He smiled sadly. "I am saying you know who you are today, but things are ever-changing. You might be a different person in a week from now. Maybe even tomorrow."

"If I stop trying to suppress the chimera magic and explore how it works."

He didn't acknowledge my words and instead abruptly changed the subject. "Tell me, Evangeline. Do you know who your father is?"

I jerked my attention to him. "Excuse me?" My heart leapt in response to his question. I assumed my father was some poor human man my mother had seduced. She killed him shortly after coitus like some fucked up praying mantis and told me so while we were sharing pizza one night during one of her thankfully rare visits.

I have no idea who he was or even his name. The only thing my mother ever told me about him was that "he was so very pretty, darling." As if that wouldn't give me nightmares for the next thousand years.

"Your Floromancy comes from your mother?"

I shrugged, suspecting he already knew the answer. "Mom isn't exactly forthcoming with information. I assume so. She has powerful healing abilities, so I believe those came from her."

"Perhaps. But Cliona does not have true power over flora. She can do the small magics common with all the fae, but powerful plant life and earth magic are beyond her capabilities."

"So that's a no on the Floromancy," I said dryly.

His smile was enigmatic. "Floromancy is an ancient magic, Evie. Far older than much of your maternal line. Have you ever questioned what you gained from your father?"

I laughed. "My addiction to British baking shows and weakness for baked goods?"

At his silence, I sobered. "My father was mortal."

Cernunnos rose to his feet. "Was he?"

I stared at him as he hopped off the rock.

"Cernunnos." My throat went dry. I stared at him in horror. My father was mortal. Mom had always said…

No. No she hadn't. I'd drawn my own conclusions, hadn't I? I swore viciously under my breath.

The fae king turned and strode away.

"Cernunnos!"

An iridescent portal opened before him. He turned and studied me for a brief second. "You will never lose yourself once you discover who you're truly meant to be, Evangeline."

Cernunnos took a step backward, the portal swallowing him in a flash of bright light.

My eyes snapped open.

I was lying in bed, covered in a cold sweat.

Inside my palm lay an oak leaf the color of burnished gold.

A flower bouquet lay before me, but I didn't want to touch it. Malevolent energy wafted from the wilting blooms. Tess, Moira, Ash, and I all stood in a semi-circle around the spelling table, staring down at it.

"Who brought this in?" I asked.

Moira flipped through the clipboard she held. "Um. A woman named Amy."

"Marriage date."

Moira's eyes skimmed down the page. "One week ago. Her mother dropped off the bouquet for her daughter. The daughter's name is Chloe."

"Do we have the groom's name?"

Ash shifted uncomfortably. "I don't like this," he murmured. "Those flowers are...tainted."

Moira shook her head. "No place for it. I can add it to the sheet for next time."

"Please do," I murmured.

Tess rubbed her hands over her arms. "He's a bad man. A very bad man."

"I'm not sure he's a man at all."

Three sets of wide eyes swung my way. "You can tell that?" Moira asked.

I tipped my hand back and forth. "Sort of. There's a magic imprint soaked into the blooms, but it's faint. Men don't normally handle their bride's flowers." Odd that he handled them at all. "Do you know if the couple is on their honeymoon?"

Moira shrugged. "I assumed so since the mom dropped the bouquet off, but I didn't ask." She took a step back, eyeing the flowers warily.

"Should we call her back and refuse the job?" Moira made a note on the clipboard. "She left her cell and an email address."

I thought about it, but shook my head. "It's not the bride's fault. When is she expecting the flowers back?"

Moira consulted the clipboard again. "Two weeks."

"Good. Let's pack this back up." I turned to Ash. "Can you grab one of the magic dampening sacks?"

"I'll get it," Tess volunteered. She floated away in a hurry.

"Chicken," Ash muttered.

"Don't be jealous you didn't volunteer fast enough," Moira chided.

I laughed. "Once Tess gets back, we'll secure the flowers. I didn't sleep well last night, and I don't want to work on them while my head is fuzzy."

Ash leaned over and felt my forehead with the back of his palm. "Feeling alright, Evie?"

I brushed his hand away. "You know I've never run a fever since you've known me."

The dryad shrugged. "First time for everything. Some illnesses of our kind manifest in a higher body temperature."

"Nothing but weird dreams plaguing me," I confessed. More than a dream, but I wasn't ready to tell them the fae king had popped up and had a disturbing convo with me.

"You're off tomorrow and should take it easy. You've had an interesting few days."

At Ash's curious glance, Moira winced. "With the number of customers coming in, we've been busier than normal."

Ash didn't say anything, but he gave us both an odd look.

The bell over the door rang, announcing a new customer. Tess and Moira went to the front while I wrangled the evil bouquet. Ash winced when I picked it up, which made me laugh.

"It's not a bomb," I teased.

He shuddered. "I'm glad you're wearing gloves. Touching that with bare skin seems unwise."

I tucked the flowers into the magical pouch and carefully zipped it up, ensuring all the blooms were carefully tucked in. I couldn't leave it for too long. Even with the magic in the shop, fresh flowers still needed to be looked after or preserved as soon as possible if they'd already been cut. "I'll look at it in a couple of days."

"When you catch up on your sleep," Ash said as he probed but pretended he wasn't.

"Yes," I said and smiled sweetly. Handing him the bag, I waved and went to help Tess and Moira.

"Evie!" Ash gasped. "You are the worst!"

I laughed and pushed through the connecting doors.

Moira spun around, eyes wide. "Go!" she mouthed, frantically waving me back.

I stopped and blinked, about to ask her what was going on, when a staggering and familiar magic washed over me.

Tess's face brightened when she spotted me. "Oh! Here she is now." She came out from behind the counter, her cheeks pink and eyes sparkling, a look I had never seen on her. Tess put the 's' in morose.

"Evie Quinn is the owner and knows everything about flowers. I'm sure she can answer any questions you have."

Moira squeezed her eyes shut and exhaled before slapping a smile on her face and turning around.

The Shifter Lord and a small blonde woman with smiling

green eyes walked by Tess's side. My heart leapt in my chest, and I quickly moved to control my breathing.

Caelan was one of the most powerful shifters in the country. If I had an extreme physical reaction, he would get suspicious. A suspicious shifter was the absolute last thing I needed.

Moira didn't have to worry about it because she had no heartbeat, and Tess, bless her dark little heart, was clueless.

I smoothed my hands down my floral apron and smiled. "Hello. Welcome to Little Shop of Florals. Is there something specific you're looking for?"

The small woman smiled and stuck out her hand. "I'm Simone Ashmoore, The Shifter Lord's Omega."

Her handshake was firm and dry. Comforting magic rolled over my skin as we touched. Omegas were rare and prized within their packs for their unique, blissful magic, but rarely rose high in the ranks. It was odd she was with Caelan. From what I knew of Shifter Lords, they rarely left their compounds without their second. If Simone was a second, she was extraordinarily powerful.

"Evie."

Caelan stared at me, his eyes not missing a thing. He was tall and powerfully built, his entire presence feeling like a warning. Even the plant life inside my shop had gone still and wary. He was well over six feet, with broad shoulders and a trim waist. Everything about him screamed restrained violence, and he stood with absolute stillness.

The Shifter Lord was a storm in waiting, barely held together by human skin.

His hair was dark, longer on top and slightly tousled, the only thing even a little messy about him. But the most stunning thing about him was his eyes. Storm gray and gold-flecked, a rarity in human form.

Only Lord's eyes glowed gold when they shifted or used their power, but Caelan's magic was held firmly in check. His power was so tremendous, it had manifested into physical traits.

His clothing was made less for style and more for function. Today he wore well-used blue jeans and a charcoal-colored t-shirt with a flannel jacket over the top. His boots were leather and scuffed. Steel-toed and heavy, if I had to guess.

Caelan, for all his power, looked to be a working man. A sliver of admiration wound through me before I squashed it down.

As he looked at me, he catalogued weaknesses, searching for ways to hurt or subdue. I don't think he meant anything by it, but Caelan was a man who constantly scanned for threats. In his line of work, he had to.

Power hummed around him, a magnetic field that brushed against my skin. I wrapped my power tightly around me, keeping it pushed deep down inside. This would be the true test to see if Caelan recognized me—if my thistle tattoo worked as it should when a threat like a Shifter Lord appeared.

Tess broke the tense silence. "The Pack needs flowers for a funeral," Tess said.

I blinked and tore my eyes away from Caelan. "Oh!" I put a hand over my heart. "My sincere condolences."

Get it together, Evie. He probably didn't think anything of my perusal. I bet everyone stared at him like that. "I'd be happy to help. Would you like to step into my office?"

Being enclosed in a small space with Caelan wasn't ideal, but I had to pretend everything was normal. Speaking about funeral arrangements in the open was the height of unprofessionalism.

Caelan stepped forward and held out his hand. "Caelan Wolfe."

His last name was Wolfe? My lips twitched.

Moira sucked in a choked gasp of air.

Simone's eyebrows lifted, her bright eyes sparkling with amusement.

To cover my faux pas, I smiled and mustered up my old high school theater skills. "A Shifter Lord," I breathed, piling on false admiration. "Thank you so much for choosing my shop."

When our hands touched, magic sparked between us, unseen by the others but felt by us.

Caelan's eyes went wide. His nostrils flared as he tried to fully scent me. That's where the power of my tattoo came in. All someone could smell was a low powered Hedgewitch. But there was one fatal flaw. It didn't do a thing when someone at Caelan's power level touched me. He wouldn't know what I was, but he would know I wasn't just a Hedgewitch.

And that might prove to be a huge problem.

His skin was warm and calloused, and for a brief second, I wondered what those hands would feel like running over my bare skin. I swallowed hard and pulled my hand away.

Caelan's eyes narrowed. "Evie Quinn, you said?"

I nodded and cleared my throat. "Would you like to come into my office?" I asked again.

Caelan smiled, the effect devastating, and I wondered if he knew what I'd been thinking about a second before. "Lead on, Evie."

He wouldn't let me lead him. Caelan walked up next to me, his gray gaze scanning the shop with a thorough eye. "Every Shifter Lord takes on the surname of their beast, though we don't always announce it."

So, he had noticed my amusement. Great. But I couldn't stifle my curiosity. "Is it given to you at birth or do you have a different surname before you're named Lord?"

His brow crinkled, and I wondered if no one had ever asked him that question. "Different. It's Hawthorne."

My breath caught as I stumbled. Caelan caught me by the elbow before I went down, steadying me. I righted myself as a nervous laugh escaped me. "Sorry about that. I'm a total klutz sometimes."

His hand burned into my skin. "Quite alright."

But he didn't let go until Simone cleared her throat, then he jerked his hand away like he'd burned himself.

I turned away and led them through the back into the office, where I kept the book of floral selections. My mind spun. Hawthorne. Caelan's last name was Hawthorne? Of all the surnames for a Shifter Lord to have, I never would have expected it to be so...witchy. The Hawthorne represented love and fertility and had a direct connection to the fae realm.

I also hadn't expected it to relate so directly to my powers.

Shaking my head to ward off those thoughts, I held open the door, but Caelan took it and gestured for me to go inside.

Simone gave me a strange look as she brushed past, but her expression morphed into one of awe as she stepped in.

"Whoa," she breathed. "This is your office?"

I pulled a couple of chairs up to the large carved table to the right side of the room and went around to the other side of my desk to get the book with all the selections.

"It is. Every plant in here was grown either by cutting or seed. The ones on that shelf over there—" I pointed to a set of large, polished mahogany shelves Ash had made from a fallen tree. "Those are hybrids I've created over the years."

Caelan had stopped in the middle of my office, his mouth slightly open as he took everything in.

I rarely felt self-conscious about my magic, but even I had to admit my office was a little...extra. Plants were arranged on every available surface, and where there wasn't a surface, I'd added shelving. Or a table. Or a wire rack.

Even the top of my credenza was crammed with plants. Vines climbed the lamps and light fixtures, tangled through the curtain rods, and hung with lush green leaves. I'd even placed three string of pearl plants inside my ceiling chandelier.

I had multiple varieties of pothos, Monsteras, ferns, and orchids blooming in every color in the large bay window over-looking the town square. There were African Violets and peace lilies, multiple types of succulents, Easter and Christmas cacti in full bloom, and dozens of others.

Simone wandered over to the hanging rod by the window and

gawked at one particular plant. "This," she breathed. "What is this? It's stunning."

I walked over to her and grinned. "It's called Callisia Repens Pink Lady. It's a turtle vine."

She reached out and jerked her fingers away. "Oh, sorry. I just—"

"Feel free to touch anything you want. Plants crave contact just like we do."

Simone's lips parted as she reached up to stroke its leaves. "I've never seen anything so beautiful. How do you keep it alive?"

I shrugged. Floromancy was a rare magic and not usually dangerous, but I rarely discussed my gift with anyone. "A strong green thumb and lots of research."

I watched as Simone marveled over the plant. "Would you like a cutting?"

Simone gasped. "Oh no. I couldn't."

Caelan came over and stood beside Simone. "You should accept her offer. It's good for the plant and an excellent way to brighten up your rooms."

I blinked in surprise. "You grow things?"

Caelan's teeth flashed. "Nothing like this, but I have a few houseplants I enjoy."

Interesting. So many people dismissed green things inside the home, claiming they were too much work, or they had a brown thumb, but houseplants oxygenated the air, soothed anxiety, and helped calm the atmosphere. Plus, they were beautiful to look at. I wondered if Caelan felt the same.

Tearing my attention away from him, I refocused on Simone. "I'll take a few cuttings for you and root them. It will take a couple of weeks, but when they're ready, I'll call you for pickup if that's alright. If you see anything else you'd like to try to grow, I'm happy to take any cuttings you'd like."

Simone's smile grew. "That's incredibly generous. Thank you."

Her bright gaze swept the room. "Can I ask for one of everything?"

Caelan huffed a laugh. "How about we keep it under five today? We don't want to take up too much of Evie's time, and we still haven't looked at the flower selections."

Chastened, Simone's cheeks went pink. "Of course."

I smiled at her. "I'll see what I can do. Until then, please sit down so we can talk about what flowers you want for your service."

CHAPTER

Eight

One week had passed since the Shifter Lord had come into my shop, and I was just starting to calm down after his visit. If he'd recognized me, something would have come of it by now. Even Moira had been as nervous as a cat around tin foil, completely unlike her.

A shout of dismay came from the back. Moira and I glanced at each other in alarm and hurried toward the sound.

Ash stood in front of the flower cooler holding the remains of the metal door—the door usually hinged to keep the cooler closed. He stared at it with dismay.

I cleared my throat. "Ash?"

He jerked and blinked. "Err. Hey. Umm. This is not what it looks like."

Moira snorted. "So, it's not you holding the cooler door that you apparently ripped off the hinges like some kind of wooden superhero?"

Ash sighed. "Well. Yes. Then I guess it's exactly what it looks like." He gently set the door against the wall with a booming thud. "I've been chilling those bonsais for weeks now, and it was time to collect them." He shook his head. "I got so excited I forgot my own strength."

I'd forgotten about how strong he was, too. Ash was always so kind and gentle I sometimes forgot he was a male dryad. He had the strength of a mighty oak and the occasional stubbornness to match.

"I'll replace it," he said. "Until then, I think I can rig it up to keep the cool air in." He grimaced. "I hope."

The tainted wedding bouquet was in there. Allowing it to thaw wasn't a good idea. "I'll call some repair places today. Until then, see what you can do."

The dryad nodded, misery all over his face. I reached out and pulled him in for a hug. "Not your fault. Whenever you think it is, just remember the Great Pothos Debacle of 2023."

That got a chuckle out of him.

I'd still been learning how to juggle my mixed magic when my Floromancy went wild. Every single pothos I had in the shop grew several feet and tangled everything up in vines. They grew so fast and so long, they'd broken the front door and the main window. We'd taken several thousands of dollars in damages and had to explain to a group of handsome, confused firefighters that we were developing a new fertilizer for the market, but the experiment had gone awry.

Pretty sure they didn't believe us, but since we hadn't hurt anyone and damaged nothing except my own property, they helped us sweep up the glass and let us be.

"Moira banned pothos up until this year," Ash reminisced with a hearty laugh.

"Moira should have banned them forever," the vampire muttered. "I still get PTSD flashbacks when I walk past one."

We helped Ash carry out his bonsais before assisting with the replacement of the door. It didn't seal all the way, but it should be okay until we got a repairman in.

"No one opens this door again without a buddy," I lectured, making my voice loud enough for Tess to hear.

The banshee's sad moan of agreement filtered back to us.

I slapped the dust from my hands and headed toward the

front, making a mental note to set aside the funds for the repairman.

WE STOOD around the phone waiting for it to ring. A lot rode on this call. At first, when Mr. Jeffers started contacting the shop, no one thought anything of it. Every two weeks, he ordered a huge seasonal bouquet for delivery to an address about twenty miles away, far away from the downtown area.

We all, like the emotional saps we were, assumed the flowers were for his wife. Joy Springs was full of paranormals. Few of them were dumb enough to cheat on their wives, simply because the wives were just as deadly as their husbands. There was no way to tell what Mr. Jeffers was—human or paranormal—so we assumed he was a good dude being a great husband.

Oh, how wrong we were.

Moira took the calls at first, and I'd work putting the bouquets together for delivery. Every time, he'd ask for a different message on the card. Most messages were sweet, but over time, things had gotten progressively spicier. Again, no big deal.

But then, a woman came into the shop looking for some flowers for a vow renewal cake. Her last name was Jeffers. One of the big rules in our shop was to never, ever speak about any past orders or deliveries if a spouse came in.

For this exact reason.

Also, Jeffers wasn't a rare name, but Tess had spotted a picture of the woman's husband when the wife opened her wallet, and it was the same guy we Googled when we got curious about all of those deliveries.

However, she gave us a completely new address that got us curious, and we'd huddled around as Tess accessed some website that gave us a bird's-eye view of the address the husband had given us and then the apartment address the wife gave us.

So we were nosy. Sue us. We had to do something to keep things lively around the shop, and this one ended up being way more interesting than we could stand once we brought up the property records for the first house and linked it to a powerful mage with suspected ties to organized crime.

Ash guessed the home was a paranormal brothel and Mr. Jeffers was availing himself of the talents there, showing his appreciation through bi-weekly flower donations, in addition to the no doubt substantial amount of money he was dropping there.

Moira thought Mr. Jeffers had a single mistress who was either one of the workers or the Madame who ran the place.

Tess was more into the investigating part of it and didn't care a whit what Mr. Jeffers was or wasn't doing. She wasn't great at board games, either, but that was Tess.

I, after thoroughly researching the house, thought he wasn't cheating and maybe the woman we thought was his wife might be a familial relation. Everyone groaned at that because, and I quote, "Seriously, Evie, where is your sense of drama?!" So, we decided to make a bet.

If Mr. Jeffers was cheating, Moira had to wear the enchanted bee suit, and Ash had to turn into a Honeycrisp apple tree and grow enough apples for a week.

Ash grumbled about it because he hated when we used him for his fruit growing abilities. Moira balked at the thought of wearing that suit around, but was so convinced she was right, she finally agreed.

I kept the suit in a locked closet because it was a huge distraction. And a little terrifying. Originally designed by Marnie and Twila, the owners of the cafe I loved so much, as protective gear to wear while they maintained their poison garden, the enchantment had gone...wrong. They'd offered it to me, and I'd accepted because I had a soft spot for the weird and faulty.

The phone rang.

Moira hip checked me. I swore and stumbled over a potted plant, landing on my tailbone.

"Moira!"

She gave me a fanged grin and snatched up the phone. "Little

Shop of Florals, this is Moira. How may I assist you with your floral needs today?"

Tess waved a hand, and the speakerphone turned on. Moira shot her a dark look. I stuck my tongue out at her and pulled myself up with the help of the edge of the counter.

"Hello, Moira. This is Wayne Jeffers. I'm calling to place my weekly order, but I wondered if there's any way you could have it done and delivered today. For a generous rush fee, of course."

Moira grimaced and looked my way.

I gave her a thumbs up and a wicked grin. After that dirty play by Moira, I'd do anything to see her miserable in that bee suit.

She paled at the look in my eyes. "Err. Of course we can. What would you like, sir?"

Mr. Jeffers rattled off an ambitious flower order. We charged him an arm and a leg to have it done and delivered today, and when he hung up, I clapped my hands together. "We're all doing the delivery today, so no one can cheat."

Moira gasped in mock offense. "I would never."

Tess burbled a warbly laugh. "No one wins Park Place and Boardwalk every single game of Monopoly."

Ash laughed. "True story."

"I'm heading to the back to get this done. We'll leave right when the shop closes. Tomorrow morning, first thing in the a.m., Moira is in the bee suit, and Ash is apple central." Tomorrow was going to be epic.

"Hardly," Moira scoffed. "I can't wait to see you trying to handle cash wearing that thing."

But I knew in my bones I was going to win. "I guess we'll see." Flicking my hands, I waved them away. "Everyone back to work. We've got two hours before quitting time."

THE TEAM rarely did deliveries together. Tess and Ash were

crammed in the backseat, each holding on to one side of the massive basket of flowers I'd made for Mr. Jeffers.

I was in the driver's seat, and Moira quivered with anticipation in the passenger seat.

"You really outdid yourself with this one," Ash commented. "It's gorgeous."

"Thanks!" I'd added a few extras in because I was feeling generous. The basket spilled over with roses, daisies, peonies, baby's breath, and numerous other flowers. A heady fragrance rose in the air, calming my nerves as we exited the highway. Fredericksburg and the surrounding areas didn't usually have a ton of traffic, but I'd always been a nervous driver. There was something about being responsible for a two-ton vehicle while also being responsible for everyone and everything else in the vehicle with you and ensuring you stayed alert for anyone outside of the vehicle making mistakes.

I preferred taking my bicycle for most deliveries, but some, like this one, required a vehicle. Moira offered to drive, but I declined. Getting over my fear required immersive therapy. Even if my knuckles were bone white as they clenched the steering wheel.

"You can afford a driver, you know," Moira said quietly, as I took a corner going about 15 miles per hour.

The temp dropped about ten degrees—Tess's way of silently agreeing. I'd never heard her wail, and I hoped I never would, because being in an enclosed space with her required sweaters and sometimes gloves. Hearing a full-on banshee wail might require a healer.

"She drives like a grandma on downers," Ash muttered under his breath.

"Shut it," I growled. "This is necessary."

"Is it though?" Moira asked.

"I'll get over my fear one day. I just need to take more out-of-town deliveries."

"Or you could leave them to us and save us from your bad driving," Ash said helpfully from the back.

"When you lose, I'm going to harvest all those apples and not give you a single slice of pie later," I muttered.

"Cruel mistress," Ash said with a sigh.

"I'm immortal, but I feel like I'm dying in slow motion," Tess whined.

Moira barked a laugh. Tess so rarely made a joke, my lips twitched.

"Very funny." But I added a bit of pressure to the gas pedal to keep the peons quiet.

It took twice as long as it should have, but we finally pulled up in front of a massive estate with wrought-iron gates. I gawked at the entrance as we slowly pulled up to the speaker and keypad.

"State your business," a dry voice crackled over the speaker.

"Delivery for Mr. Wayne Jeffers. I'm Evie Quinn from Little Shop of Florals."

The keypad beeped, and the gate swung open, revealing a large circular driveway.

"Guess we're good," I whispered.

"Make sure you go fast enough so the gate doesn't close on the van," Ash said.

"Piss off, tree." I rolled through the gate in more than enough time, sending Ash a dark glare through the rearview mirror.

He snickered.

Moira rolled her window down and put her head out, gaping at the expansive house. "This place is crazy," she breathed.

"Still think he's cheating?" I asked.

"Oh yeah. More so now than before."

I pulled up to the front door. Moira and Ash got out, but Tess elected to stay in the car. The sun was out today, though it was just setting behind the tree cover. Summer was Tess's nemesis, and she rarely went out unless she had to. I never asked if it was a banshee or a Tess thing, and she never offered any information.

Moira and Ash each took a handle, gently extricating the basket from the seat.

"Watch the steps," I cautioned, staying close behind them just in case one of them lost their balance. When we stood at the massive blue door, I gave the arrangement a last critical eye, providing a boost to a few petals a little worse for the wear after travel. Once I was satisfied every bloom was in the best possible shape, I turned, smoothed my hands down my blouse, and rang the doorbell.

While we were waiting for someone to answer the door, a shiny BMW pulled through the gate and parked behind our van. A tall, handsome man exited the driver's side and hurried up the steps.

"Oh shit," Moira whispered. "That's Mr. Jeffers."

"Here we gooooo," Ash said with glee.

A strange moan came from the van. Even Tess was getting into the drama.

"I'm so glad I timed this correctly," the man breathed as he stopped next to me. "Have you rung the doorbell yet?"

I nodded stupidly.

"Good." He took a deep breath. "I hope this works." Mr. Jeffers glanced down at the flowers. "Oh. Wow. Impressive. Worth the extra money."

His eyes crinkled when he smiled, and I was charmed in spite of myself. I hoped this guy wasn't a cheater. He seemed like a good dude.

Moira and I gave each other a confused look. Footsteps sounded from inside, and the door creaked open, revealing a lean, dark-haired man. He had bright blue eyes and salt and pepper hair, and offered a polite smile when he saw me, which widened when he saw the basket.

"Goodness. He outdid himself this time, didn't he?"

Mr. Jeffers stepped forward. The man looked up, eyes widening when he saw who stood before him. "Wayne," he breathed.

"Liam." Mr. Jeffers reached out and took Liam's hands.

I winced and motioned for Moira and Ash to set the basket down. "Come on," I whispered. They set the flowers to the side and walked down the steps.

"I am so sorry. For everything." Mr. Jeffers inhaled and bowed his head. "This is the last delivery. I'm here to see if you'd consider giving me a second chance." He dropped down to one knee and pulled something from his jacket pocket.

"That woman wasn't his wife," I said with quiet glee.

Moira swore viciously under her breath. Ash let out a long sigh. And we stood there and watched Mr. Jeffers propose to the apparent love of his life, who accepted with a shout of delight.

Tess leaned out the window. "Mrs. Jeffers is his sister."

Ash and Moira spun, identical looks of astonishment on their faces. I let out a loud laugh and opened the van door.

"You little—you knew the whole time?" Moira sputtered.

Tess gave a tiny little grin, leaned back, and rolled up the window.

"She's a menace," Ash muttered.

I waved at the two men, but they were so wrapped up in each other they didn't notice. I was glad they'd already paid me.

When I started to get back into the car, Moira nudged me. "Nope. I'm driving home."

"I need to stop at least once," I tried to argue. Even after making the bouquet for Mr. Jeffers, I hadn't expended enough magic.

"Then we'll stop. Just point out the place, and I'll pull over."

"Fine." I dropped the keys in her hand. Once we were settled in, she pulled out of the driveway and back onto the country road.

"How'd you find out about Mrs. Jeffers?" Ash asked Tess a few minutes later.

"The internet," Tess said simply. "There's a picture of them together on her social media and the caption is congratulating her big brother on his promotion. Of all people, I wouldn't think you'd assume she was a traditionalist and automatically took her husband's name. Mrs. Jeffers kept her maiden name." The banshee paused. "I guess it was an easy assumption to make. If you're living in 1955." She smiled sweetly at him and popped her headphones in.

Ash stared at her open-mouthed, then shook his head. "Why didn't I think of that?"

"I didn't either," Moira said darkly.

Fingers of dusk brushed across the sky as we drove, streaks of orange and purple turning the sunset into a glorious riot of color. Now that I wasn't white knuckling the steering wheel, I could get a better look at the landscape on either side of us. This part of the state was an odd mix of wide-open spaces, scrubby plants, and rolling hills crammed with native plants and wildflowers.

"Over there," I pointed. A large hill filled with flowers of all colors lay about half a mile ahead. It'd be the perfect place to release some magic. As a bonus, or maybe not for the locals, by tomorrow it'd be a picturesque stopping point for tourists heading into wine country.

Moira pulled the vehicle over, and I slipped out. "Give me half an hour."

"Be careful." Moira turned the car off and unbuckled her seatbelt. "If you're not back in forty-five, we're coming to find you."

I smiled. "You know I can take care of myself."

Moira grinned. "It's not you I'm worried about."

I laughed and shut the door. Fresh, hill country air ruffled my hair as I kicked off my sandals and set them on top of the hood. I loosened my hair from my ponytail and shrugged off my cardigan, neatly folding it and setting it beside my shoes. In just my tank top and a pair of loose linen pants, I walked off the side of the road and up the hill.

No traffic passed by. Moira turned off the headlights and darkness fell, but I had no trouble seeing.

Cernunnos' words—the words I'd shoved away for over a week now—surfaced in my mind. Embrace who I was meant to be.

But who was I?

As I strolled, flowers bloomed under my feet. Vines stretched from below the surface and slithered along the ground. Tree branches reached down and gently brushed strands of hair away from my face. Magic poured from my body, soaking into the earth, the release weeks in the making. Once I reached the top of the hill, I sat cross-legged on the ground and closed my eyes, content for the first time in weeks.

CHAPTER

Nine

CAELAN

She was so fucking beautiful. I lay low to the ground in wolf form, peering through a canopy of wispy flowers. Her power beat through the earth, pulsing all around me, peaceful and content. The air was charged with magic, unlike anything I'd ever felt before.

I'd been following her for a week now, with absolutely nothing to show for it. Evie went to work. She went home. And she went back to work. I hadn't even seen her go to the grocery store.

It was maddening. Evie was young, beautiful, and powerful. Why was she living such a lonely existence?

Her hair had grown at least three inches. Brightly colored flowers wove through the dark strands. Evie's eyes glowed a swirling mix of pink and green, and a soft smile rested on her lips. Blooming vines curled around her wrists and arms, and her bare feet were buried deep into the soil.

The trees stretched and groaned as Evie's magic fortified them, the leaves a dry rattle in the gentle wind. Owls hooted and swooped through the air. But then the strangest thing happened.

A raven cut through the air on wings of ebony, heading straight for Evie. My muscles bunched, but I waited. If it came close enough to attack her, I would act, but it would ruin any hope of peace between us if she caught me stalking her.

Just as I was poised to leap, the raven's cry shattered the night air, and it banked, slowing its flight until it lowered its feet and landed right on Evie's shoulder.

What in the world?

Evie reached up and stroked the raven behind the neck. "Hey Poe. Haven't seen you in a while."

"Called home."

"Mmm. You okay?"

"Hurt."

"I know," she said quietly. "Glad you're back."

The raven nuzzled her cheek.

"Moira and the others are in the van if you want a ride home."

"Stay."

"I'm almost finished." Evie inhaled and raised her hands, palms up. Swirling balls of magic rose from her fingers, and she gently batted them into the air. With a soft sigh, she rose, gently extricating herself from the flora. The floating balls of power swirled around her as she headed down the hill, the raven still on her shoulder.

I rose and slowly crept behind her, carefully navigating all the extra plant life.

When she reached the van, she flicked her hand and the glowing balls rose and flew in different directions, painting the ground in a wash of tourmaline colored magic.

Evie turned, giving one last look to the land she'd cleansed and refreshed, and locked eyes with me.

Shit.

Evie's raven shot into the sky in a blur of feathers and wings. Magic boomed, flowing from her body like a percussive blast. The ground under my feet shifted and buckled, tossing me off balance.

I hit the ground, landing hard on my side. Grunting in pain, I scrambled to my feet.

Evie's eyes had gone from the soft colors of a watermelon tourmaline to the color of a blood ruby.

I backed up a few steps in surprise. What the hell?

A soft cry escaped her lips before she turned, hauling her shoes and cardigan from the top of the vehicle's hood, and scrambled into the van.

The driver peeled out, gravel flying in all directions. Seconds later, the only thing I could see were headlights disappearing into the horizon.

CHAPTER
Ten

"Put your head between your knees and breathe." Moira's voice was low and urgent.

A strangled cry escaped me. I bent over, my entire body shaking.

The vampire's cool hand rested on my back. "Deep breaths, Evie. In and out."

I dragged in a ragged breath and exhaled.

"Good. Keep going."

We raced down the highway, the vampire barely braking as we flew around curves.

I'd almost shifted. It was so close I felt the Chimera magic overpowering my Floromancy. Fangs had slipped from my teeth, and the first stirrings of fur rose on the back of my neck.

So close. Too close.

"Someone was out there," I croaked once I could speak.

"Who?" Moira demanded.

"Shifter. I think. Glowing eyes." I let out a deep exhale. "I couldn't make out a form. The foliage was too high, and the beast was crouching. I can't believe I didn't sense it the entire time I was out there. Stupid of me."

Ash leaned forward, hands on either side of the seat. "No.

Never. I wouldn't have expected anyone out here. We're in the middle of nowhere."

"Do you want me to see if I can find out who it was?" Tess asked.

Banshees had a mist form. She could easily track the shifter or whatever it was. Shifter didn't feel completely right. The eyes weren't right for a shifter, but its magic had been locked down, probably to keep me from sensing its presence. I hated to think I'd allowed the creature to get so close because I was distracted. Being distracted could get me killed.

"You don't mind?" I asked, finally able to sit up now that the threat of shifting had passed.

"Not at all. It's a nice night."

"Then please see what you can find out." I turned and gave Tess a grateful smile, but the banshee had already turned to mist and slipped from the car.

Ash stared at the window she'd disappeared from. "She's unnerving sometimes." He rubbed his hands over his arms and sighed. "Think she'll be okay?"

Moira laughed. "You worrywart. She's a banshee. I think she'll outlast us all."

"You're probably right." But he didn't stop looking out the window trying to catch a glimpse of her.

TESS POPPED BACK into the shop an hour later. She was silent as the grave anyway, but when she was in mist form, you couldn't hear or see her coming, especially if the lights were dim.

Moira's yelp of fright and subsequent swearing made me and Ash laugh.

"Tess is back," he announced.

"No shit!" Moira called. "Tess. Moan or something next time."

The banshee rolled her eyes and reverted to human form. "Like I can help when I moan."

I hid my smile behind my hand and poured her a cup of tea from the carafe sitting on top of the table we were sitting around.

She took it with a grateful smile and curled into her favorite chair. Ash got up and arranged a fuzzy blanket around her. Tess never complained, but her mist form took quite a bit of energy, and when she came back to her human form, it took her several hours to warm up to normal temperature. Curling her hands around the mug, she inhaled the brew and sighed.

"My sense of smell is not as acute as yours and Moira's, but I believe you're dealing with some kind of shifter. Unfortunately, he or she was long gone by the time I went back to the area."

"Could you tell if it was a lone wolf?" Moira asked.

"No way to tell, but what faint scent I picked up was new. The spot you chose does not have any other shifters who've visited recently."

"It's Caelan," I muttered, scrubbing a hand over my face.

"Let's not jump to conclusions," Ash warned.

"It has to be," I insisted. "He might not know who I am yet, but he suspects." It took a while for the clues to click into place. The golden eyes were a dead giveaway.

Moira's lips thinned. "I agree with Evie. He hasn't been in power for this long by being a fool."

"Even if it is, his presence is not our biggest problem," Ash said, his eyes on me.

I groaned. "I can't help it. If I'm in danger, the power always rises up."

"Maybe you should let it." Ash's eyes held no judgment, but I looked away all the same.

"I can't." Memories of my time in Hazel's cabin assailed me. "I'm too dangerous." I'd almost killed her several times during those first two treacherous weeks. "Hazel should have left me to my own devices. She's lucky to be alive."

"Hazel made her choice," Moira said. "No one deserved what happened to you."

"Maybe not, but sometimes I wonder if it would be better for everyone if she'd put me out of my misery instead of carrying me back to her place."

Moira's eyes flashed emerald. "Don't ever say that. None of us would be here if you'd died."

Ash scooted closer. "She's right, Evie. You aren't a monster."

I snorted. "That's where you're wrong. I'm more than a monster. I'm the thing that nightmares are made of."

"That seems like an overly dramatic statement," Tess observed.

Moira burst out laughing and tried to cover it with a cough, but it was too late. I sent her a dark look. She ducked her head and gave me an apologetic look.

"Maybe it seems that way to us," she said to Tess, "but we never had to experience what Evie's going through."

Tess lifted a slim shoulder in a shrug. "Why shouldn't we be who we are? Isn't that what Evie always tells us?"

You know...getting your good advice tossed back into your face during a low moment was not awesome.

Moira sent me a look. "I think Evie is a little frightened of who she might become if she were to fully embrace the Chimera's magic. That's why she's suppressing it."

Tess stared at Moira. "I'm a banshee. Everyone who knows what I am is scared of me. I've never had a boyfriend, much less an orgasm, because making any noise other than regular conversation must mean I'm trying to kill them, right? If I can still be myself, when the whole world is terrified of what I might do, why can't she?"

The banshee rose and poofed into mist again, slipping through the front door of the shop and disappearing into the darkness.

No one spoke for a long time. Ash gave me a look dripping with judgment and rose, hurrying outside after Tess.

Moira, who'd been my friend the longest, sat there silently for a moment before clearing her throat.

"Tess is right, you know."

I closed my eyes and flopped my head back against the couch

cushion. "What the fuck," I whispered to myself before letting out a loud groan. "You're going to be really sorry when I finally shift and eat you all like a BOGO appetizer special."

Moira chuckled. "First lesson, Evie. Friends are not food."

I cracked an eye open and glared at her. "As worrisome as my issue is, are we not going to talk about Tess's lack of orgasms?"

Moira's lips pursed. "I don't think it will be a problem for much longer," she said cryptically.

My eyes narrowed as I tried to figure out the cryptic tone to her words. Then I looked at the door and my mouth fell open. "You think?"

My gaze went back to Moira. "No way."

"His heartbeat picks up every time she's in the room." Moira's lips tugged up. "And when she wore that cute little fifties dress for Halloween last year—"

I held my hand up. "Nope. That's enough of that."

She laughed. "I'm not even sure Tess realizes Ash is smitten with her."

I blew out a breath. "We will not be the ones to tell her, either."

"Not a chance. Those two will have to figure their own stuff out."

I mulled it over. "A dryad and a banshee. You think it will work?"

"Stranger things have happened," Moira said cryptically. She rose and picked the tea carafe up. "No more for you. This blend will help you sleep and make it easier to interpret your dreams."

I stared down at my mug. "Dammit, Moira! You dosed me again?"

She rolled her eyes and picked up my empty mug. "Every blend I have is magical. It's your own fault, really."

"How am I supposed to get home?"

Moira washed out the teapot and mug, carefully setting both on the drying rack. "Your ride home is a bicycle, and the tea is mild. It's not like last time."

Last time was when I fell into a dead faint about thirty seconds after my last sip. Moira aptly named that blend "Coma," but didn't tell me until the next day when I rolled into work two hours late feeling like I'd gone three rounds with a pro boxer.

I gave her a dubious look that made her laugh. She threw her hands up in surrender. "I promise! You'll be fine."

Shaking my head, I rose and stretched. Every muscle in my body felt tense. "Beekeeper suit is in the locked hall closet." I grinned. "See you tomorrow for our weekly market trip."

"I hate you," Moira muttered, but the words held no heat.

"Sore loser." I pulled out my brand-new cell phone as I walked to the door, and had a moment where I wondered if I should go back and try to find my old one. "I'm going to text Ash and Tess to make sure they remember." A frown marred my brow. "And apologize."

"Good idea." Moira wiggled her fingers in a wave. "See you tomorrow. Meet at the gate?"

"You know it."

THE RIDE HOME WAS UNEVENTFUL, but my nerves wouldn't settle down. It felt like someone was watching me the entire time, which should have been impossible unless they were running across the rooftops to keep up. Bicycles could squeeze through places cars couldn't, so I picked up my speed, dodging any darker areas in favor of well-lit roads, until I was inside my locked gate. I left my bike on the porch and hurried inside, triple-checking all the locks and windows.

Even with Moira's tea, it took a while to fall asleep. My anxiety was higher than it had been in years, and I couldn't help feeling like I was barreling toward something I wasn't ready for.

When sleep finally came, I dreamed of golden eyes and spring breezes.

CHAPTER

Eleven

Ash and Tess stood at the market gate the next morning. The banshee hadn't responded to my text from last night, and relief filled me when I spotted her. Tess was the youngest of all of us, early twenties, and was still learning to deal with her emotions in a healthy way. Screaming, like most banshees did when they were angry, would injure us all, and it was one of the few rules I'd laid down when Tess came to work for me. The only time she could use that particular deadly power was in a life-or-death situation.

Our eyes locked. I dropped the basket I held, gave her a hesitant smile, and when an answering one tugged her lips up, I let out a small sigh and hurried over to bring her into a hug. Tess gave a huff of laughter and wrapped her arms around me.

"I'm sorry," I whispered in her ear.

"Me too."

"No. You were right, and I was wrong, Tess. It's difficult for me. I have a lot of feelings surrounding what happened to me and what it caused." I stepped back and held her by the arms. "But I promise, I will try."

Silvery tears glittered in her eyes. "We should all be ourselves."

I nodded. "We should."

Ash's eyes softened, and he opened his mouth to speak before something caught his attention and a hoarse wheeze sounded from his throat.

Tess's brow furrowed. I turned only to see Moira waddling up to us in a canary yellow bee suit. Glowing honeybees floated around the hood.

I pressed my lips together. Tess's soft laughter echoed around us.

"Shut it," Moira growled as she stomped up to us. The bees angrily buzzed at the words. Her eyes narrowed. "Is there something you aren't telling me about this suit?" she demanded. "Almost every time I speak, they get angry."

I grinned.

"Evie! Dammit!"

The bees swirled around her face, bobbing and weaving, their buzzing drowning out the sound of conversation around us.

"If you lie or curse, the bees get...reactive."

Moira closed her eyes. "How long do I have to wear this stupid suit?"

The bees buzzed again.

"Stupid is not a cuss word!"

The bees did not agree.

"Until the end of the day," I said through my laughter.

She made a disgusted noise. "Which is?"

I glanced at Ash. "How long before you can grow those apples?"

"Once we finish up here, we'll go back to the shop. Should be a few hours. No more than five." He shrugged. "Nature is on its own schedule."

"Okay weirdo," Moira grumbled.

The gates to the market opened. I shook my basket at my friends. "You know what to do. Meet back here in an hour?"

Ash gave a little salute. Tess rolled her eyes. Moira swatted angrily at the magical bees buzzing around her.

"Right." Rolling my eyes, I headed inside.

The Joy Springs Market was only open on weekends, and if you didn't get there right when the gates opened, there was a good chance the shops would be out of stock when you finally arrived. I headed straight for the egg guy first because he was always out of duck eggs if I got here even half an hour past opening time.

March, my egg guy, was an odd bird. He wore mismatched clothing, old sandals that had looked like they were on their last legs for at least the past three years, and a pristine Rolex. His hair was sandy blond and pushed back with a brightly colored bandana, and he had a perpetual California surfer tan. His teeth were blinding white, and when he smiled, it reminded me of Ross on that episode when he bleached his teeth and they glowed under UV light.

"Hey March," I greeted.

"Heya Evie!" He reached into his cooler. "Two dozen today?"

He set them on the fold-out table separating us, and I picked them up and put them in my basket.

"Yup. You got anything else I might be interested in?"

March looked shifty on a good day, but today he made an odd little slouching motion and held up a finger. Intrigued in spite of myself, I leaned over the table to see what he was doing. He hissed and waved at me to get back.

I held up both hands and leaned back, curious but not willing to risk his wrath. March was always a little weird. Not unstable, but poking the bear seemed unwise.

Shuffling noises came from the bag that he dug in, and when he straightened, he held a small box.

I looked at him. "What is it?"

"Something special," he promised. "You interested?"

Why was he acting so weird? "Err. Sure?"

March set the box down and carefully opened it. "I know you have the magic," he whispered. "So you're the only one who should have this."

I froze. The Joy Springs Market was not a magical market. We had one, but it only came once a month, and it was a process to get into. This market was for humans only. An awkward laugh escaped me. "Okay, March. I'll bite. What is it?"

Once he opened the box, he slid it across the table. I peered inside and sucked in a gasp. "Where did you get this?" I asked urgently as I shut the flaps of the box.

"A nest in a magical land." March waved his hand around and giggled. "A gift to the lovely flower lady."

"A gift?"

"Free for Evie lady. Take it, take it." He giggled again.

I hurriedly took the box and put it in my basket, then tugged the scarf tied around my purse off and secured the box so it wouldn't move around too much. "Are you sure? I can pay you, March."

He waved a hand. "No. Gift for flower lady."

I took out the money for the duck eggs and shoved it into his hands. "Then I thank you, March. And I'm glad you only showed this to me. Have you told anyone else about it?"

March put his index finger over his lips and made a shhh noise. "Magic is secret, Evie."

Yes, yes, it is. Oh March. I reached over and touched his hand. "Do you have any flowers for me today?"

He nodded eagerly and motioned for me to go to his truck. A quick sweep of the crowd revealed nothing amiss, so I stepped around the table and headed back with him.

March had tons of plants, but not a lot of money for nutrients or fertilizers. When I first started visiting, he noticed my presence boosted his plants, something no one else would have put together. After the first couple of visits, he brought even more plants and asked me to touch them.

I sensed nothing magical in March, but he had an odd gift for seeing things, magical things, and I hoped it wouldn't one day bite him in the ass.

March pointed to the back of his truck. I peered over and

laughed at the dozens of potted plants reaching toward me. "Did you bring all of them today?"

He grinned. "They're hungry." His smile faltered. "But so am I."

My heart squeezed. "Well, how about I juice them up really good for you?"

March's face lit up. "Will you? For how long?"

I smiled. "How about a month? Will that work?"

"A whole month?" He nodded eagerly. "Thank you, flower lady!"

"My pleasure. Keep an eye out for me, will you, March? Make sure no one is coming?"

His head bobbed, and he turned away and crossed his arms like a tomb guard. I swept the area one more time to make sure there were no prying eyes around and called up my power.

His plants loved him, but they, as March had known, were nutrient deficient. They had plenty of light, plenty of water, and plenty of care, but March didn't have access to good soil.

He only had what the ground provided, and with current farming and agricultural practices, as well as the human footprint, even the earth was deficient in nutrients. I sent a thread of power out and touched each plant, boosting the soil's health and adding nitrogen, calcium, and phosphorus where needed. Some needed more magnesium and sulfur than others, and so I spoke quickly to each plant until they were all well fed and satisfied.

When I called my magic back, the plants let out a collective sigh, their leaves stretching away from me and toward the sky. I smiled and shook the excess magic from my hands.

March was still facing away when I hopped out of the bed of his truck.

"All done. You may see some rapid growth and even some odd blooming. No need to worry. They haven't been properly fed in a while, and all they're doing is adjusting."

He turned around and peered inside the truck, a wide smile

turning his lips up when he spotted how green and glossy his plants were.

"Thank you, lovely Evie!"

"You're welcome, March." I fished inside my purse for another twenty and handed it to him. "I want you to get something for you to eat tonight. Do you have somewhere to cook?"

March stared at the bill in my hand. "I can't. You keep it. I have enough."

I took his hand and pressed the bill into his palm. "I insist. Besides, I should be paying you for letting me hang out with your plants."

His eyes widened, and he shoved the bill in his pocket. "Th—thank you. I'm going to get some beans tonight and make a big pot! It will last me a whole week!"

"You do that, March." I gathered my basket and patted him on the back. "See you next week."

"Okay, lovely flower lady!"

I left him standing over his plants, cooing to them.

AN HOUR LATER, I waited by the front entrance, feeling nervous as a cat. I'd gotten what I needed for home as well as for the shop, but March's box had me antsy. I shouldn't have taken it from him, but if anyone knew what he had, they'd kill him for it. At least with me, I'd have a fighting chance if someone came after it.

Ash was the first to return. His canvas bag was filled to the brim with dried fruit, herbs, and fresh greens. Tess came next, her bag filled with fresh bread and baked goods.

Moira didn't show up for another ten minutes, still swatting at those bees.

Her bag was empty.

"Uh. Moira?"

She made a disgusted noise. "I can't pick anything up! Every time I do, my gloves stick to it! I am walking flypaper!" Moira huffed and threw her bag down. "I'm never making another bet for as long as I live."

The bees' buzzing rose in volume.

"Oh! Piss off, bees!"

Ash snickered. Tess dug into her bag and offered Moira a scone. I turned so the vampire wouldn't see my grin.

"How am I supposed to eat that, Tess?" Moira screeched. "Hoooowwwww?"

"You take that hood off and eat it," Tess explained, like Moira was a recalcitrant toddler.

"I'm scared of getting stung," Moira grumbled. "Can we go home now?"

I bent down to pick up her bag. "We can go, you big baby. Meet you back at the shop. There's something I need to talk to you about."

Ash's brows went up. "Everything okay?"

I glanced down at my bag. "I'm not sure yet."

CHAPTER

Twelve

We all stared down at the pearlescent glittering egg nestled on a bundle of hay inside the box March had given me.

"Holy shit," Ash breathed. "Is that what I think it is?"

"Yup," I said unhelpfully.

Tess moaned and floated away, tugging at a lock of her hair.

Moira whistled low. "Your mother is going to shit a brick when she finds out."

I hesitated for a moment before saying, "What if she doesn't find out?"

Ash's attention jerked from the egg to me. "You want to do what? Become an incubator for a magical bird and keep it hidden from your mother? The owner of the only three magical birds whose song can resurrect the dead?"

I grimaced. "Umm. Yes?"

Ash threw his hands up. "Madness, I tell you."

I didn't keep many secrets from Tess, Moira, and Ash. They knew about my attack, the pertinent bits of my past, and that my mother was Cliona, a Tuatha fae and Queen of the Banshees.

While it was a cool tidbit for mythology trivia, no one wanted my mother around. Getting involved with the gods was a real quick way to get dead.

"I won't keep it here," I promised. "I'll keep it at the house."

"Why don't you just give it back to your mom?" Moira asked.

I shook my head. "It's hard to explain. The way it came to me...I don't think I'm supposed to." I looked up at them help-lessly. "Call me crazy. I feel like this bird was supposed to come to me."

A flap of wings sounded seconds before Poe landed on my shoulder. We never knew how he got in, but he always managed to find me, no matter where I was.

"She barely let you get away with that one," Ash said, his eyes lingering on Poe.

I reached up to stroke the raven's ruff. "She didn't have a choice. Poe broke away of his own free will."

"Cliona," Poe croaked.

"Yeah." I craned my neck to look up at him. "What do you think we should do?"

The bird ruffled its feathers and peered down at the egg. "Stay."

"And my mother?"

"Bad mother," Poe croaked.

Ash snorted. "Understatement of the year."

Poe hopped off my shoulder and flapped to the table. I sucked in a hissing breath, and Poe turned to peer up at me as if to say, "Really?" He hopped right into the box, ruffled his butt feathers and sat right on top of the egg.

"Baby cold."

Ash's eyes softened. "Aww," he cooed. "You're going to be a good mother, Poe."

Poe squawked. "Better than Cliona."

The vampire laughed. She stroked Poe's silky head and stepped away. "I think we should raise it in the shop."

Ash blinked. "And if Cliona shows up?"

Moira lifted a shoulder in a shrug. "She's never shown up before, and our shop is warded against her. We can hire Marnie to put a glamour on the bird so she can be out when the customers are here. Lots of places have parrots."

"And when she doesn't sound like a parrot?" I asked, wondering if this was a terrible idea.

"Parrots are known mimics, and humans like to believe what's easiest." Moira shook her head. "The way the egg came to you is bizarre, and I don't believe in coincidence. Poe says it should stay, so it should stay. The raven has been right more times than I'd care to admit."

I looked at Ash. He sighed and threw his hands up again. "Fine. If one of us is grievously injured, maybe it can heal us."

Tess moaned from her place by the register.

Moira's lips twitched. "We need a yes or no, kiddo."

The banshee sighed. "I want to see the egg one more time."

"Poe." The raven stood and hopped from the box. Tess floated over and hovered close. She leaned over and held her hand over the egg. Silvery gray magic glittered from her fingers and floated down to settle over the egg.

I held my breath. Tess rarely used her other magic. She'd warded the shop against other spirits and ghosts and had once created a death sigil she wouldn't discuss, but I'd never seen her do anything like this.

Her eyes flashed white. "Cliona has not touched this egg."

Ash's brow furrowed. "How?" he breathed.

Tess's power saturated the air. "The mother smuggled the baby out. It was meant to find you."

The power abruptly snapped off. Tess floated to the ground. "I put a silencing spell around the egg. Its magic hums and will attract curiosity." She gave me a tight smile. "The baby will be safe here now."

And with that, Tess floated away.

No one said anything for a long moment.

Ash shook his head and exhaled a shaky breath. "Well. Guess it's staying."

Poe hopped back into the box and settled back onto the egg.

I rubbed a hand over my face. "Does anyone know where I can find an incubator?"

Guess I was going to be a bird mom.

MONDAY MORNING CAME WAY TOO bright and early. The egg was secured in my office with Poe acting as incubator. I wasn't too worried about it right now. Once it hatched, it would be a different story. Tess was off today, and Ash was in the back growing apples because the bird and the weekend got in the way.

With Moira manning the register, I was walking around the shop, siphoning my magic and giving everything a boost. My orchids were in full bloom, purple, white and pink flowers on full display in the shop's window. African Violets bloomed on one of the floating shelves, and I had grow lights on a couple of things that shouldn't be indoors. I was a lot of things, but not sunshine, so even with my magic, some things still needed a boost.

I gave extra attention to those and then went over to the pothos. As I was tending the soil, the bell rang, announcing new customers. Power prickled over my skin.

Moira was usually quick to greet anyone walking into the shop, but when I heard nothing, I poked my head from around the corner to make sure everything was okay.

Caelan stood there with Simone and another shifter, a lean, tall man with amber eyes who did not look friendly. At all. His hair was blond and shaggy, and his jaw, dusted with five o'clock shadow, could cut glass.

"Lord," Moira said evenly.

I wanted to disappear around the corner and pretend I'd never seen them, but they were shifters. As one, three sets of eyes found me. Simone grinned.

"Hey Evie!"

I came out from the corner and smiled. "Hey, Simone. I have something for you."

She gasped. "My plants? Already?" Her eyes lit up.

The strange wolf gave her a weird look.

Caelan held a hand up. "Let's discuss other business first, Simone."

I swallowed hard. This didn't sound good. "Sure!" I chirped. "How can I help?"

"Can we speak in your office?" Caelan's expression was unreadable. My magic flared in response to the question. The surrounding plants didn't feel anger from him, which was good to know, but I still felt unnerved.

The bell rang again, announcing another customer. Moira gave me a warning look before turning to greet the newcomer.

"Sure." I sent a whisper of power to the office. Poe would feel it and hopefully hide the egg. With Tess's silencing spell, Caelan and the other shifters shouldn't feel anything strange.

I led them to the back. Simone smiled when she walked in, her gaze skimming over the room, eyes alight with pleasure. The other wolf gave it a once-over for threats, but green things did not seem to impress him. Caelan was all business, though. He went straight to the table and opened the book of samples.

"We're having a Pack gathering and would like to hire you for the floral arrangements." Caelan gestured for Simone. "Come and look through this. I'd like the focal piece to have crimson flowers."

Simone hurried over to flip through the book.

The Shifter Lord turned to me. "This is my Beta, Garrett."

I nodded to the shifter.

"Garrett, this is Evie Quinn. She's the owner of this shop and a talented…" Caelan paused. "Plant mage."

My lips twitched. "Floromancer, actually," I corrected.

Garrett's teeth pulled away from his lips. "Your magic is flowers?" The way he said it pissed me off. Like flowers were beneath him. Magic rumbled in the room. My magic. And not my Floromancy. There was a beat of silence before I spoke.

"Nature is the most powerful force on earth," I said evenly.

Garrett's eyes narrowed on me.

Caelan's eyes flared gold. "Don't be rude, Garrett." His voice came out in a raspy growl. "Evie is the most talented florist in town."

My nostrils flared. I was far more than a florist. Was this insult Evie day? I cleared my throat. "What day is your event?"

Simone answered. "Two weeks from today."

I had zero desire to work for Caelan again. He'd paid quickly when the funeral flowers were delivered, but I had a rare opening on the books, and I was trying my best to stay on good terms and get him out of my shop. But I didn't want him coming around all the time.

I winced. "I'm so sorry. I don't have any availability for at least the next sixty days."

Garrett's eyes widened. Simone turned away from the book and stared at me. Caelan's fists clenched at his side. I slapped a polite smile on my face. "I was able to accommodate your last request due to a last-minute cancellation, but I normally have a three-month waiting list."

"You refuse the Shifter Lord?" Garrett growled.

"I'm a private business. I have the right to refuse service to anyone." I gave him a tight smile and walked to the shelf behind my desk. I'd put almost a dozen starter pots in a box lid for easy carrying.

Since Simone seemed so excited about the possibility of having a piece of all of my plants, I took cuttings of the ones that were easiest to grow and had been nurturing them to stay strong and hardy. She'd be hard pressed to kill anything I gave her.

I took the box down and tested the soil in a few of the pots with the tip of my index finger. "These won't need any water for at least the next few days," I said as I put the box down beside Simone.

Her eyes lit up. "Thank you—"

"Omega!" Garrett barked. "Do not accept gifts from this...this..."

"Florist?" I said dryly.

His eyes flashed silver. "Your disrespect is going to get you killed one day."

I blinked. "Excuse me?" My power rumbled through the air. Simone jerked her hand away and stood, an apologetic look flashing over her face. "Are you threatening me?"

Garrett took a step toward me. "I don't need to threaten you. If I wanted to kill you, you'd never see me coming."

I grinned, letting a little of the Evie who was not a Floromancer out, my mother's daughter and enough Chimera to make him stop and blink. "I'd like to see you try, dog."

Simone sucked in a breath.

"Garrett!" Caelan barked. "Stand down."

The Shifter Lord got between us, his back facing me. "Peace, Garrett."

"She's a tainted bitch," he spat.

My stomach dropped. What did he mean by that? My magic was mixed, yes, but my tattoo protected the truth of my tainted blood. Had it failed?

"Garrett," Simone said softly. She walked over to him and touched his arm. I saw no magic coming from her, but his aggression rapidly cooled until it was almost completely gone. "Evie is not harmful."

He scoffed. "If you could see how she looks at me, you'd rethink that statement."

"I didn't come into your house and insult you multiple times," I snapped.

Caelan turned to face me. "My apologies, Evie. My Beta meant no harm."

I laughed. "The hell he didn't."

His jaw tightened. "I'm asking for your patience."

"I'm still standing here with my magic leashed, Shifter Lord.

Today, it's all the patience you deserve." I glanced at Simone. "Besides her. Simone is cool. Maybe just send her next time."

Simone closed her eyes as if she were asking for patience, and I almost laughed.

"I'll remember that," Caelan said, a touch of exasperation in his voice, before he turned to me. "We need your services, Evie."

"And I told you I was booked." I had no idea if I was or not, but the odds were good we'd have something on the books. If not, I'd find something to occupy us to keep from working with him again.

"Do you not want to work with the Pack?" he asked.

"I have no quarrel with the Pack. There are two other florists in the local area. Perhaps one of them might be available."

Gold flashed in Caelan's eyes. His jaw tightened. "There are no other Floromancers in this area." A short pause. "As I'm sure you know."

"One doesn't need to be a Floromancer to provide flowers for an event." My tone was polite but firm. "If that's all, I have several orders I need to fill. I'm happy to show you out."

Garrett snarled and turned on his heel, storming out of my office. Simone gave me an imploring look. I really did like her but having Caelan in my shop wasn't great for business.

Everyone just assumed I was in trouble or worse. Looky loos had already started peeking through my windows after his first visit. I couldn't imagine what would happen after this one.

"Simone, please give us a moment."

The Omega's face went white. "Of course." She hurried out of the room, leaving only me and the Shifter Lord.

He took a couple of steps until he was less than a foot away. His crackling power sparked against my skin. My heart beat like a frightened deer, but I stood my ground. Caelan's proximity bothered me more than this confrontation, and I was having trouble focusing my thoughts with him so close to me.

"While my Beta's reaction was regrettable," Caelan said, the timbre of his voice deeper than before, "it is in your best interest to accept this job."

"Oh?"

"You will find being in the good graces of one of the Shifter Lords will open doors."

"I have all the doors I can stand," I said through gritted teeth.

His storm gray eyes were clear and calm. "Perhaps. But you will find rebuffing one of the Lords comes with consequences."

My lips pulled away from my teeth in an angry snarl. "Are you threatening me, Lord?" Chimera power swirled in my veins begging to be used. I slowed my breath and calmed my beating heart. Giving any secret away to him would be deadly.

Caelan's eyes narrowed. "Why do you spurn me so, Evie?" His gaze flicked over my face before he took a step and walked a circle around me. "You stand there appearing as nothing more than a woman. A Floromancer as you say. Someone with the power to command plant life. A simple magic compared to mine. And yet, you stand before me and defy my will."

Defy his will? This arrogant, chauvinistic …

"Do you have a death wish?" My skin tingled everywhere he looked as he walked around me. When he faced me again, there was genuine curiosity on his face.

"Few people have death wishes."

"Then why won't you take this job?"

I studied him for a long moment. Caelan was angry, but he was also genuinely curious. He couldn't fathom why I didn't want to work with him. "Most people may fall at your feet to do your bidding, but my shop does well enough on its own."

His smile didn't reach his eyes. "Lovely Evie, you did not answer my question."

He called me lovely. I swallowed hard. "Why don't you want to use one of the other florists?"

"Again with the non-answer. Fine. One answer in exchange for yours. Fair?"

My nod was short.

"Simple. They are not you."

"They are talented and have good reviews. They'd fall all over themselves to do a job for you."

Caelan's scoff dripped with derision. "Everyone does."

"Humble," I remarked, my mouth too fast for my brain.

He grinned. "And that is why I want you. Because you don't want me. Do you know how refreshing that is?"

"Can't say that I do." I shook my head. "People who have power don't understand how it affects others. I don't want the extra scrutiny on my shop. I don't want to answer questions about you or have people try to cozy up to me because they think I have sway with you."

The entire thing bugged the hell out of me. "I also don't like the Pack coming into my shop and trying to strong arm me into doing your bidding."

Caelan's eyebrow went up. "You don't seem to understand how royalty works. I ask and I receive."

"You receive because people are afraid to refuse."

He took a step closer. Too close. "Are you afraid?"

I was already in it. Might as well say what I mean. "I'm more pissed off at your arrogance than anything."

His teeth flashed in a quick grin. Caelan reached out and tilted my chin up with his index finger. Our eyes met. "Your eyes remind me of the sea," he murmured.

"The sea is the most dangerous place on the planet."

His lips twitched. "Are you dangerous, flower girl?"

Caelan's thumb caressed my chin. Desire and awareness of his proximity rolled down my spine. He could snap my neck if he wanted to. I'd live, but if he thought I was pissed off now...

"Force me to do your event and you'll find out," I said breathily.

His chuckle danced along my skin. Warm and sensual, it held a promise. "How do I convince you to take this job? A promise of wealth? Prestige? A favor perhaps, saved for a rainy day?" His thumb brushed across my lips, lighting all my nerve endings on fire. "Tell me, and I will make it so."

Why didn't it feel like we were talking about flowers anymore? "I want for nothing."

"Liar," he whispered. "I sense something lying in wait deep inside you. Like an eye cracking open after a long period of rest. What awakens within you, little Floromancer?"

I tugged my chin out of his hand and changed the subject. "Simone forgot her plants."

He took my arm when I turned to get the box. "Leave it. I will get it for her."

"A Lord carrying an underling's things?"

"She is not an underling, Evie. Nor is Garrett."

"A friend then?" I asked, curiosity getting the better of me.

"Family," Caelan said.

"A Shifter Lord claims family not of his blood?"

"We are not like the other regions. You think me a brute. I see it in your eyes. Is this why you won't allow me to hire you?"

"I am not attracted to power, Lord."

"Caelan."

I held up my hand. "Absolutely not." A crack of laughter escaped me. "That right there is what I mean." I pointed at him and wiggled my finger in a circle. "You attempt to disarm me through warm familiarity. If I call you by your first name, I will feel special, *included*. More biddable."

Caelan's eyes crinkled at the edges before he let out a delighted laugh. "Biddable is the last word I'd use to describe you." He stepped closer, invading my personal space once more. "Tell me what I must do to secure your time and effort. It is only flowers, Evie."

We both knew it wasn't, but I felt myself caving. "You'll pay triple my fees and the cost of supplies."

"Done." Zero hesitation.

Dammit, Evie. Know when to reach for the stars.

"You'll provide a truck and send a representative to pick up the arrangement when I'm finished. I'll allot one employee to set up your displays, and you will pay whomever I choose double overtime."

"Done." He wiggled his eyebrows. "With a caveat."

"You aren't in the best bargaining position here, Lord."

Caelan's eyes glittered. This bastard was having a grand time. "You'll create one showpiece for the center of my table. I'll provide exact measurements when I return to the Keep but expect it to be at least two feet wide by four feet long. It should be a showcase of your talents, both mundane and magical."

I blinked. "You want a magical centerpiece."

"I do."

"It's—I can't. It's against the law. You know this." Joy Springs had quite a lot of flexibility when it came to practicing magic around humans because most dismissed what they were seeing as sleight of hand or trickery rather than the real thing. But if I created a floral centerpiece showcasing my Floromancy, everyone would realize it was real.

"Yes, if humans were there to witness it. This is a gathering solely for Joy Springs paranormals which means it is allowed."

I stared at him for a beat. On one hand, I loved the idea. Floromancers were one of the most dismissed types of mages. But on the other hand, my Floromancy was different from others, probably due to my demi-god heritage. My eyes narrowed. "A centerpiece that size is going to be astronomical."

Caelan shrugged. "I'm paying the cost."

"What kind of magic?"

He spread his hands out. "Don't care."

I snorted, a wicked idea forming in my mind. "I can do anything I want."

A grin tipped his lips up. "Anything at all."

"I don't want any credit for it. If anyone asks you who did the centerpiece, you will give anyone else but me the recognition."

His lips thinned. "Why." It was a demand, not a question.

I didn't want to get a reputation for being a Lord's sycophant. "Those are my terms, Lord."

"Caelan." He exhaled a heavy sigh. "Difficult woman. Fine. But I expect your best work." He handed me a business card. "My email and cell phone are listed. Text me the invoice once you have it."

"I require half up front—"

"Don't care. I'll pay the entire thing once I receive it."

"And if I make an error on the invoice?"

He waved my concerns away. "I'm good for it." Caelan stepped away and went to pick up the box. His sharp gaze skimmed over the plants before he looked at me. "Do you have any extra of the pink one?"

I blinked. "You want a plant from me?"

A slow grin curved his lips. "I want much more from you, flower girl. But I'll settle for a plant to begin with."

Color bloomed in my cheeks. I spun on my heel and hurried to my cutting shelf.

Caelan's wicked chuckle stiffened my spine. I squeezed my eyes shut, mentally pushed his suggestive laughter from my mind, and took one of the Pink Lady turtle vines down. Even though I was pissed, it wasn't the plant's fault. I bent over the little round ceramic pot and pushed a thread of power through the roots and soil, fortifying the cutting for the journey to Caelan's castle. Then, because I was feeling a little salty, I leaned and whispered a command to the plant and tipped my palm over the pot, depositing a glowing kernel of magic. Nothing naughty or mean, but something that might freak Caelan out.

When I turned, all traces of embarrassment had faded from my face. "I'll email you the care instructions."

He looked down at the teal pot I held. "The rest are in plastic. Are you sure I can take the pot?"

"She's still too young to move. Consider it a truce." I smiled tightly and handed him the cutting.

A tanned finger brushed over one of the small leaves. "Hello."

If he were anyone else, my heart would have melted, and I would have thrown myself at him for treating my plant like a sentient being. That's what people don't understand. All plants are sentient. They feel things, maybe not in the same way we do, but plants know love and pain and hunger and thirst.

The little turtle vine reached up and curled around Caelan's finger. The Shifter Lord gasped and, instead of freaking out, burst into delighted laughter.

Dammit.

"Is this your doing?" he asked, still fascinated by the plant.

"Yes and no. Plants require a lot of energy, and most of it is used for growing. They don't have any extra for other things."

His gaze lifted. "You gave it a boost?"

I tilted my head. "Perhaps."

The vine uncurled from his finger and folded in on itself. "This is amazing, Evie. I will cherish her."

Color touched my cheeks again. "You're welcome."

He offered me a tiny bow. "I will show myself out. Simone will send over the number of arrangements we need and the exact measurements for the main showpiece."

"Thank you for your business." I planned to charge him out the ass. If Little Shop of Florals was the worst deal in town, maybe the Shifter Lord would take his business elsewhere and things would get back to normal around here.

Caelan chuckled and left the room, his plant and Simone's box in his hands.

I waited until I heard the bell jingle before I let out a long groan of frustration and scrubbed my hands over my face.

A soft croak sounded. Poe popped out from under the desk and hopped onto the wrist I extended. "Hey. Sorry about that."

"Wolf man."

I chuckled. "Yes. The wolf man."

"Dangerous."

"He is." I stroked the back of his neck. "How's the baby?"

"Warm." Poe hopped off my wrist and flapped to the desk, then looked back.

"I'll get her."

Once Poe and the egg were situated close to the window, I shut the door and headed into the main area.

Moira and Ash fell silent when they saw me. A massive basket of shiny red apples sat on the counter. Break the news first. Pie second.

"We have a big job," I began.

Moira nudged Ash. "Pay up, bark boy."

I rolled my eyes as the dryad reached into his pocket and tossed a bill at her. "I thought you were better than that, Evie," Ash grumbled.

My jaw dropped. "Ash!"

"I knew you wouldn't say no," Moira said with a devilish glint in her eye. "Ash is just a sore loser."

"He sure is," I muttered, giving him a dark look. "In my defense, we're going to charge him so much that all of us can afford to shut down the shop for an entire month and take the trip to Europe we've been dying to go on." And then some, I didn't add. They'd find out when I bumped up their paychecks.

Moira and Ash stared. "Seriously?" Moira said. "You bargained with the Shifter Lord?"

"You have a death wish," Ash said with a shake of his head.

"I was trying to get him to leave. He insisted on hiring me." I shrugged. "I thought since he wasn't taking no for an answer, I could at least make it worth our while."

Moira grinned. "That's my girl."

"I'm not sure what the final numbers will be because I don't have all the information yet, but he's asking for a massive center-piece." A wicked grin spread over my face. "A magical center-piece. And I have a plan."

Ten minutes later, I found out my friends did not quite share the same sense of adventure I did.

"Are you insane?" Ash hissed.

The dryad was usually the voice of reason in our little quad of insanity.

Moira stood there frozen for a long moment. "You think embarrassing the Shifter Lord is a good idea?"

"There's no way to know if he'll be embarrassed. He asked for a display of power, and I'm going to give it to him."

My friend shook her head, but admiration glinted in Moira's eyes. "It's been a long time since someone pissed you off this much. Are you sure you want to do this?"

I rubbed my hands together gleefully. "I'm positive."

Thirteen

T he weeks passed uneventfully, and we settled into an easy, familiar rhythm once again. Normalcy was under-rated, I decided, as I dug elbow deep into a trough of perfectly balanced potting soil. I didn't normally grow every single flower for our arrangements because it would tax my magic too much on a daily basis. Or at least it used to. Before everything happened. For this, I planned to dazzle the shit out of the Shifter Lord.

Simone had sent the plans over quickly. Caelan had requested arrangements for twenty round tables and the main showpiece for several rectangle tables pushed together in a long line. I'd already finished the smaller arrangements and decided to go all out. Every piece was a living, green automaton performing scenes from The Wolf and the Fox, a little-known fairy tale from the Brothers Grimm.

Each scene told the story of a greedy, evil wolf who abused the poor little fox living with him until the fox tricks the wolf and escapes, leaving him to die at the hands of the angry farmer who catches him.

I cackled the entire time I worked on it. Every arrangement was a living, breathing work of art. Ferns curled and uncurled, swaying and reshaping themselves into the forms I coaxed them into, greenery twisting and rolling, flowers unfurling and blooming before turning back into tightly held buds.

The spell was complicated, but simple. Each scene would play repeatedly until close to the end of Caelan's event. Except for the main centerpiece. That one was a little different. While it was an automaton, I'd designed it to show one scene until 9:45, fifteen minutes until the end of his event—the fox betraying the wolf and the greedy wolf's inevitable demise at the hands of the farmer.

Once the clock hit ten, that same automaton would shift into a graveyard scene with fog created by dandelion puffs and rain created by guttation from pothos vines. A headstone would pop out of the ground, the epitaph simple and heartfelt.

Here lies the Shifter Lord.

A male who never learned

A clever fox will always rule over an aggressive wolf.

Five minutes after that, just as people were beginning to leave, the entire piece would explode in a riot of blooms and petals like a Fourth of July fireworks display.

Caelan would *murder* me. Well. He would try at least.

I put the finishing touches on the spell. The automatons wouldn't begin until fifteen minutes after the start of the event. To the untrained eye, my work appeared to be a stunning display of florals with a slight hum of magic. Unless someone was a well-trained Floromancer, they'd assume the source of the hum was a preservation spell.

True. But not the entire truth.

Once the spell clicked into place, I stepped back, put my hands on my hips, and grinned.

One of Moira's eyebrows lifted when I walked back into the main part of the shop.

"Everything ready?"

I nodded.

"Simone called earlier. They'll be here in half an hour."

I grabbed my purse. "Great. I'm running out to grab some lunch. Mind texting me when they're done?"

Moira shook her head, a rueful smile on her lips. "You sure about this?"

"Yup! I want you, Ash, and Tess to leave early this evening. The banquet isn't over until ten, but I'd rather be safe than sorry."

Tess floated over and paused. "Powerful magic back there, Evie. It's some of your best work."

Surprised by the comment, it took me a moment to respond. No one knew exactly what I'd done, but even without the automaton magic, the floral displays by themselves were stunning. "Thank you, Tess. It was nice stretching my wings. The Shifter Lord gave me free rein, and I took it to heart."

Ash wrung his hands together, his face drawn in a mask of concern. The dryad could be such a worrywart sometimes. "I don't like this, Evie."

I reached over and brought him into a one-armed hug. "What's my motto on bullies?"

Ash sighed and rolled his eyes. "The only way to stop a bully is by standing up to them."

Moira grinned.

I squeezed Ash. "Yes. Caelan is a bully."

"And he's the Shifter Lord." He grunted and tried to wiggle away, but I held tight.

"Which means it's even more important to impart this necessary lesson. We don't put up with bullies or strong arm tactics." I ruffled his hair. "Right?"

"This is not kindergarten," Ash growled. He wiggled away and glared. "He will kill you. Caelan isn't known for his soft heart, Evie. He is a predator."

I didn't speak for a long moment, but when I did, it was with conviction. "And you forget, Ash, so am I."

Silence fell. Ash's eyes widened, tears filling their mossy green depths. "Maybe," he said softly. "But if you die, it will break our hearts." He shook his head and wandered to the back of the shop.

Tess let out a little moan and floated after him. Moira plopped her chin on her hands and watched me. "I'm not going to ask you if you're sure about this again."

"Thanks," I said dryly.

Moira laughed. "He's not wrong. None of us understand why you're trying to yank the shifter's tail."

"He's the one who asked for a display of power."

"Yes," Moira drawled, "so do something bland and generic that still showcases your talent. Caelan doesn't need to know how powerful you are."

"He won't. My Floromancy is completely separate from the other."

"It is," she agreed, "but I've been on this earth for many, many years and I've met quite a few Floromancers. None of them are like you."

"It's still flowers and not mauling men to death."

Moira straightened and threw her hands up. "I can see you're past reason on this one. If this is what you think is best, then I'm with you." My friend didn't sound angry, only resigned.

I wasn't sure at all, but I wanted him to know I wasn't someone to be trifled with. If he kept coming at me, I was afraid of what I might do.

"I don't want him to pressure us again. We're busy enough without wondering if the Shifter Lord is going to come and destroy our business."

"He could do that any time he wanted to," Moira said gently. She came out from behind the register and brought me into a hug. "But since you've given me the go ahead to leave early, I'll leave you to it." She grabbed her purse. "Try to stay alive."

"I didn't say you could leave this early!"

On her way to the door, Moira winked. "Oh, you didn't? I couldn't hear you over the sound of your own self-superiority."

A surprised laugh bubbled from me. The bell over the door rang, and Moira slipped out. "Asshole!" I called.

Her cackling laugh trailed away.

Ash and Tess closed up shop, neither of them saying much before they left. Once the last light flipped off, Tess floated over and hugged me.

"Be careful," she said in her high, ethereal voice.

"Always. Have fun tonight."

Tess's pale cheeks colored. "It's just taco night," she insisted.

"I know. But remember, where there are tacos, there are margaritas."

Tess snorted and waved me away. Ash stopped by the front door and watched.

I lifted a hand in farewell, but he didn't return it. Regret curdled in my stomach. "Ash, everything will be okay. I promise."

He made a derisive sound in his throat. "Among all your other abilities, you're suddenly psychic now?"

Hurt, I blinked away the tears stinging my eyes.

"Ash," Tess said, a warning note in her voice.

He yanked the door open, the normally pleasant bell clanging discordantly. "Let's go, Tess."

The banshee shot me an apologetic look before hurrying out after Ash.

Ouch. His rejection stung, but I wasn't the type to cower from someone like Caelan. While I preferred staying under the radar, Caelan was trying to force me into the spotlight. What he didn't realize was that I'd grown up with a master manipulator.

I'd forced him to sign a contract for this particular order, and part of the contract involved keeping who created the flowers for him confidential.

To his detriment, he didn't seem concerned. Whether he figured I valued my privacy too much or didn't want my name associated with him, Caelan seemed to take the clause in stride. But it was for a specific reason. Tonight's display may very well embarrass him, and I didn't want people loyal to Caelan coming after me. They may suspect because I'm the only Floromancer close to the Keep, but they'd never know for sure as this was the first and only display of its kind. I had nothing like it in my store and didn't plan to stock anything like it in the future.

No one knew I possessed this kind of power. Caelan would shortly. And I hoped he would think twice before exerting his will on me again.

I cleaned up the register area and made a fresh pot of coffee. On most days, I'd siphon my power once more before I left, but tonight magic hummed inside me, crackling against my skin.

Caelan's event would begin soon. I had time to do some catch up before needing to be on guard. A possibility existed that Caelan would forgive this, but he was a proud man. I fully expected him to show up this evening.

My nerves buzzed, partly from all the caffeine I'd consumed, partly from anticipation mixed with a heavy dose of fear. He'd smell it on me if he came to my shop tonight. But I'd made preparations for his arrival. I would not die this night. Neither would Caelan if he were careful.

Floral fragrance hung heavy and sweet in the air tonight. The temperature was cool but humid, a result of my magic and the plants waiting in preparation. I'd brought some things from the back, plants I carefully tended but almost never used—my own creations, hybrids I'd brought to life when staying with Hazel when I felt like I was growing out of my skin.

These special flowers were deadly, dangerous things. Perfect for the deadly, dangerous thing who might later come to call. I could feel the plants' anticipation in the quiver of their thorns, poison glistening from wickedly sharp tips. These could never be allowed to grow wild, never be propagated. I'd hesitated before bringing them out tonight, but Caelan had me in brute strength. If he got a hold of me for too long, I might be dead by the end of the confrontation.

I'd made these when my magic was still settling after the attack, and some of the Chimera had bled through. Six plants sat around the shop, two with crimson red leaves and purple vines. Two more had fat, glossy green circular leaves, and an odd spotted yellow stem. The other two looked like nothing more than a common pothos vine. I called those my Chimera vines. Most of the magic I'd spilled had gone to those two plants, and they were the most dangerous of all.

Their poisons were unique and unknown to science. Discovering exactly how deadly my creations were was a memory I didn't like to think about, and after a few gruesome incidents, I'd sent a tiny amount of each anonymously to a lab because I was curious, and a few weeks later, my request for identification made the national news when the government asked for the person who sent them to come forward.

Whoops.

They wanted more samples and claimed they wanted to "contain" the poison for public safety. My mother, cruel as she was, had taught me many lessons, but the most important knowledge she'd ever imparted was to never trust the government. In her exact words, she'd said, "They make the fae look like benevolent puppies."

It was an odd stance to take since pesky things like politicians couldn't stop someone like my mother, but looking back, I genuinely believed she was trying to help me.

I was old enough at the time to know if I revealed myself, I'd either be dead or in a cage, and the plants I'd created would be used in secret and probably against other people.

Obviously, I never responded to the government's plea, and I'd sequestered the plants at home in a specially designed suitcase Hazel made for me. A few years later, they were hale and happy and just as deadly as they always were.

And tonight, they might save my life.

Nine p.m. came, then ten. At ten fifteen, I set aside my shears and tools, slipping a wicked cursed dagger I used on my most troublesome plants into the sheath at my back. I rarely wore it, but I thought it best to be prepared for anything tonight. It wouldn't do much to Caelan, but it might slow him down a bit. Seconds could mean the difference between life and death.

In my left front pocket, I had a packet of Ash's famous itching powder, potent as hell on a normal basis, but this one was charged by a Harvest moon. In my right, a pocket full of ground wolfsbane flowers.

Caelan was nothing if not meticulous. I expected him to come in, try to have a conversation with me, then threaten to kill me.

All very civilized.

But the Shifter Lord surprised me, and it almost ended before it ever began.

CHAPTER

Fourteen

I'd just brushed the last of the discarded leaves into the trashcan when the front window shattered, glass exploding into fine powdered dust. I threw my hands up in defense, the glass shredding my arms into ribbons. Pain tore through my limbs, and a scream tore from my throat.

A massive dark figure sailed through the window, one moment a wolf, the next an angry, furious man. Blood dripped from my arms onto the floor, the only thing that could betray my nature, but Caelan was too pissed off to notice.

He stalked toward me with a predator's grace, any touch of gray gone from his eyes. Golden light enveloped the room, his gaze honed on me.

"Why?" His voice was a low, graveled snarl. "Have I done something to you, Evie Quinn?"

I stayed behind the massive wooden work table, even as I knew it wouldn't stop Caelan if he wanted to reach me. He kept walking, slow and measured steps.

"Yes," I said simply.

His head cocked in a quick, even movement, an alien gesture that sent terror rolling down my spine. "Do tell," he rasped.

"I told you no multiple times, and you refused to listen to me."

He stopped on the other side of my work table and took a deep breath. One of his hands reached out, grasped the underside of the table, and flipped it into the air, sending it sailing into a display. Shattering ceramics and glass were the only sounds at first, followed by my soft breath of dismay. Suffering filled my senses, plants dying, their stems and roots damaged beyond repair.

I swallowed down my fear. "You're going to pay for that."

"Bill me," he snarled. Caelan was less than a foot away from me, glorious in his nudity, though I was too scared to admire his virility because I was pretty sure he was about to murder me. Even so, I couldn't pull the trigger on those other plants, shockingly undamaged.

I didn't back up. Why would I? He'd just keep following me. Instead, he reached for me and picked me up, massive hands spanning my waist, his fingers tipped in deadly claws. I gasped in surprise as he walked me back until I was crushed against the wall and Caelan's body.

A memory assailed me.

Pounding music, my broken heart, a handsome man with an accent made for seduction. A liaison in the woods for a picnic the next time and a shift in the air. Finn was his name, a temporary distraction from my wounded soul and ruined life, until he picked up my scent away from the crush of hundreds of bodies in that club and changed into something I hadn't even seen in nightmares.

Then the claws and teeth and pain and violation came until I was a ruined husk under the Inverness stars. I remembered the grass feeling like a soft blanket as my lifeblood pumped into the earth, and even the flowers couldn't save me as the creature's magic ravaged through my veins.

"Evie."

From a horrific divorce to a brutal assault, then death in a stunning countryside, it was about par for the course during that time of my life. And all I remembered was his hands and his breath, and the split of my skin when his claws raked through my stomach.

"EVIE!" Caelan's roar shattered the memory.

My magic erupted.

Crimson magic flung the Shifter Lord away, his hands violently ripped from my waist.

"No." My voice was a ruined bark as the shift came on. Claws extended from my fingers and toes, ripping through my sandals. I pointed a hand at Caelan. "GET OUT."

But the Shifter Lord's eyes were on my face as a crimson glow shaded the room in a wash of bloody light.

"What are you?" he breathed.

"GET. OUT." I flung my hands out and sent the Shifter Lord flying once more.

His bark of surprise was cut off as he hit the outside concrete with a loud crack.

I spun and ran to the back, snatching my purse and car keys. Magic sizzled in my veins as I fought with everything to deny my shift. I slipped on broken glass and went down hard, cursing through elongated fangs. My shirt hung in tatters, and my pants were ripped right down the side seam.

A broken sob escaped me as I staggered to my feet.

The sound of crunching glass made me freeze. "Evie."

My shoulders slumped. "Don't make me kill you, Caelan."

He huffed a sharp breath. "Let me help you."

I ignored him and bolted through the back door, my speed enhanced by magic and fury. It took me three times to open my car door, and when I got in, I hissed as glass smashed against the seat and my bare legs. When the car started, headlights illuminated Caelan's bloodied, naked figure.

I squealed out of the parking lot just as sirens sounded from several blocks down.

My entire body shook. Blood poured from dozens of wounds, and a stray thought about being forced to reupholster my car's interior brought a surprised chuckle.

I was caught in a half-shift and would stay that way until morning. I'd found no way around that particular quirk of my magic. When the Chimera shift started, if I didn't allow it to finish, I'd be stuck this way until dawn.

My cell rang.

I fished through my purse and glanced down at the screen.

Moira.

"Not a good time," I growled.

"Shut up and listen," she said urgently.

I stilled.

"Police are crawling all over the shop. They're looking for you. Caelan is speaking with them."

"How do you know?" I stopped at a red light and let my eyes flutter shut.

"I'm watching from the shadows. This is bad, Evie. Really bad."

"We'll deal with it." My words sounded garbled. The fangs. I hated the fangs.

"How?" Moira whispered.

"We'll talk tomorrow. Can you have Ash call the repairman out? The window needs repairing tonight if he can. The entire thing is shattered." I cursed under my breath when I realized I'd left those plants out. If anyone touched them…

A flash of darkness streaked by the window. I whipped my head around but saw nothing.

"Evie?"

"I promise we'll deal with it."

"Caelan is gone, but the police are leaving." She exhaled a heavy breath. "I'm not sure what he did, but he might have saved our asses." Moira paused. "Or condemned us."

I let out a half-hysterical laugh. "We'll see if I'm still alive tomorrow."

"Evie."

"I have to go. Tell Ash and Tess to take the day off. You too."

Moira sighed. "I love you. Do you need me to come?"

"No!" I pinched the space between my brows. "I'm sorry. No. I'm okay. Just rattled."

"I'll see you tomorrow."

"Moira—"

"No arguing." She hung up before I could do just that.

The ride home was agonizing. I should go to the hospital simply to have someone pick the countless shards of glass from my skin I couldn't reach, but it would bring too many questions. My body had already healed over the smaller ones.

I thought about calling Moira back, but it was late, and all I wanted was to be alone. The drive home wasn't far, but it felt like hours. When I finally dragged myself into the house, I went straight to the bathroom. I'd get what glass I could reach and worry about the rest tomorrow.

Moira always wanted to help. Maybe I could get her to pick the rest of the glass from my skin.

Freshly showered and with most of the glass gone, I sat down on the edge of the bed and took my first deep breath since Caelan flew into my shop. He'd taken me by surprise, and I wasn't sure why I was surprised by that.

"I need to get out more," I muttered through enormous fangs. The only social outings I had were with Moira, Ash, and Tess. Assuming I'd known how Caelan would behave was profoundly dumb of me.

And now I had a destroyed shop and a pissed off Shifter Lord on my tail.

Sighing, I rubbed my hands over my face. I'd get up early and head to the shop to see the damage during the daylight. But first there was one more thing I needed to do. Shifting into my original dual form would help push the worst of the rest of the glass out and keep me from trying to fall asleep in this half form. Right now, I had massive lion fangs, sporadic patches of hair all over my body, and claws on my fingers and toes. Not to mention an extreme craving for bloody meat.

The meat would have to wait. All I had in the fridge were a

couple of packets of yogurt and some granola stuffed in the pantry. I focused on my inherent magic, allowing it to wash over me. Soothing earth magic rolled over my body, and I sighed as the feeling of soft winds and blue skies tingled against my skin. A few moments later, my mass shrank, and my human form faded away, leaving me sitting alone on the bed in wren form.

I asked my mother once why I was a Fairy wren instead of a regular brown one, and she scoffed and said, "Darling, the fae does nothing halfway. Why be brown when you can be all the shades of the sky?"

Once I fell asleep, nothing would wake me until the Chimera magic faded away. I hopped onto the windowsill and pushed the blinds aside with my beak. Nothing suspicious leapt out at me, but I stayed there for a couple of minutes to see if Caelan had followed me home. In this form, he could pop me into his mouth like an hors d'oeuvre and I'd be helpless to stop him.

Time was more difficult to fathom in this form, but I stayed on the windowsill for a while until I was satisfied no one lurked outside. I nudged the blinds back into place and flitted over to the little basket I kept on my dresser, outfitted with a soft blanket and a small bowl of fresh water. Ruffling my feathers, I shook a few more pieces of glass out of my feathers and settled down to sleep.

Exhaustion settled into my fragile bones, and it didn't take long until I was swept away into a deep, healing sleep.

CHAPTER

Fifteen

CAELAN

Evie had a pet bird. An intelligent one, it seemed. I lay low, nestled in the fertile ground around her property. Magic permeated the soil and everything growing inside and out.

The grass was soft and lush, and I felt comfortable lying here, even though I was staking out her place. Everything was fertile and green and smelled like the world had before man destroyed much of the land. The health of this soil and the overactive plant life were unsurprising with...whatever the hell Evie was. Floromancer, yes, but she was far more than that.

And she was injured. I followed her vehicle as far as I could, and when I'd lost her in the swarm of downtown traffic, I followed the scent of her blood.

Evie's blood was curious. Disturbing. Interesting. I'd gone to her shop tonight to—well, I wasn't sure what the hell I planned to do when I got there—but things had gone downhill fast. Something happened to her, something traumatic. I'd stalked her, and she was bleeding, and I couldn't stop myself from getting so close to her. In doing so, I triggered some deep memories inside her that paralyzed the poor girl.

I was an asshole of the largest caliber.

Evie's bird stayed at the window for a long time, far longer than a normal bird should have. I'd never seen one like it around here. It had a mix of electric blue feathers interspersed with black around the eye and was extremely small. The creature could fit into the palm of my hand.

Sometime later, the bird nudged the blinds closed, but I waited an extra half hour before making my move. Skulking from the shadows, I crept down the small hillside and into Evie's front yard, sniffing around the porch before I went into the back yard.

She had no pets that I could tell and no male at home, nor had there been any male here other than her companion dryad.

The thought sent a disturbing flash of satisfaction through me. I brushed it away, shifted to loosen the small bag around my neck, and shifted in a flash of bright light.

I dressed quickly in a thin pair of joggers and a t-shirt and reached into the bag again and withdrew two long stainless-steel picks.

Most people had a misguided sense of security. They refused to believe things like me prowled the night, or that it was this easy to get into their house. A few careful turns of the picks, and Evie's lock clicked open.

I opened the door, pleased to see Evie kept her hinges oiled. Bad for her, great for me. But then something else occurred to me. What if someone else tried to break in? I stepped inside and closed the door, vowing to have someone over soon to reinforce her doors and windows.

She needed to keep things like me out of her house.

The thought made me still. Why was I so worried about her? She'd humiliated me in front of the Council, my Pack, and many power players within the state. I'd been furious when I burst into her shop, ready to punish her for what she'd done, but when I smelled her...

I let out a soft breath. She'd done nothing except for what I'd asked her to do, and she'd protected herself with that damn contract I'd blown off. My lips twitched. She was right. The fox had outsmarted the wolf.

Not only had she shown me a display of her power, she'd gone above and beyond and showed me not only how staggering her magic was, but that she had finite control. I'd never seen anything like those automatons, even if she'd pricked my pride.

I stood by the door for a long moment, sniffing out any threats, but the only person who lived here was Evie. For some strange reason, there was no avian scent.

Maybe there was an exit I hadn't noticed. The bird was teeny tiny and could have made a quick escape. But it was odd I couldn't smell any trace of its presence. Not that a bird would be a danger to me, but I liked knowing where anyone and everything was when I was in a new place.

A quick scan of the room told me a lot about Evie. She was far from a minimalist. Every space was crammed with books or soft things or knickknacks. Or plants. She had plants anywhere a flat space existed and even where there was no flat space. They hung suspended from the ceiling, from curtain rods, piled on shelves and tables. They grew haphazardly from cheap pots on top of the fridge, on the kitchen island, on the coffee table, on top of the television shelf and fireplace.

They were everywhere.

Every seat and couch in the living room had fluffy pillows and soft blankets. My fingers trailed over one on the back of the loveseat. A discarded mug sat on the coffee table next to a book placed face down. I peered down at the title and almost laughed out loud.

The History of Werewolves in America—Fad or Phase?

Straightening, I prowled through the house searching for her. She'd fled the shop seriously wounded, and I wouldn't be able to sleep unless I knew she was okay. Even if she thought I'd gone to her shop to kill her.

I followed her scent to what I assumed was her bedroom. Pausing at the entrance, I waited but heard nothing except for the faint whir of a fan. It almost seemed like she was gone, but that couldn't be right. Her car was in the driveway and her blood was dotted all over the concrete and porch. Evie was somewhere in this house.

Frowning, I stepped away from the door and explored the rest of the house, searching every room, but there was nothing except faint traces of her presence. When I went back to her bedroom door and searched again, I still couldn't hear any breathing. But something told me she was in there.

I reached out and turned the handle.

Bloodstained, ruined clothing lay discarded on the floor, her sandals lying at opposite ends of the room. I moved further into the room and looked around. Her forest green comforter was darkened at the foot of the bed. I peered closer and inhaled. More blood. But the bed was empty. I moved toward the closet and peered inside, thinking maybe she had collapsed. Nothing there either.

A lamp on her dresser cast a warm, golden light over the room. If her living room and kitchen looked like a jungle, this place looked like a fairytale forest. Orchids of all types sat on multiple shelves and all over her nightstands. Vines curled through the blinds and around the curtain rods, some with fragrant purple blooms. She'd chosen a dark blue paint color, giving the bedroom a comforting, peaceful vibe.

Something in the heart I'd thought long frozen thawed. Had Evie lived a life of war and sought solace in the things she could control? A stack of books lay haphazardly on her nightstand, a mix of romance and mysteries, along with a glass carafe half filled with water. A Tiffany lamp sat beside it, the stained glass a mix of blue and emerald. She had about a dozen pillows scattered across her bed, and what looked like a hand knitted wool blanket that held an odd tinge of strange magic.

But where the hell was she? I spun in a circle, feeling her presence. She should be here, and yet, there was no trace of Evie, only the strong scent of her magic and her presence soaked into the very marrow of this house.

I sat on the edge of her bed, avoiding where she'd bled, and closed my eyes, opening all my senses. Once the room fell completely silent, a faint, tiny sound pricked my ears. The noise came from around her dresser.

Confused, I rose and went over to the old, scarred wooden dresser and looked around. A silver necklace with an acorn charm rested in an abalone shell. Next to it lay a leather necklace with a silver goat charm tied onto it. I'd never seen her wear either, but I'd only been in her shop a couple of times. A pair of leaf earrings lay next to the necklaces, and a wrap-around ring in the shape of a laurel wreath lay on top.

A half-burned candle, another small stack of books, and a vase of fresh-cut flowers sat in the middle. But on the edge, there was a small oval basket with part of a soft blanket hanging out. There. That was where all the magic came from.

I stepped over and peered down. My heart stopped in my chest.

The blue wren from the window lay there, deep in sleep. My mouth fell open. Evie was a shifter. Or something. I'd never seen someone who could shift into such a small form. With every ounce of magic in my body, I kept as quiet as I could as I studied her.

Opening my senses as wide as possible, I bent down and listened. The faintest sound of a rapid heartbeat was evident, but I had to strain to hear it. As I focused on her, I noticed shiny bits reflecting the light. When I realized what it was, I swore under my breath.

Glass. Tiny shards of shimmering glass lay scattered all over the blanket and inside her body. I spun abruptly and on silent footsteps went into her bathroom and dug around until I found a pair of tweezers and a small cup. I set those down on her nightstand and picked up a small chair close to the window and set it beside the bed. Then I reached in gently and picked Evie up, along with her blanket, gently shaking the glass from the fabric, and knowing I wouldn't wake her.

She might not be a full shifter, but she'd fallen into the deep, almost comatose, healing sleep all of us found when we'd been seriously injured.

Once I had settled into the chair, I placed her on my lap, careful not to jostle her too much. The human part inside me screamed I was violating her territory and if she found out, she would never speak to me again, but the voice was overshadowed by the snarling wolf screaming I must protect her.

The wolf always won.

I picked up the tweezers and gently spread one of Evie's delicate wings out. She didn't move an inch, still locked in sleep. Oh so carefully, I began picking glass out of her body, marveling at the delicate bones and soft feathers.

It took me a couple of hours to find every single piece of glass, and when I was finished, I gently tucked Evie's blanket back into the basket and set her in the middle, going by memory to ensure nothing was different from when I arrived.

Once I put the tweezers away, I folded the small paper cup full of glass over and tucked it into my pocket. When I stood at the back door, I did one more sweep to ensure I wasn't being observed and sent a pulse of magic through her house, wiping my scent and my presence from the area.

Later, when I stood on the small hill overlooking her house, I sank to the ground and buried my face in my hands. Where we'd be tomorrow, I couldn't say, but tonight had escalated so far out of my control, I couldn't think about it without feeling a deep sense of shame. She'd be well within her rights to never see me again.

But I'd do everything in my power to ensure that wouldn't happen.

And the thought bothered me more than I could say.

CHAPTER

Sixteen

I awoke much sooner than I expected, still in my wren form. Rising, I stretched my wings, expecting a tugging pain.

But there was nothing. No pain, only a delicious stretch. Confused, I looked around my basket, expecting to see a pile of broken glass shards, but there was nothing there either.

I hopped onto the edge of the basket before leaping off and onto my bed, shifting as I landed. A deep sigh escaped me, and I lay there for a moment, staring at the ceiling.

It was early enough in the morning that darkness still stretched across the land. A quick glance at the clock made me blink. Five a.m. Holy crap. Why was I up so early?

I rolled out of bed and went into the bathroom to mark the places I'd need to have Moira extract glass from, but when I examined myself in the mirror, my skin was smooth and unmarred.

"What the hell?" I breathed. Moving my body to the left and right, I lifted my arms, then my legs, then got a hand mirror to look closer, but there was nothing. No glass to be found anywhere.

Bemused, I turned on the shower and got ready for the day. Getting to the shop early was a good thing. I could clean up the worst of the damage before the other shop owners got to work and started asking too many questions.

FILLED with caffeine and half-stale scones, I pulled up to my shop less than forty-five minutes later, lucky enough to get a spot right by my front door. Ash and the others usually got here before I did, so ninety percent of the time I had to park at least a block away. Being the owner, I could push it and insist on a front parking spot, but the exercise was good for me, and downtown parking came at a premium.

I grabbed my travel mug and got out of the car, not paying attention until I turned to walk inside and saw...nothing.

No evidence of any damage existed. A brand-new window complete with the exact hand drawn logo I had before was in the place where the shattered window had been last night.

I stood on the sidewalk, dumbstruck. All the glass on the sidewalk had been cleaned up, and the shattered pots were replaced, the greenery from before carefully re-planted. My heart sped up, thudding painfully in my chest.

I opened the shop door and peered inside, sending my senses out to see if anyone else was in the shop, but there was only me. Bewildered, I hurried inside and set my purse down on the register desk, then inspected the shop.

Every stray piece of glass had been collected, every broken pot repaired, though some of the plants were seriously damaged, and I'd have to see if I could nurse them back to health later this morning. The wooden work table was still broken down the middle, though someone had hastily repaired it with duct tape.

Another repaired potted plant sat on top of the surface. Multiple shelves were repaired the same way, a couple of them lopsided enough to concern me. I thought for sure I'd be shut down for several days, but all I needed to do was move some shelves and plants to the back and replace the table, which, all things considered, wasn't as terrible as I thought it would be when I got up this morning.

I loved the work table, but I was still alive. One of those things was more important than the other. Shaking my head at the odd turn my morning had taken, I made a cup of coffee and went over to the work table to see if it was truly beyond repair. The plant was stressed but better than it was last night, but when I moved the pot, I spotted a folded piece of paper underneath.

When I picked it up, a familiar scent rose. My heartbeat spiked as I unfolded the note.

I did what I could. You have a new table on order with the same dimensions and material, and several replacement shelves are scheduled for delivery today. I cannot apologize for what happened because an apology will never be enough to repair the damage, both material and immaterial. I'd like to speak with you soon. If you allow it.

The note was signed simply: *Caelan.*

I sank down into the chair next to the table and stared at the paper. Hating him would be much easier than feeling whatever I felt. He'd come back sometime after I'd left, after sending the police away, and did his best to repair the damage that he caused.

As much as I wanted to pretend I was innocent, I'd knowingly pushed his buttons because he pissed me off.

Ugh. Being a grown-up was so ridiculous sometimes. Folding the note carefully, I tucked it into my back pocket and chewed the side of my lip as I pondered what to do. When my mind stayed blank, I tried to push the Shifter Lord from my thoughts and focused on my shop.

My shop was here and inanimate, and I didn't have to do anything other than some clean up. The plants were a different story, but most of them should be okay.

So that's what I did. The work table wasn't steady enough to balance all the plants I needed to heal, so I pushed it into the back and pulled out a large fold-up table. The shop wasn't scheduled to open for several hours, so I topped off my coffee and got to work.

Magic buzzed against my skin as I worked. Two hours in and most of the plants were on their way to being good as new, and I had a ton of cuttings to start. As I worked, I whispered apologies, telling them I was dumb to do what I did and that, while they didn't deserve what happened to them, I might have.

Of course, my plants were loyal, and they vehemently disagreed with my low opinion of myself, which made me smile. Once all the plants were fixed, I went to the back for seedling pots, rooting hormone, and potting soil, then got to work making new plant babies.

An hour before the shop was scheduled to open, a large van parked in front of the shop and two burly men hopped out. One, a massive blond guy with muscles for days, knocked on the shop door. When he spotted me through the window, he waved and pointed at his van.

"We have shelves for you, courtesy of the Shifter Lord. Mind if we drop them inside?"

Would there be a price for accepting these? If I opened the door, was this one more crack in my resolve to keep Caelan away? I couldn't open the shop with the janky ones I had now. Maybe I could set them up and send Caelan a check.

"Miss Quinn?" the man said, his brow furrowing.

Yes. I'd write him a check for everything. Resolved, I opened the door.

The man presented a clipboard. "If you wouldn't mind signing for everything, we'll bring them in, get them set up, and remove your damaged shelves."

I scanned the paper, but there were no prices listed. "How much are the shelves?" I asked, glancing up.

He blinked. "Err. I was instructed not to say, ma'am."

I gritted my teeth. "If you don't tell me, you won't be bringing those shelves in." My gaze flicked to his name tag. "Jeff." I smiled to soften my words.

"Miss Quinn—"

"I understand you're under pressure from the Shifter Lord to do as he bids, but I think it's worse if you return to him with a truck full of shelves than it is for you to tell me how much these are. Don't you think?"

The second man stood like a statue, a blank expression on his face. Jeff flicked a glance at him, but his partner stayed silent. Finally, Jeff blew out a breath and pulled out his phone. He scrolled to something and turned the screen to me.

I made a mental note of the price. "Thank you. I'll move the plants off the shelves."

"No need, ma'am. We'll take care of everything. Just tell us where everything goes."

The two men had the shelves installed in less than half an hour, and just as they were finishing up, another truck pulled up. A woman hopped out and waved when she spotted me.

"Evie Quinn?"

I stifled a sigh. Was this what it felt like to be a female main character in a billionaire romance? Completely bowled over and helpless to do anything? "Let me guess. You have a delivery from the Shifter Lord?"

To her credit, the woman winced. "I do."

The other delivery guys nodded and headed out the door with little fanfare.

"I'm Jennifer Markham. There's a truck full of pots out here for you." She pointed over her shoulder. Jennifer was tall, dark-haired, and lean. She wore adorable floral overalls, a white tank, and scuffed leather boots, and her hair was done in a long, thick braid she'd slung over one of her shoulders.

The sigh escaped me this time. "Do you have prices for everything?"

She opened and shut her mouth before a rueful laugh escaped. "Like a bulldozer, isn't he?"

I grinned. "Have you ever delivered pots this early to a random woman before?"

"No, but I redid his landscaping and didn't sleep for a full month because he kept me on call at all hours of the night."

"For a landscaping job?" I couldn't keep the disbelief from my voice.

Jennifer laughed. "Yes! That man has serious opinions about salvia." She grimaced. "And sometimes those opinions come after midnight."

We grinned at each other. Jennifer peered through the window. "I don't get downtown too much, but this looks like a cool store. What kind of events do you do most?"

I opened the door and let her in. "All kinds, but we get the most requests for weddings. Fredericksburg is a popular place to get hitched, and we get good word of mouth from there."

Jennifer's jaw dropped. "Holy smokes. All these plants are yours?"

I nodded. "It's easy enough having cut flowers in a cooler, but I want people to know I have a green thumb twenty-four hours a day."

She laughed. "Smart."

I let her browse for a bit before she came back, holding out her clipboard. "Gotta have you sign. Shifter's orders."

Once I handed the paperwork back, she jerked her head toward the truck. "Come on out. I stacked everything I had. You can pick whatever you want up to twenty pots."

I followed her out and meticulously sorted through everything, and when I was finished, I insisted she write up an invoice for me with the prices and taxes, so I could write Caelan a check. When I saw the total, I sucked in a gasp.

"I'm the potter," Jennifer said with a chuckle. "And that's the wholesale price. I'm not sure what Caelan did, but from the last delivery truck and mine, I'd guess your shop took some damage. It's none of my business, but I'd let him pay for this one." She winked. "Because I'm very expensive."

"A potter and a landscape designer?"

"Blame the economy." Jennifer shrugged. "I have a touch of plant magic, and my parents convinced me it'd be a terrible idea to skip college to be a potter full time. As much as it pained me to listen to my parents, I went to college for landscape design and sell ceramics on the side."

She rolled the truck door down and hopped off the tailgate. "Unfortunately, my parents were right. I sell enough pottery to keep the shop lights on and pay a few bills, but the vast majority of my income comes from resident and corporate landscaping."

I blinked at her casual mention of magic. Noticing my expression, she chuckled. "Magic beats from you like a furnace, Evie. Anyone with a hint of power can feel it."

"Well. Um." I waved the paper. "He already paid you, right?"

She snorted and pulled her keys from her pocket. "Oh yeah. While I'm more inclined to do favors for the Shifter Lord, I require payment up front, no matter who it is."

I held a finger up. "Wait a minute."

Hurrying back into the shop, I grabbed a business card and scribbled my cell number on the back before heading back outside. "Call me sometime. Maybe we can grab a cup of coffee or something."

She waved the card at me. "I just might, Evie Quinn." Jennifer winked and hopped into the truck. "Not sure what you did to him, but he was mighty remorseful when he called me last night."

I groaned. "You don't want to know."

She grinned. "Oh, but I do. Maybe we'll grab a drink instead of coffee." Jennifer waved and started the vehicle. "Be careful out there. And watch out for Caelan. He's a charming sonofabitch, but you don't want him fixated on you."

Good advice, but I was beginning to worry it might be too late. "Don't I know it."

Jennifer drove away, her words ringing in my ears.

I didn't call in Moira and the others, though she popped in a few hours after normal opening time and walked in with her mouth agape.

Moira's eyes scanned the room, a furrow of confusion forming between her brows. "Did your mom come in and clean up or something?"

We locked eyes and started cracking up. My mother probably didn't even know what a broom was. "You wouldn't believe me if I told you."

The vampire grunted. "Oh, I bet I would. This has the Shifter Lord written all over it."

My shoulders slumped. "Yeah." I shoved Jennifer's price list at her. "I thought I'd write a check for everything, but the asshole hired a talented potter."

Moira took the invoice, scanned the paper, her brows slowly inching higher with each line she read. "Whoa."

"Yeah." I laughed. "You can check out her work in the back. I brought in twenty new pots."

"Still writing a check?"

"Thinking about it. He's the one that broke them, but writing a check prevents me from owing him anything, and I didn't have to report it to the insurance company." But paying him in full would take a chunk out of the payment from the floral arrangements I made for Caelan and that chapped my ass.

"Meh." Moira flicked her fingers. "You have plenty of money, and we'll all chip in to keep him off our back."

I wasn't a millionaire, but I did alright. Writing the check would pain me, but it was the wise thing to do. "I'll decide tonight."

Moira grabbed an apron from the hook by the door, one of the few things that survived Caelan's wrath without damage and tied it around her neck.

"You don't have to work," I chided. "Why don't you take the day off?"

"Nothing else to do, and you know how much trouble I get in when I'm bored." Moira tied her long hair up in a high ponytail, then dug around in her purse for a small, leather cosmetic case. "Now, let me see your back so I can pick the rest of the glass out."

"About that." I'd been thinking about it all morning and still couldn't figure out what happened. "I went to sleep full of glass, and I woke up without any. It's the damnedest thing."

Moira stared. "Even in your ass?"

I barked a laugh. "Even in my ass. I'd feel it in there, but I can't feel a thing."

Her brows drew together. "Let's go in the back. I want to double check."

It was about time to close for lunch, anyway. After flipping the sign to closed, we headed to my office.

Moira twirled her finger. "Assume the position."

I turned around and tugged my shirt off. This wasn't the first time Moira picked glass or thorns or burrs from my skin, and I'm sure it wouldn't be the last. The vampire hummed, her cool fingers skimming down my back, pressing in certain areas, before moving to my hips.

"Hmm. Tug your pants a little lower."

"Your obsession with me is getting a little weird," I drawled.

Moira laughed. "Yes, skinny pale asses totally do it for me."

I tugged the side of my joggers down. Moira pressed a few more places, then clicked her tongue. "Nada," she pronounced. "Should we be worried about that?"

"I didn't sense anything in the house." I pulled my shirt back on and fixed my joggers. "Maybe Mom showed up?" She could erase every trace of her scent if she wanted to.

"Yeah, but she digs through your shit because she's a nosy bitch. You'd know if she'd been there."

"True." Mom had no ability to be stealthy. She moved through the world like she had the right to be anywhere at all, and the concept of private property did not compute in her fae brain.

"Plus, she wouldn't heal you without making you pay for it."

"Also true." I slumped onto the couch and kicked my feet up. "So what happened? Did I fully absorb the glass and turn it to slush or something?"

"Mmm. I'm more inclined to lean toward a benevolent fairy godmother."

We laughed again. Benevolent fae was fairy-tale cinema marketing and not based in real life whatsoever.

A key in the lock turned and Moira's head jerked toward the sound. Her eyes narrowed. "It's Ash," she said before she plopped down in one of the chairs.

He popped his head in a moment later and jerked his thumb over his shoulder. "Thought you said the shop was destroyed?"

Moira grinned. "Our murderous Shifter Lord felt guilty. He paid to have everything fixed."

Ash blanched. "In a period of twelve hours?"

"Try five or six. Almost everything was fixed before I got here this morning."

The dryad and Moira exchanged a look I chose to ignore. He came in and took one of the other chairs. "I heard something I think you'll be interested in."

Moira sat forward, dark eyes gleaming. "Oooh. Gossip. Spill the tea, wood boy."

Ash snorted. "As always, your nicknames are both demeaning and endearing."

Moira grinned. "I try."

"The Shifter Council met last night." I met Ash's eyes, and my stomach dropped to my toes.

"Oh shit," I breathed.

Moira let out a cackle of laughter. "That was what the flower arrangements were for?" She put a hand over her mouth but couldn't stop her belly laugh. "Oh, Evie. You beautiful idiot."

"No wonder he was so pissed." Guilt speared me. I knew there'd be important people at his banquet, but we usually heard rumors when the Council of Lords gathered. I assumed it was only local power and not Lords from all across the world.

"They're fracturing," Ash continued. "Rogue packs are beginning to form, and Caelan is under extreme pressure to either bring those to heel or expand his territory."

"Or step down," Moira murmured.

"Yes," Ash confirmed. "Our Shifter Lord is progressive, and some in the Council don't like his policies. The gathering was meant to be an informal peace summit."

"Informal?" I blurted. "With all that money he spent on just the flowers?"

"He's filthy rich, Evie," Ash said, rolling his eyes. "The cost for him is equivalent to a drop of rain."

"Still." I thought about it. "Maybe I should have charged him more."

The vampire reached over and patted my knee. "That's our Evie. Business woman 'til the end."

"There's one more thing." Ash rubbed his hand over his face. "I've heard some rumblings about divine magic popping up in some of the smaller towns."

I froze. "What kind of divine magic?" Was my mother acting up again?

"No idea. But I think we should all be on guard. We all know what happens when the gods start walking the world again."

Silence fell. Yes, we did. And I knew more than most considering one of them was my mother.

Eighteen

CAELAN

"You're an idiot," Simone breathed.

"He's a stupid motherfucker, is what he is," Garrett growled. "Are you insane?"

I sat at my desk glaring at my Omega and my Beta. "You're very lucky you're my closest friends."

Garrett scoffed. "We might be, but it doesn't mean you listen to a single word we say."

His tone pissed me off. Garrett always said what he meant, and I usually appreciated it, but not when I fully realized how badly I'd fucked up over the last twenty-four hours.

Simone didn't say much, her direct stare unnerving.

I decided not to tell them I'd broken into Evie's house. The damage I'd done to her store was bad enough. Trespassing and breaking and entering were felonies. So was destruction of property, but as Shifter Lord, I had much more discretion about how I handled issues.

And Evie, like it or not, was becoming an issue.

"It's taken care of," I growled.

Garrett made a disgusted noise. "How is it taken care of? Did you threaten the girl or throw money at the problem?"

I gritted my teeth.

"Garrett," Simone cautioned.

He waved a dismissive hand. "You should have killed her the second she moved here. What were you thinking?"

I tamped my rage down. Garrett was my oldest, dearest friend. His temper was an issue, but he was a born strategist and could one day be a Lord. If he reined his temper in.

"Just like everyone else, she applied to live here as a florist. A Floromancer. There was no reason to look twice at her application, and you know it."

"That display was more than Floromancy," Simone said quietly.

"I agree." I scrubbed a hand over my face. "But this was partly my fault." I bit down on the smile threatening to form. "I baited and threatened her, assuming she would roll over and do what I wanted."

Simone chuckled. "And she did."

I inclined my head. "Yes. Her stunt was the textbook definition of malicious compliance. I'd all but forced her to be our florist, and I specifically requested a display of power. She went above and beyond."

Power flared in the room. "She embarrassed you!" Garrett snarled.

"She made me eat humble pie, Garrett. I deserved it."

Simone's brow furrowed. "Oh, Caelan." She closed her eyes and let out a breath. "You're smitten."

Garrett snapped his attention to me. "No. Caelan. Of all the people in this state, you cannot possibly want that...that..."

"Be careful how you speak of Evie," I said quietly, magic snapping against my skin.

Garrett's nostrils flared. "She is not right. Something lurks within her body, and it is not Floromancy."

"Garrett is right." Simone looked away. "I like Evie. A lot. But there is something about her that doesn't quite fit."

They might be my closest friends, but Evie's secrets were her own. As long as she wasn't a danger to the Pack, I would not betray her. "Then she is in good company," I said after a moment. "We cannot stand here and judge her for the magic lurking in her bones when all three of us are not quite what we seem."

Simone's eyes sparkled. "I agree."

Garrett huffed. "I do not agree. You should put her down before she becomes a threat." Without waiting to be dismissed, Garrett turned and stormed from the room, slamming the door behind him.

Simone didn't speak for a long moment. My Omega had always been a thoughtful person and a nurturing wolf. Her magic could calm even the angriest beast, and Garrett rarely traveled without her. She wasn't a woman of many words, but when she spoke, I listened.

"What else did you do?"

I sank into the chair and groaned.

Simone laughed softly. "That bad?"

"Worse." I reached for the decanter of whiskey and two glasses, pouring us each a small glass. When I started speaking, I waited for Simone's judgment, and even though her eyes widened a couple of times during the story, her face was more thoughtful than anything.

I told her as much as I could and divulged Evie's other form but didn't tell her how I'd plucked each piece of glass from her body. It felt too intimate, and I was still ashamed of what I had done. Not for helping her but helping her when she couldn't consent.

When the story was done, Simone shook her head. "You like her, don't you?"

I wasn't sure how I felt, but I didn't hate her. When I said as much, Simone laughed. "She's not a wolf. Evie doesn't have to obey you, and it bothers you."

She had a point. I was used to being obeyed without hesitation. Evie basically told me to fuck off in a hundred different ways, and I had yet to do it. I didn't want to disappear from her life, and that thought bothered me far more than I wanted to admit aloud.

"I am curious about her," I admitted.

Simone's eyes flickered. "So are the other Shifter Lords. Tread carefully, Caelan. Evie won't be anyone's prize."

She threw back her whiskey and rose. "She won't accept your payment for her shop, either."

I snorted. "Of course she will. I did thousands of dollars in damage but saved her from an insurance claim and from paying out of pocket."

"Mmm," Simone hummed. "I don't think she will reject it outright, but she will attempt to pay you back." She brushed a kiss over my cheek and headed toward the door. "Possibly in a way you won't expect."

I smothered my grin. Anticipation filled my veins at the thought of what Evie might come up with. The automatons were hands down genius—one of the most creative things I'd ever seen —and I was one of the oldest shifters in the country. Not much surprised me anymore, but when that headstone popped up with the epitaph, I'd seen red.

But I also felt something for the first time in a long, long time, other than cold numbness.

CHAPTER

Nineteen

I closed up late that night, giving the damaged plants one extra boost before heading home. There was one I needed to worry about, so I scooped it up and carried it with me to the front. I'd take it home and see if it did any better there, where the energy was more stable.

I stuck my key in the door to unlock it, only to see a figure standing outside.

Male. Tall. Lean. Dark haired. A choking amount of magic. Gorgeous.

Shit.

"What do you want?" I called through the door.

"I'm only here to talk."

"And if I don't want to?"

"Then I'll leave." His expression remained blank, though his gray eyes burned.

I snorted. "Are you alright? No veiled threats or I am the Shifter Lord, you must obey me nonsense?"

Caelan's lips twitched. "I wouldn't call it nonsense."

I made no move to open the door. "I'm tired. It's been a long day, and I want to go home."

"Then allow me to walk you to your car."

I barked a laugh. "My car is right behind you."

"Then I will be quick."

A sigh escaped me. "Fine," I growled. Struggling to open the door with my hands full, Caelan stepped up and extricated the plant from me, using his foot to hold the door.

"Will this one be alright?" he asked.

My heart cracked a little at the concern in his voice, but I steeled myself. Don't be weak, Evie. That way lies madness.

"It needs some extra care, so I'm taking it home."

His massive hands wrapped with such care around that small pot did funny things to my insides. Caelan bent his head and peered at the small succulent. String of pearls was difficult enough to keep alive, that even I, the Floromancer, wasn't convinced I could salvage the poor thing. These plants were supposed to be easy to care for, but I always felt like these things had three modes.

First: Oh no, I added a single drop of extra water. Plant: *I'm dead.*

Second: I moved the pot a quarter of an inch. Plant: *Hisssss. I'm dying!!*

Third: I did absolutely nothing out of the ordinary. Plant: *Aargh. You've killed me.*

Even Caelan staring at it made me nervous. He was an intimidating guy. Was he going to scare the plant to death?

But to my surprise, the plant shivered and lifted one of its vines toward Caelan. He blinked in surprise and gasped softly.

"Evie!" he whispered. "It—does it like me?"

I pressed my lips together to keep from laughing. "It seems so."

He lifted a finger but hesitated and didn't touch it. "Go ahead," I encouraged. "It's giving you permission."

With a gentleness I didn't know he possessed, Caelan touched the small, trembling vine. The String of pearls reached out and curled around his finger. An awed smile touched the Shifter

Lord's lips, and at that moment, a piece of the stone encasing my heart cracked.

This man, this Lord, was dangerous. To my body, my soul, and my heart. He could kill me if he wanted to, and yet he stood there awestruck by the dying plant in his hands.

Tears shimmered in my eyes, and I blinked them away before he noticed. "You can have it if you want to. Once I nurse it back to health."

He lifted his stormy gray eyes to me, surprise lighting their depths. "Truly?"

The vine hadn't let go of Caelan's finger. "I think she's chosen who she wants to go home with."

"She?" he questioned.

I lifted a shoulder in a shrug. "Most plants hold both sexes. Some plants are only male or only female, and others have the ability to change their sex. I gauge mostly by their energy, and the one you're holding possesses a strong feminine energy."

"Does she have a name?"

I couldn't hold back my smile. "No. I just cut her from the mother plant today. You can name her if you want. Once she gets better." A frown marred my face. "I hope I can help her, but I can't guarantee she'll be okay."

"I understand." Caelan turned. "Want me to put her in the car?"

I clicked the unlock button. When the car beeped, Caelan opened the passenger door and set the pot inside the small tub I usually kept on the passenger side floor for occasions just like this. I freshened the potting soil at least once a week, but today I added additional nutrients and an extra shot of magic because I suspected I'd be taking at least one plant home today.

"On top of the dirt?" he questioned.

"Yes. Wiggle it down a little more so the pot won't topple."

Caelan did as I instructed and dusted his hands off once he'd shut the door.

I stood on the opposite side. "Did you need something?"

Caelan stayed silent for a long moment. "I'd like to start over."

The shifter had rendered me speechless. I stared at him mutely before opening and shutting my mouth. What could one say to that? "You strongarmed me, then got pissed at being outwitted, and decided to retaliate by destroying my shop. So no, Caelan, I don't think we can start over. Starting over would be us in a coffee shop, and I trip and accidentally spill my drink on your shirt and ruin it or saying something weird because I was nervous!" My voice was rising, and I couldn't seem to help it. "You don't get to start over when you single-handedly try to ruin someone's livelihood!"

Without waiting for a response, I got into my car and slammed the door. A moment later, I was out of the parking spot, headlights reflecting on Caelan's somber face, before I hit the gas and sped away.

The nerve of that man.

He wanted to start over? I would never forget the fear I felt when he backed me against the wall. My hand trembled against the steering wheel, and I willed myself to squash those memories down.

The human part of me suggested I simmer down, that Caelan had paid for the damage and seemed contrite for what he'd done. But that was the part of me that made my heart beat when a man walked behind me on a dark evening, or when one wouldn't take no as an answer. In those instances, I had to remember who I was and what I was capable of. Even if I didn't use my Chimera magic, I could still use the earth as a defense, and I could turn into a wren and escape, a talent that was decidedly inhuman. So, I had to tell that little part of me to shut it.

What Caelan deserved credit for was attempting to rectify his mistake and his sincere note. But none of us had the ability to go back in time, and that was my biggest issue. Why did some people think if they apologized or tried to make amends, it automatically erased everything that happened? It didn't. It couldn't.

Shaking away those thoughts, I turned into the driveway and

once I parked, I reached for the plant, gently lifting it onto the passenger seat. I'd take it in the back way so I could quickly repot it into something that had more room for root growth.

With the back door opened and the tub in my hands, I stepped inside, but an odd scent on the wind made me freeze. Frowning, I set the tub on the kitchen table, then hurried back outside.

Nothing seemed out of the ordinary, but the hair on the back of my neck stood up. The scent was faint but familiar. I went down the steps and paused, lifting my face to the air and taking a deep inhale.

There. I fished my cell from my pocket and turned on the flashlight. My night vision was better than most, but whatever it was seemed small, and the flashlight would help. Following the scent trail led me around the side of the house. Sweeping the light back and forth revealed nothing until I spotted something darker in the grass. It was a small, fluffy bundle that resembled a dandelion puff, but when I got closer and bent down to peer at it, I realized it looked just like a tuft of fur.

Confused, I reached for the small tuft and held it up to my nose and sniffed.

Caelan's familiar scent, along with the unmistakable tinge of wolf wafted up. My jaw clenched as I realized the implications of what I'd found.

Sonofabitch.

The question of why I had no glass in my skin when I woke up had been answered.

I was going to murder that nosy, meddling werewolf.

Twenty

Ash, Moira, and Tess were already at the shop when I
arrived the next morning. I opened my office to see Ash
sprawled on the couch, his nose in the pages of his
newest fantasy obsession. Moira was at my drawing desk, a pot of
tea and all the fixings scattered around her, while Tess was
conversing with one of the pothos.

The banshee liked talking to my plants, and I didn't have the
heart to stop her, though I made a mental note to move the pothos
closer to the window and give it an extra boost before I left for the
day. Tess tended to depress the poor things.

"Why's everyone here so early?" I asked as I tossed my purse
onto the desk.

Ash lowered his book. "I take it you didn't check the email."

I was too busy plotting revenge against everyone's favorite
wolf. "No. I was busy repotting a plant, and I went to bed early."

Moira fixed me a cup of tea and passed it over. "We've been
invited to the Night Market."

I almost dropped my tea. "What?"

"You heard me." Moira smirked. "The notice came in last
night."

"I—I didn't even apply this time." The Night Market came to

Joy Springs twice a month, and I'd spent the last four years trying to get in, only to be rejected every single time. Last month, I decided to stop trying. A girl could only take so much rejection before it felt personal.

"We know," Ash said. "So, we did the application for you."

Moira snapped up a sheet of paper and waved it at me. "Three days from now, you have one of the front spots at the market, renewable without an additional application for the next twelve months."

I gave her a dubious stare. "We have a front spot for the next twelve months?" That seemed far-fetched. Or...like someone had pulled some strings.

"Sonofabitch," I growled. "Caelan."

Moira grinned. "Seems that way, but we shouldn't look a gift horse in the mouth. You've been trying to get into that market for years now. It's great for us, great for the store—"

"And one more way Caelan owns us," I finished.

Ash made a humming noise. "He does seem way too interested in you, Evie."

Tess moaned and floated over. "I think I should talk to Caelan's ghosts."

Three pairs of eyes swung her way. It took me a moment to unscramble my brain so I could formulate a response. "I'm sorry. You just said Caelan's ghosts? Does he have ghosts?" Sometimes Tess said the weirdest shit and expected us to react like everything about it was normal.

Tess nodded. "Everyone has ghosts."

Moira choked on her tea.

Ash sighed. "Tess."

She moaned. "Am I being weird again? I'm sorry. I always assume people know things only to find out they don't."

I pinched the space between my brows. "Let's get back to the ghost comment. What do you mean, everyone has them?"

"Spirits linger close to those they love. When someone passes over, sometimes their ghosts don't travel on like they're supposed to. Stronger bonds make it harder for spirits to pass on to their afterlives."

"Shouldn't we be able to see them?" Moira asked.

"None of us have any," Tess pronounced. "I made sure of it."

None of us knew how to respond to that ominous announcement, so I chose to ignore it. "Can you get close enough to Caelan without him sensing you?"

Tess nodded. "Easy peasy. Shifters ignore spirit traffic because there's so much around. One more won't bother him."

I shook my head. "Too dangerous. I'm new and shiny. That's why he's interested."

Moira's lips quirked. "And your solution is to not be so interesting?"

I shot her a dark look. "Time is the solution. We ignore him, and eventually he'll find something or someone else to obsess over."

Ash set his book down. "I don't think our Evie understands how obsession works."

"If you're thinking about turning the market invite down, it's a terrible idea." Moira poured herself another cup of tea. "Caelan might have secured the invite, but he doesn't get any of the extra money you'll pull in."

"Who knows?" I muttered. "Maybe he takes kickbacks from all the vendors."

"Like a wolf mafia?" Ash drawled.

"I've seen stranger things."

The market would be great for our shop. Practitioners visited from all over the state, and few people could pass up fresh flowers when they spotted them. Since it was a magical market, I could enchant the bouquets I sold, and people could request specific charms. This might lead to more business and more connections in the magical community.

As much as I hated that Caelan pulled some strings, Moira was right. Saying no out of stubbornness would be foolish.

"Fine," I sighed. "We'll do the market."

At my words, Moira and Ash hooted. "Finally!"

"But," I interrupted their celebrating, "all of you have to work late until market night."

"We planned on it," Moira said.

AROUND LUNCH TIME, another delivery truck pulled up, this one labeled with the local luxury furniture maker's mark. Two burly men hopped out, one with a clipboard, and headed toward the door.

"Must be the replacement table," Ash said. "Want me to intercept?"

I'd spent most of the morning working in the back enchanting bouquets and had only come out to get another cup of coffee. "I'll take care of it. The table has to be made in a specific way, so I'll send it back if I need to."

Ash nodded. "You should know the furniture maker is a dryad. Doubtful you'll need to send anything back. He's well-versed in Floromancy."

Many years ago, I commissioned a well-known Amish furniture maker to create a massive wooden table for me. The wood had to be untreated and unstained, sealed with only natural materials like oil and beeswax. I refused to work on any projects involving flowers or plants on a chemically treated workspace.

The craftsman had asked no questions about the reasons why and seemed to appreciate the parameters. He charged me a fair price and delivered a stunning table two months later. The legs and supports were made of stainless steel, but the main workspace was a large piece of mahogany, polished to a high shine and treated with beeswax and olive oil.

I cherished the table and brought it with me when I moved. When Caelan destroyed it, a little piece of my past had died with me. The maker was only in Washington for a brief time before he moved out to be with his family in the Midwest. Tracking him down might prove difficult.

"I really loved the table I had."

Ash gave me a sad smile. "I know you did, but I think you should give this one a chance. I know his work. You might be surprised."

I nodded and followed him to the door. "I hope it's not too expensive."

Ash snorted. "Oh, it will be. This guy has a waiting list a year long. He must have set everything aside to work on this project."

Ash didn't see my wince. I could see my bank balance going up in flames.

The men entered, their eyes lighting on me as soon as they walked in. "Miss Quinn," the taller one asked. "We have a delivery for you." He handed the clipboard over for my signature.

"Do you have a bill?"

They exchanged a glance. "We do not."

"No bill, no signature," I said sweetly.

"Ma'am, we're under strict orders to deliver this to you today."

"And I need a bill." I smiled. "It's easy enough. Just send me the invoice the maker sent the Shifter Lord. Once I have it, you're more than welcome to come in and drop off the table."

We stood there in a polite stalemate until the second one nudged the first. "We have a tight schedule today, Rick. Just send it to her."

I smiled at the guy who was not Rick.

But Rick shook his head. "We were told not to tell her the price."

Not Rick scoffed. "Would you rather stand here and argue about this and be late to every one of our next appointments, or just forward her the email?"

"Dan!" Rick hissed. "We aren't supposed to send it."

"I won't tell if you won't tell," I said sweetly.

Dan lifted his eyebrows. "See. The lady won't tell. Now send it and let's get the hell out of here."

I laughed. "I like your style, Dan."

"If he asks, this is on you," Rick muttered as he took his cell phone out and scrolled. A moment later, my phone dinged. I opened my email to see a message from Rick Colby. Once I opened it to see there was indeed an invoice attached, I gestured for them to come on in.

Dan gave me a friendly wink and brushed past Rick. "Where do you want it?"

I showed them the spot where my old table used to sit. "Here, but I'll need to inspect the table before you leave."

Rick snorted.

Annoyed, I stopped and put my hands on my hips. "If you don't stop being an ass, Rick, I'm going to kick you out of my shop and give all the credit to Dan."

Rick's eyes widened, and I felt a little guilty about my subtle threat. But damn, I hated men like Rick, who couldn't be bothered with any kind of change or inconvenience, no matter how tiny.

Dan slapped Rick on the back hard enough to make him wince. "Let's get this inside for the lady, shall we?"

Rick winced and nodded. Both men disappeared outside and got to work.

Ash's eyebrows lifted when our eyes met. "Subtle," he drawled.

Moira cackled from across the room. "Let's see what Rick does if he has to haul that table right back out."

The odds were high that's exactly what would happen, but I'd give this craftsman dryad a chance.

Rick and Dan hauled a massive, wrapped piece of wood over the sidewalk. I held open the door for them, trying to make out any features of the table, but it was wrapped too thoroughly. They headed back out for the legs while I got busy inspecting the table.

Dan shooed me out of the way when he got back inside. "I have the right tools. Allow me."

I stepped away and let the man do his work. A few minutes later, a stunning piece of mahogany with a faint tinge of magic sat tipped on its edge against the wall.

Dan handed me an envelope. "From the maker. He asked for you to be the only one who opened this note."

Curious, I loosened the wax seal and pulled out a piece of sandalwood scented parchment.

Miss Quinn,

I must confess I was quite surprised when I received a request to recreate your work table. The Shifter Lord brought me a large piece of the top and sketched out how the original looked. Please send my compliments to the original craftsman who created it. I recognize quality work when I see it, though I could also tell the creator possessed no magic. I hope you won't mind, but I took some liberties with this new creation.

I know you are a Floromancer, and from Caelan's words, one of quite impressive power. The magic ingrained in this table is subtle. First, you will rarely need to condition and oil this table, once a year at most. Second, any cut flowers you store on top or are working on will no longer require a preservation spell while you work.

It is the least I can do for someone who took in my nephew and showed him such kindness.

If you ever have need of my services again, please reach out to me directly.

The note was signed *Septimus*, and a phone number was written in painstaking print below the signature.

I tucked the note into the envelope and turned to the dryad. "Nephew?"

Ash had the grace to look abashed. "I didn't realize he'd send a note."

Dan and Rick handled the table carefully, gently screwing in the base and legs. When it was finished, and they'd turned it right side up, a gasp escaped me.

This was a true piece of art. Shaped almost identical to the original, this one was also made of mahogany, polished and smooth to the touch. The legs were different from the original, hand-turned, and allowing the natural whorls in the wood to shine. But what was so different was the faint hum of magic vibrating from the top.

Moira and Tess came over.

"Stunning," the vampire murmured.

"It's a shame such a beautiful tree had to die for you," Tess said, which was high praise indeed from the banshee.

"My uncle does not cut down trees for his work," Ash said. "Every tree he uses has fallen naturally on his land. Mahogany trees don't grow here, so he most likely sourced it from another dryad in another territory. No dryad kills trees for their own use."

Tess turned to look at him, not saying anything for a long moment. "Everything dies, Ash. Even trees." She paused.

Ash looked crestfallen.

"Though I will say it is nice to know they'd met their natural end before being made into such a beautiful creation." Tess gave Ash a hesitant smile and walked back to the register area.

The dryad's brow furrowed before a wide smile tilted his lips up.

I ducked my head and turned away. Moira winked and went back over to the coffee area.

Banshee/dryad romance. Weird, a little depressing, but also very cute.

Dan cleared his throat. "Would you like to take a final look before you sign off?"

I nodded, even though I had no uncertainty about using the table in my practice. Running my fingers over the wood, the dryad's power hummed against my skin, friendly and welcoming. I'd like to meet Septimus one day, if only to see Ash around another family member.

The wood responded to my touch, and I almost jerked my fingers away. It was alive, but not. My first table was inert, only a table. This one was a living piece of art.

I signed my name and handed the clipboard back to Dan. "Thank you. Everything looks great."

Dan nodded and pulled Rick away. "We'll get out of your hair then. Have a nice day, ma'am."

When they were gone, everyone gathered around the table.

"I'm not sure I should look at that invoice," I said in a hushed tone.

Moira chuckled. "Yeah. Your bank account is in danger."

I had a plan to return Caelan's money, but it would take a few days to get everything ready. The tuft of his fur had changed things. He'd get his money and a little payback in return.

And if he messed up my table again, I might have to let him see the beast living under my skin.

CHAPTER

Twenty~One

T he Night Market came much faster than I was prepared for, but we all pitched in and finished the preparations a few hours before we had to be there to set everything up. None of us had any idea what to expect, but we'd all attended the market multiple times and knew the crowds would be diverse and heavy.

We'd brought as much as the van would hold, every available inch stuffed to the brim with corsages, boutonnieres, bouquets, wreaths, and all shapes and sizes of vases filled with flowers. Each of us wore a small flower pinned to our chest, primed with separate charms. Mine was a charisma charm. Every word that fell out of my mouth would loosen a customer's purse strings, only if they were leaning that way in the first place.

Tess's charm was for patience and forgiveness. She was efficient and competent, but sometimes my girl was dark. If she said something about the dead or someone dying while wearing the charm, customers would be more apt to show her grace.

Moira's charm was for beauty, not that she needed much help in that department, but men were more apt to buy when charmed by a beautiful saleswoman.

Ash's charm was one for aesthetics. People who talked to him would want to buy something natural to liven up their space. Green things made you feel better, though most people, even magical, dismissed their power.

Was it cheating? Nope. Every single vendor there would be wearing something similar to ours, and some of their compelling charms would be much more powerful than ours, borderline black magic. We knew this because we frequented the market quite often as customers, and all of us were too powerful to fall prey to such a spell. And we avoided the sellers who strayed too far away from giving someone a gentle nudge versus a punch in the face.

We might not continue wearing them after our first market, but I wanted to start out with the best chance for success I could.

The sun had set about an hour ago, though the sky was still filled with streaks of pink and purple. Summer temps in this area were hot, but the humidity wasn't as bad as it was closer to the coastal areas.

Think of Houston as a swamp, and this area more like a summer picnic at a lake. Night time is when Joy Springs really shone. Temperatures and humidity dropped even lower, and it was comfortable to walk outside without breaking into a sweat. I'd spent time in Houston during the summer, and I'd rather be waterboarded than do that again.

The Night Market was hidden from prying eyes by mysterious magic no one could quite decipher. A few days before the market was held, each shop chosen to attend would receive a postcard with a magical QR code you had to scan for entrance. To avoid forgeries, you also had to submit a single drop of blood for every attendee that would be matched with the QR code. The market had never been infiltrated by anyone who wasn't invited. I was safer here than I'd ever been in my shop.

Even with the lights, the stars were still visible above. Magic hummed in the air, every flavor of power skimming over my bare shoulders. I sensed shifters and sirens, plant mages, dryads, and others. Marnie and Twila were here somewhere, hopefully with a new coffee blend.

Ash was first out of the van. He let out a happy sigh, stretched, and allowed his arms to form multi-knobbed branches. The sight made me grin. The dryad rarely shifted in the shop. He wore a day-to-day glamour because of all the human tourists, so it was nice to see him feel comfortable enough to shift at will.

Moira was next. She carried a water boiler by the handle so she could serve hot tea blends. We should have power at the booth to keep the water at proper temp, but she'd have to constantly refill it. We'd see how that went. A larger water boiler might be on the list soon.

Tess didn't bother stepping out of the vehicle. She reverted to her half wisp form and floated out, stopping beside Moira. Her pale eyes were wide as she watched all the vendors setting up.

"Alright," I said when we were all at the back of the van. "Looks like we have one power strip for mundane appliances and fae lights to string up around the tent if we want them."

"We want them!" Moira said.

"Then I'll let you set them up with Tess. Let's get unloaded, starting with the things we think will sell the fastest."

We'd backed right up to our booth, so unloading wasn't a huge hassle, and we could grab things as we sold out.

True to their word, the organizers had put us toward the front. We were sandwiched between an earth witch selling herb and incense blends and a wand maker. After polite greetings on all sides, we got to work beautifying the booth.

An hour later, and half an hour before the market opened, we stood before the booth, critiquing how it looked.

"I like it," Ash said, "though it's a little too girly for my taste."

Tess's breathy laugh surprised us all. "Did you forget who you worked with?" she asked.

Ash stared at her with an open mouth. His cheeks went pink, and he looked away before clearing his throat. "No. I could never forget."

Dude had it so bad.

I pressed my lips together and looked away. Moira was a little more shameless and wiggled her eyebrows at Ash, who snorted and waved her off.

Tess, bless her banshee heart, noticed nothing. If Ash wanted her to know he liked her, he might have to be extremely blunt with her. As in showing up with flowers, escorting her out the door, and saying something like, "Tess, this is the first step of a seduction. Do you know what a seduction is?" And if the poor girl said no, he'd have to present a bullet point presentation, complete with phonetically spelled definitions.

And if she still didn't get it, Ash might have to resort to grabbing Tess and laying one on her, à la Rhett Butler and Scarlett O'Hara.

Until then, I didn't mind watching this adorable, awkward one-sided courtship.

"Maybe less pink," Moira said, steering us back to the issue at hand.

I tilted my head and narrowed my eyes, trying to see it through my team's eyes and not mine. Pink was one of my favorite colors, but with the white tablecloth and the other mix of blush flowers, the display had a bit of a wedding vibe.

"How about magenta?" I said, tapping my finger against my chin.

"Yes," Moira agreed. "Deep hot pink and maybe add some deep blues or purples in. Did we bring another tablecloth?"

I bent to rummage through one of the tubs. "Black and green."

"What color green?" Ash asked.

"Forest."

"Do the green," Moira said. "If we have a black table runner, we can add that too."

In ten minutes, the set up was finished, and the booth had taken on a deeper, more ethereal air.

I studied it, both hands on my hips. "I like it."

The earth witch next to us leaned over. "Much better. Beautiful." She gave us two thumbs up. "First market?"

I nodded. "Yes. We want to do it right the first time."

"I'm Emmy. Don't be afraid to switch it up during or for the next market. I've done this one for years and went through at least six set ups before I found the one that works for me."

Emmy was short and had a riot of curly brown hair pinned up in no discernible order atop her head. She had friendly blue eyes and dimples at the edge of her mouth when she smiled. As was the case with most witches, I couldn't discern her age. She could be anywhere from thirty to eighty. Witches weren't immortal, but they were very long lived.

"Do you have a shop in town?" I asked. I'd never seen her before, but I was a creature of habit and didn't often venture too far away from the town square.

"No. I live in Dripping Springs, so I only do the market once a month. Me and my best friend switch spots." She smiled. "You'll meet Yvonne next time if you're here. She's a besom maker."

"I look forward to it."

"Once things slow down, feel free to browse my wares. I offer a substantial discount to the vendors."

"There's tea over here if you want some," Moira called. "Only three blends today because of our small water boiler, but I'm happy to make you a cup."

"I'd love one," Emmy said. "Once the market opens and things stop being so crazy, I'll pop over."

The wand maker was a tall, thin man who said very little, and only offered a polite smile by way of greeting. He had small, round glasses, and a sharp jawline, but even with him sitting several feet away, I could feel his aura of power. Wands weren't my thing, and I never used them, but much like my new work table, his wares felt alive.

We each grabbed a chair and sat down, taking one last break before the market opened.

When the bell rang announcing the market's opening, a sense

of anticipation and giddiness filled me. As much as I hated us getting in here because of someone else's influence, our shop's talent would see us through. And if it didn't, at least we had the opportunity to experience it once.

"Places, people," I said quietly as I stood and tightened my apron.

Our booth was a riot of color, bright flowers blooming at their peak. Each glass vase was a different color and shape, and we'd used stacked shelving to display each one at different heights. Moira and Tess had strung fairy lights all over the booth and around the table, casting everything in a soft, ethereal glow.

Ash had the best handwriting out of all of us, so he'd taken on the responsibility of writing up clever descriptions of each product. I don't think we could have done it better, not for our first time. Maybe when it was over, we could do a hotwash and discuss improvements for the next one, but pride filled me with what we'd already accomplished today, even without a single sale yet.

People of all shapes and sizes piled into the market.

"Here we go," murmured Moira.

Twenty~Two

"Holy crap," I groaned as I kicked my shoes off and dug my bare toes into the earth.

"That was awesome," Tess breathed.

Moira sipped a cup of blood-laced tea. "We might need to hire more help."

Ash had turned his bottom half into a tree and was soaking up some of the extra magic permeating the earth from the market denizens. "Do we have stock left in the shop or does one of us need to change next week's order?"

I accepted a cup of non-laced tea from the vampire. "Bump up next week's stock order. I may need to remodel the greenhouse."

We sold everything. None of us could believe it. And not only had customers decimated our stock, we'd given out every business card we brought and booked two weddings.

"You've needed to remodel that thing for ages now," Moira remarked. "The greenhouse looks like an abandoned asylum."

"Har har," I drawled. "It came with the house, and it has some odd energy, so I haven't done much with it. But now that we're doing these markets, I might have to start growing more stock to keep us in business."

Ash frowned. "You'll deplete yourself too soon."

Moira and I exchanged a look. "I don't think that's the case, but if I start feeling drained, I'll notify you to scoop up more stock for the week."

Ash gave me an odd look but nodded and slowly pulled his roots from the ground. A dryad couldn't perform magic like most of us. I could snap a spell off in seconds. Dryad magic was slow and thoughtful, much like a tree. Their magic grew over centuries, not weeks, and Ash was a perfect example. It would take him a good half hour before he extricated himself fully from the ground.

Tess, Moira, and I busied ourselves with taking down the display and cleaning up our area. One of the tenets of the market was to leave the earth in better shape than you found it. As a Floromancer, I tended to take rules like that to the extreme. Once everything was packed neatly into the van, and Ash was in human form again, I went back to our booth space, settled myself on the ground, and dug my fingers into the earth.

By now, almost every vendor was gone, and the market had settled into a quiet, comforting hum. Fae lights still glowed in the booth shells, but the noise had died down to a murmur.

"We'll wait in the van," Moira whispered, gesturing for the others to follow.

I shot her a grateful smile and closed my eyes. Magic thrummed against my fingers, itching to be commanded. The noise died away as I sent a pulse of power into the ground, finding life shoved too far down. I nudged those seeds closer to the earth and sent nutrients into the surrounding soil. Wildflowers that never had the chance to grow soon sprouted from the ground in a twenty-foot diameter. I fixed the dry patches of ground by rerouting water that wasn't serving anything, and around the black magic practitioners, I repaired the dying life close to their booths. As much as I disapproved of the practice, the Night Market allowed them in, so I did what I could.

When I opened my eyes, I had a curious audience giving me a careful berth. Around ten magic practitioners were watching me. I blinked and smiled awkwardly until one stepped forward.

"I'm Ruth." She was a tall redhead and had a friendly smile. "None of us have ever seen Floromancy in action. We were curious, that's all."

I touched my chest. "Evie. I own Little Shop of Florals."

"Oh! That's the place right in downtown?" Ruth asked.

I nodded. "We've been there a little over four years now."

"I'm in Fredericksburg, but I've heard of your shop. We've been involved in weddings where you did the flowers."

I rose and wiped my fingers on a towel Moira had laid on my lap while I was out. What a thoughtful vampire. "Do you have a business card?"

Ruth dug in her pocket and handed one over. She quickly introduced everyone else, but I was still magic groggy, and all the names blurred. I gave everyone a polite smile and handed them business cards from my private stash if they wanted one.

We said our goodbyes, and it wasn't until I turned around that I spotted what I'd done to the market.

"Oof." Flowers were everywhere. "Shit," I whispered.

Moira came up and linked her arm through mine. "You're a regular fairy-tale princess."

"Think they'll be mad?"

"Only Hitler would be mad about wildflowers."

A surprised laugh escaped me. "Well, I'm all about pissing Hitler off, so I guess we're good."

"That's my girl," Moira cheered. "Let's get you home. You look wiped."

She dug the van keys from my pocket and opened the passenger door for me before jogging to the other side.

I was asleep before Moira had pulled out of the market parking lot.

Ash nudged me awake. "We're back at the shop," he said quietly.

I yawned and let Moira help me out of the van. "That's the first time I've napped in a long time."

"You needed it," she said. Moira handed me my purse. "Got your phone?"

I patted my back pocket. "Yup."

She narrowed her eyes at me. "Will you be okay driving home?"

"Yes, mom." I gave her a little shove. "We've had some late nights. I'm fine."

Tess floated next to Ash. "This was so much fun! I can't wait until the next one."

"Glad you like it," I said. "We'll chat about what went right and what went wrong in a few days. I think we all need some time to recover."

"On that note, I'm ready for bed," Ash said. He brushed a kiss across my cheek. "Be careful."

We waved goodbye, and I got in my car, wishing I had a cup of coffee to wake me up. Once I flipped on the radio and pulled away from the shop, I rolled down the window to let some cool air in and pulled the braid from my hair. Happy exhaustion settled into my bones, and a slow smile pulled my lips up. I felt useful today. Every day I opened my shop, I felt helpful, but today, people were interested in our booth, drawn to our display, and ninety percent of the customers who stopped by actually purchased something. The other ten percent had placed special orders.

This was the first time I'd ever taken specific charm orders for people. Normally, I gauged what someone needed based on my intuition and responded accordingly without their knowledge. Today, I listened to people and what they needed and had sold dozens of made-to-order charms. The next few days would be busy.

And that meant even more money coming into Little Shop of Florals.

Lost in my thoughts, I missed the first low snarl. As I slowed for a red light, a lone wolf howl rended the air. My fingers tightened on the steering wheel. When a second howl tore through the night, I leaned my head out the window and listened.

When the third came, I pulled my vehicle off the road and parked. A sharp, pained yelp and the sounds of animals fighting had me barreling from the car.

Caelan was my first thought, followed by Simone. He could take care of himself, but the memory of him lying in the dirt mortally wounded flashed through my mind, and I bolted toward the sounds of fighting.

A quarter mile later, I peeked around the corner. Several wolves surrounded each other, a massive dark wolf at the head of one side, wolves of all colors behind him in a semi-circle formation, facing off against a pack of all white wolves. Getting involved right now would be dangerous for everyone, so I stayed downwind and observed. I'd never seen Caelan in wolf form, though I assumed he was the large wolf based on the coloring of the tuft I'd found in my yard. A smaller, reddish wolf stood tensed on his right side, and a huge gray wolf stood on his left.

The others stood tensed behind him, heads lowered and fangs bared, protecting his back and flank.

I wasn't worried about any of them as long as I stayed far enough away to avoid them scenting me. The one I was worried about lay prone on the ground next to Garrett, bleeding heavily from a stomach wound. Life still flickered around the wolf, but I could tell she was close to death.

My magic itched to heal, power sputtering at my fingertips. I waited for my moment, every second one taken away from the wolf's life.

When Caelan's mournful howl ripped through the air, and all the wolves lunged at each other, ripping and tearing, I saw my moment.

Keeping my head low and my body closer to the ground, I stayed near the wall. The fight had spilled away from the wounded wolf, but one, a smaller white and gray wolf stayed close, protecting her. I'd have to deal with that one before I could help the other.

Once I came within ten feet, the second wolf turned, a low, deadly snarl rumbling from its chest. I held my hands up and stopped. "My name is Evie. Your Lord is familiar with me. I can help her."

For a moment, I thought the wolf was going to lunge. My muscles tensed, and I ripped magic from the stone, holding it in stasis until the wolf decided how big of a threat I was.

"I'm a Floromancer, and I can heal your friend. But there isn't much time. Decide now, or it will be too late."

The wolf snarled once more before dipping its head and watching me warily.

I nodded and hurried toward the wounded shifter. Going to my knees, I dug my hands in the wolf's fur, searching for the worst of the wound.

"You need to shift," I said urgently.

But the wolf, a she I decided, was too far gone. I'd never helped a creature shift, but I took the magic I'd gathered and gently touched her on the edge of her wound. Earth magic soaked into the wolf's body. She glowed green and pink, and a low whine came from deep in her throat.

I put a touch of command in my voice. "Shift." Channeling more power into the shifter's body, I searched for the source of her magic, and when I found it, I gave it a good zap.

The injured wolf yelped, causing the other one to snarl. I held a hand up. "Not helpful," I barked. "I promise you I'm helping her."

The second wolf whined and came around to my side and sat down. "Keeping guard? Alright then. Just don't interfere."

A slight huff made me smile. "Your friend needs to shift. She's dying."

The wolf yipped and bent to gently nudge the other. I pushed more power into my voice. "SHIFT." Power rumbled the ground as magic shimmered around the wolf. A yelp of pain tore through the wolf's yips, and a few seconds later, a young, nude woman lay before me.

"Good," I breathed. "I'm so sorry. This is going to hurt."

I laid both hands on her and pulled power from the ground. Cement cracked around us as vines rose from the ground, curling around the shifter's arms and legs. Magic the color of watermelon tourmaline flowed from my fingers and slowly knitted the edges of the jagged wound in her stomach back together.

Yips and snarls and yelps of pain rang all around us as the packs continued fighting, but I tuned them out, focusing only on the female shifter. When I felt her blood stabilize, I withdrew, allowing my vines to stay wrapped around her. They'd continue pumping the healing magic of the earth within her until Caelan was ready to take her home.

"The vines will stabilize her," I said to the watcher wolf. "Don't remove them until you have to, and I ask that you not cut them. Touch them and gently ask them to let go. They will. Be careful not to jostle her too much. She will be okay if you get her back to your keep soon, okay?"

The wolf whined and nudged me with its cold nose. I reached out and scratched it behind the ear. "If Caelan asks, maybe say you have no idea who I was?" I smiled hopefully, but the wolf gave me a baleful look.

"Right. Fine. But if he doesn't ask, you don't have to tell him."

The wolf huffed which I took for a yes. "Alright. Be careful." I eyed the other wolves still involved in what appeared to be a fight to the death. "Good luck." I rose and carefully crept back along the wall until I disappeared around the corner and hurried the rest of the way to my car.

I might regret this later, but my Floromancy was a magic of life, and if I had the opportunity to save someone, I would always find a way.

CHAPTER
Twenty~Three

CAELAN

B attle always set me on edge for hours afterward. I had a rival pack in my territory, and it had taken me by surprise, a fact I needed to sit with once I was sure we were all out of the danger zone. Other wolves were beginning to test the boundaries of what I'd put up with. This one hadn't ended well, but there'd be no repercussions as the wolves had encroached on my territory. A clear case of defending what was mine.

Tired and sporting a dozen wounds, I shifted back to human form and leaned my head against the wall. Garrett and Simone were fine as was almost everyone else except for Lena, who'd been ambushed earlier, fortunately able to call for aid before they killed her.

I turned to see how the wolf fared. During the fight, I'd felt an oddly familiar magic in the area, but it hadn't felt harmful, so I ignored it. All my focus had to stay on the fight.

Jack, Lena's mate, sat beside the wounded wolf, who'd shifted back to human form. My gaze swept down her body, and I froze, breath catching as I spotted the source of the familiar magic. My mind went back to that day in the woods when I'd been ambushed and had damn near died, only to wake up naked and alone the next morning, fully healed and wrapped in vines and wildflowers.

Pushing off the wall, I stalked over to Jack and crouched. "Who was here?" I already knew, but I needed it voiced.

Jack shied away at the harsh rasp in my voice. "She knew you'd ask and pleaded for me not to tell you."

I gritted my teeth and stared at him, gold light flaring over the other shifter's face. Jack abruptly dropped his eyes. "Evie," he whispered. "She said her name was Evie and asked to help Lena."

All this time I suspected it had been Evie in the woods that night. This solidified it. Lena's once mortal wound had healed to a thin, pink line, Evie's healing power still glowing around her.

"How is she?" I asked.

"Evie said she will live if we get her back to the keep quickly. She asked for us not to cut the vines if we could."

My eyebrows lifted. "How do we free her?"

Jack swallowed hard, his eyes still on his mate's still form. "She said to ask them nicely."

I barked a laugh. What a little hippie Evie was. "Fine." I touched one of the vines on Lena's ankle. "My name is Caelan. I'm a...friend of Evie's." She'd piss her pants with laughter if she heard me right now. "Do you mind letting go of Lena? We need to take her back home so we can call the doctor."

At first the vines did nothing, but Evie wouldn't tell Jack to ask if she hadn't meant it, so I waited for a few moments. Eventually, the vines pulsed with that familiar pink and green magic I remembered from that night in the forest, and slowly unwrapped from Lena's body, retracting back into the ground. Evie had destroyed the cement around Lena's body, but we were in an alley. The city could fix it if it became an issue later.

I touched the ground. "Thank you."

Nodding to Jack, I rose. "Bring her and let's get home."

"Should I stay back and dispose of the other wolves?"

"Let them rot." It was the highest insult I could pay to the lower Alpha who'd sent them here. If he wanted his people back, he could trespass on my territory and try to take them.

A vicious smile crossed my lips. I couldn't wait until he tried.

CHAPTER
Twenty-Four

I did not mention the detour to Moira or the others when I got to the shop a couple of days later. All was quiet on the shifter front, but the morning after, I awoke to a small basket on my front porch filled with heirloom seed packs from one of my favorite places to order from and a hand-embroidered apron that read: *I like big buds and I cannot lie.*

A purple hand-blown glass vase filled with Belgian chocolates and a stainless-steel hand shovel topped everything off.

The sender had tucked a card inside that read simply:

You surprise me, Evie. You didn't have to, and yet you did. Again.

Lena fares well and sends her sincerest thanks. Her mate, the guardian wolf, also wishes to express his deepest gratitude for your actions.

It was signed *Caelan.*

An aggrieved sigh escaped me. He knew it was me in the woods. I realized I probably couldn't keep that secret bottled up forever, but more time would have been nice. Her wound was mortal, but she had very little power compared to the Shifter

Lord. My magic didn't require me to go as deep to help her as it had with Caelan.

I triple checked the basket to ensure he hadn't slipped anything weird in, like a camera or listening device, but as I carried it in, an idea formed. The basket and thank you card was a nice gesture, but it didn't absolve him of responsibility for him coming into my house and creeping in my bedroom. I'd been working on a little side project for Caelan so I could send him the check with style. But I had a plan for a little payback while I was at it.

After I'd finished a cup of coffee and chatted with everyone, I headed to the back to check on the Venus flytrap I'd nurtured from a tiny seedling. But...I'd given it a little something extra.

Caelan was going to have a field day with this one. I chuckled to myself and reached for the bucket of handmade compost.

The Red Dragon flytrap greeted me by clicking dozens of its traps, the main, larger one stretching out to reach me.

"Hey Seymour." I gently gave it a scratch underneath the main trap. It made an odd cooing noise that made me laugh.

"Hungry?"

All two hundred of the baby traps snapped in unison. "Okay. I brought you something extra today."

After a few freeze-dried worms, Seymour settled down and allowed me to freshen up his potting soil. I'd experimented with the flytrap in a way I never had any other plants before. He was a project of my Floromancy and my rage at Caelan. I'd chosen a carnivorous plant for obvious reasons, but Seymour was a distraction while I enacted my true revenge.

"You ready for a new home today?" I asked Seymour.

The flytrap tilted itself the way a dog tilted its head when curious.

"Remember what we talked about?"

Another head tilt the opposite way.

"It's okay if you don't remember, just toss the check at him." I smiled. "Then bite him if you can."

I fed Seymour another worm and gave him a tiny bit of water to tide him over, then carefully packaged him up, adding an envelope with a check so large it made me hyperventilate, and note that simply said:

Check & Mate.

I also checked the seeds I'd placed in a spelled container and tipped them out into a small brown baggie to take with me this evening.

Satisfied with everything, I tucked the bag into the transport box, tossed Seymour another worm, and carried it to the front of the store.

"Don't touch Seymour," I warned. "He's got an attitude."

Tess peered into the box. "Aww. He's adorable! I've never seen one that color."

"Special variety." I grabbed my purse and hugged Moira who was giving me a thoughtful look. She knew something was up.

"Spelled how?" Ash asked as he looked into the box and physically recoiled. "Why is that thing so large?"

I pointed to the bag of worms. "Those and lots of love."

Ash's brow furrowed. "Flytraps are notoriously angry plants, but..." His voice trailed off, and he barked a laugh. "That's why you named him Seymour."

I grinned. "Yup. Except he can't sing, and that's a real shame."

"I'm sure you could figure that one out if you really tried." Moira's voice was droll.

"Every plant is musical. You just have to possess the right frequency to feel it."

Tess blinked at me. "Really?"

"Of course. Don't you feel better when you're in the shop versus when you're in a place that has no green space?"

Tess thought about it. "Huh. I guess I do."

"Your subconscious hears the music," I explained.

She stared at the flytrap. "That's so cool."

"Want to hear it?" I asked.

Her attention snapped to me. "How?"

"Through me." I held out my hand.

"Ooh! Me too!" Moira said.

"Alright. Put your hand on my arm," I instructed.

Ash heard the music every day. He was already part plant and more connected to the earth than I ever would be because it had literally birthed him. Once a quarter, Ash returned to his main tree to refresh his magic, and when he came back, the music in the shop was boosted for weeks.

"Ready?"

Both women nodded. "Alright. Close your eyes."

I had to be careful not to use too much magic. Once Moira had her hand on me, and I was clutching Tess's hand, I slowly opened my senses and sent a trickle of magic into each woman. Moira laughed and Tess gasped.

"Listen," I commanded and slowly turned the volume of music I always heard a little louder until the store was suffused with sound.

"Oh," Tess breathed, silvery tears shining in her eyes as the music swept around us.

"My god," Moira murmured. "Is this what you hear all the time?"

"It is." The inherent music of the earth used to be overwhelming until I learned how to control the volume. Now it acted as a barely noticeable background soundtrack to my life unless I was tangled in the earth communing. Then I opened my senses wide and let the sound cleanse and purify my body.

"Plants don't technically make music. It's sound and vibration translated into musical notes, so we can better understand." Tess and Moira gripped me tightly, their eyes squeezed shut as they continued listening.

"It's like new age music combined with techno," Tess said in a hushed voice.

"I could listen to this for the rest of my life," Moira breathed.

"Maybe we can get a few of those devices that translate the

sound. I think you can buy them online." I'd seen a few that seemed legitimate.

"Yes!" Tess said. "I want to hear what those carnivorous beasts you keep in the back sound like."

Speaking of the deadly plants, I was worried Caelan had absconded with them, but I later found them tucked in the back by the cooler. Why they didn't attack him was curious, but maybe he wasn't the one who moved them. Maybe Caelan had let a sacrificial lamb do his dirty work.

I'd been meaning to call another repairman for the cooler door as our regular one was booked solid, but someone had fixed the door sometime after our confrontation, probably at the same time he'd had the window fixed.

When the music crescendoed and faded into a slight hum, I let my magic go, and the plant sounds faded away.

Moira let go and wiped her face. Tess gripped my hand for a moment longer before she let go and sighed.

"It sounds the exact opposite of death."

Moira and I stared at her dumbly before the vampire gathered herself. "What does death sound like exactly?"

Tess shrugged. "Kinda like that noise when you stub your toe really bad. Like a sharp intake of breath before the inevitable wail, followed by a lot of screaming."

Poor Tess would have a tough time finding another job if she ever left the shop. Her personality was frightening on a good day.

"Well," Moira said. "That's good to know."

Tess smiled and floated away. Moira and I exchanged a wide-eyed look.

"Wow," she mouthed.

I loved the banshee, but she always strayed far too close to death for my comfort. Shaking my head, I grabbed my purse and the box. "Heading out. I'll see you in a couple of days."

The shop was closed for the next two days. One was our normal off day, and the other was a Joy Springs holiday celebrating the town's founding, aptly named Day of Joy. Any day off was a day of joy, and no one kept their shop open that day.

The first year I'd arrived and had just opened the shop when I realized it was almost eleven in the morning, and the town was a ghost town. One of the other shop owners took pity on me when she spotted my "open" sign and stopped to inform me about the holiday.

The town put on a small celebration every year, complete with food and craft booths, a live band, and a magic show for the unsuspecting humans. I'd only gone a couple of times and found it a bit too peopley for my tastes, so tonight, I planned to drop off Caelan's check, then go home and soak in my tub for an hour.

I was behind on my mental and physical exercises for the month and needed to catch up on those—otherwise Hazel would have my ass—*if* she found out. Having your mentor in another country wasn't always ideal, but it did allow for more slacking than normal.

The witch had given me a rigid schedule but stressed the mental exercises were the most important to keep the Chimera magic at bay. A strong mind equaled a strong will, and only a strong will could control the magic that threatened to overtake me when my emotions got the best of me.

A quick stop at one of the local apothecaries netted me a bottle of my favorite lavender vanilla bubble bath and some of her new rose and neroli body oil. One last stop at the in-town winery to grab a bottle of their famous blueberry wine, and I was on my way home, with Seymour happily nestled in his box awaiting his new quarters.

Tonight promised to be epic.

CHAPTER

Twenty~Five

Wards are a powerful tool to keep people and creatures off one's property, but they have one major failure.

They can't be tuned to keep nature out, or they'd never work properly. This meant they can't keep Floromancers out, and since our kind are normally peaceful and content to keep to ourselves, no one had yet discovered how someone could use magic like mine to not only trespass, but to wreak utter havoc.

I'd tested this a few times over the years and had discovered I could use my wren form to travel anywhere, no matter how powerful someone's wards were. Most had successfully blocked me from entering in human form, but whatever magic I had in my wren form, the wards ignored. Whether it was my fae blood or something else, I'd rarely found a ward that could keep me out.

Such was the case this evening.

My wren form was too light to carry the box holding Seymour, and a courier might clue Caelan or his staff into suspecting something was up, so I'd grown a few thick vines right at the edge of the keep. Carefully guiding them, I encouraged them to wrap around the tightly packed roots of the flytrap and sent them and Seymour sliding onto Caelan's property, past the unsuspecting wolves on the second-floor balcony and gently set the plant right in front of the Shifter Lord's door.

Then I guided the vine up and rang the doorbell, quickly sending the vines hissing back across the yard and back into the earth.

It only took a few moments for the door to open. A confused shifter looked around, stepped outside the house to scope the area, only looking down when he saw nothing concerning.

When he spotted Seymour, the look on the shifter's face almost made me laugh. He let out a shout of alarm, then called for Caelan. When the Shifter Lord arrived at the door looking annoyed by the interruption, only to find a large Red Dragon flytrap at his door holding a sign that said *For Caelan's eyes only*, his face went carefully blank, but his eyes showed his agitation. A golden glow shone over the porch.

I crouched even lower, right outside the boundaries of his property. The next phase of my plan relied on him taking the plant inside. If he decided not to and tried to destroy Seymour, I'd have to spring into action, both to save the plant and show him exactly how I felt about that.

"Take it," Caelan barked.

The other shifter balked. "You want me to carry that thing inside?"

"It's harmless."

"It has teeth. Everywhere."

"So do I," Caelan snarled. "Now get it inside. It has a message she wants me to see."

Seymour didn't reach out for a bite, but I could see the flytrap quivering. The shifter reached for it, carefully holding the plant at arm's length, and went inside, Caelan following behind.

I waited for a long moment to ensure no one would pop back outside before shifting to my wren form. A few seconds later, I sat atop his roof, inspecting the area to ensure nothing nasty would happen when I shifted back.

That was another thing about property protections. A lot of

people forgot to protect the roof. Caelan had installed no less than a dozen cameras, and that was okay. I wanted him to know it was me.

But I didn't want him to see exactly what I was going to do next, so I encouraged some mold to grow in one of the small puddles of water atop the roof and sent it crawling in different directions until every camera facing me was covered with a layer of green growth. Time was of the essence now. Someone would quickly discover the covered cameras.

I fished in my pocket for the small bag of charged seeds and pulled out a handful. They sparkled and glowed in the moonlight, ready to serve their purpose. I cupped my hands together, blew into my palms, and cast the seeds off the roof, sending them scattering across Caelan's property. I turned in the other direction and did the same, ensuring every inch of his property was covered.

Then I did the thing that horrified every red-blooded American male obsessed with lawn care. From my other pocket, I pulled out a handful of charged dandelion seeds and scattered those in all directions.

Once I scanned his property and felt the seeds waiting in anticipation in every direction, I settled in to wait, knowing I didn't have long.

The first horrified scream rang through the property a couple of minutes later, quickly followed by several more, until I heard Caelan's low snarling curse.

A grin spread across my face.

Game on, asshole.

Twenty-Six

CAELAN

"Stop being such a sissy," Simone snapped to the shifter lying in the fetal position, holding his bleeding hand.

"It attacked me," the shifter whined.

"You're lucky it didn't do worse. The note warned you not to get too close." I eyed the angry flytrap. "There's something else inside the traps."

"I'll get it," Simone said, reaching for the folded piece of paper.

"No. I'll do it." Evie sent the rabid thing to me to prove a point, but I don't think it was making the one she'd wanted.

"Lord." Simone reached out to me, but at my look, she lowered her eyes.

"Apologies."

I stood before the plant—Seymour, she'd named it—and studied the traps. There was the main one, far larger than it should be, and somewhat sentient. The other traps lay closer to the soil, watchful and wary. The envelope was tucked into several of those traps, and if I reached in, I'd leave my hand vulnerable.

The shifter, still lying on the floor, moaned. "Lord. It's poisoned."

"I'm aware." My shifter was still alive. In pain and in a piss poor mood, but still alive.

"The healer will be here momentarily," Simone said. "If she wanted anyone dead, you wouldn't be lying there bitching about everything."

I schooled my expression into blankness. A mother hen, she was not.

"But what kind of poison?" I murmured to myself.

"Paralytic," the shifter said. "Can't move anything below my waist."

Simone's lips twitched then. The study doors opened, and a massive shifter walked in.

Ben had been with me for over fifty years. He was not a wolf and had never revealed his animal form to me or anyone else that I knew of. Though I suspected maybe Simone knew since I'd caught them making moon eyes at each other a couple of times.

He wasn't 100% shifter either. Ben had a gift for healing and had stayed on with the Pack when I offered him a job after seeing him in action when a rogue cat shifter caught one of my shifters unaware on a camping trip.

His sharp, dark gaze swept the room, snagging briefly on Simone and betraying his emotions when I caught the sound of his heart rate briefly rising. Simone carefully did not look at him. Instead, she pointed to the ground.

"Poisoned and cut. Says it's a paralytic." Her voice was short and to the point, but I'd known her for years and heard the slight tremble in the words.

More power to them if those two got together. Ben never showed a hint of interest in anyone in my Pack or outside. Out of anyone in my Pack, he could use an Omega the most.

Ben was taller than me by about three inches and outweighed me by at least fifty pounds. If he got his hands around me, he might be able to take me in a physical fight, but that had never happened. As a sparring partner, he kept me on my toes.

The healer crouched, a soft blue glow pulsing at his fingertips. "Hold still," Ben growled.

The shifter obeyed, lying still as the grave.

Ben's eyes glowed the same color as his fingers as he swept through the body, looking for the source of the poison.

He stilled when he found it. "Oh," he breathed. "Clever girl."

My brows went up at the admiration in his words. A sharp pang zinged in my chest, and I brushed it away.

Ben rose and dusted his hands off. "He'll be fine in an hour or so. I'll have someone carry him to the clinic." He turned to examine Seymour.

"Don't get too close," I warned.

"I'm a healer," Ben said. "It knows I'm not a threat."

I wouldn't be so sure about that, but Ben reached a finger out as he bent and started speaking in a gentle voice. "Hello, you beautiful little monster. What are you?"

"Red Dragon flytrap," Simone said.

Ben made a humming noise. "Yes. And no." With a glowing fingertip, Ben stroked the back of the main trap's head. Seymour craned its stem up, almost like it craved the attention.

"I'll be damned," I breathed.

"This is a gift from your Floromancer, isn't it?" Ben asked.

"Evie, yes."

"She's brilliant," Ben murmured.

Simone went still, but not before a look of despair crossed her face before she schooled her expression into neutral interest.

The healer rose. "This is a Red Dragon, yes, but she somehow crossed it with Gelsemium DNA while still keeping all the physical properties of the original plant. Still looks like a Red Dragon, still carnivorous, but mildly poisonous to those unfortunate enough to get bitten." He turned to face me. "Did she leave you with any food?"

I held up the bag of frozen worms. Ben shook his head. "That will tide it over, but I guarantee you your Floromancer has given it her blood." He chuckled. "If you keep it, you may have to make periodic...offerings."

"Shit," I muttered.

Ben pointed to the folded-up paper. "Need me to get that?"

I sighed. "If you would."

But when Ben reached under the main trap to get the paper, Seymour reacted, snapping at Ben's wrist. The healer jerked back with lightning-fast reflexes and held his hands out in surrender. "Ah. Okay. For Caelan's eyes only, I understand." He stepped back and gestured for me to go ahead.

With a muttered curse, I reached toward Seymour. When it made no aggressive move, I reached further, my fingers curling around the check. Just as I pulled it away from the pot, Seymour reacted, trap opening wide, poison dripping from its teeth as it lunged for me.

I swore and jerked away. "Asshole."

Ben chuckled. "Shifter Lord, have you ever heard the old saying about attracting more flies with honey?"

"I'm not stroking a plant's ego," I snarled.

"Plants don't have egos. This one is genetically modified to be aggressive, but it only reacted that way to me when I tried to take something meant for you. Perhaps kindness is the way to this thing's heart."

"Seymour," Simone said quietly.

Ben's brow furrowed before a deep, barreling laugh rumbled through his chest. "Its name is Seymour?" He chuckled again. "I need to meet this Floromancer."

Hot rage spiraled through me. Simone and Ben turned to me, one of the healer's eyebrows rising. "Oh. It's like that, is it?"

"It's not like anything," I snarled.

Simone pressed her lips together and took the paper from my hand. "Just in case it's poisoned," she said.

"It's not," Ben said. "I'd smell it. The only thing on the paper is ink."

Simone unfolded the paper, and another paper fell out. When

she retrieved it, a rush of air expelled from her chest, and she winced. "You aren't going to like it," she said.

"What is it?"

Simone held up a check made out to me, written for an extraordinary amount.

The exact amount I spent restoring her shop.

"There's a note," Simone continued.

"Read it," I growled.

Simone cleared her throat. "It just says 'Check and mate.'"

A low snarl rumbled from my throat. I spun away and stalked from the room, reaching out and swiping a chair up, breaking it in half. Wood splinters shattered, but it wasn't enough. The urge to destroy overwhelmed me. I swept the glass centerpiece from the table, shattering the Murano hand blown bulbs.

"Lord," Simone said urgently.

I reached for one of the bookshelves, picked it up with one hand and tossed it through the window, the feeling of uselessness screaming through my veins.

Ben murmured something to Simone, so low I couldn't make it out.

Why won't she let me protect her? Why must she continually spurn my advances?

I threw my head back, an enraged howl spilling from my throat, and burst through the front door, intent on finding her.

Twenty-Seven

The second the furious howl rang out, I sent magic spiraling into the ground. Full-grown trees burst from the earth, ripe with fruit. Flowering vines wrapped around the house's columns. Bushes in a riot of colors popped up, ruining his perfect landscaping, but the most perfect part was the mix of native wildflowers and dandelions that sprang up, obliterating Caelan's perfect grass in a carpet of stunning blooms.

I sat cross-legged on his roof, waiting for him to spot me.

Caelan stalked down the porch, stopped at the edge of the yard, and put his hands on his hips. A litany of curses blasted from his mouth. I put my hand over my mouth to keep from laughing and watched as he stepped onto the wildflower carpet.

A massive man behind him followed, his deep, rumbling chuckle making my lips tilt up. "You gotta admit she has style."

"Shut the fuck up, Ben." Caelan went to the middle of his front yard and swept the area. I'd deliberately sat where he'd scent me and waited for the gentle breeze to reach his nose. Once it did, Caelan's eyes snapped up.

The large man barked a laugh when I gave Caelan a little wave and dropped my fingers one by one until only the middle one was left. Then I waved that one at him, turned into a wren, and leaped from the roof. My car was parked a mile away, far enough to avoid suspicion, close enough for me to fly with ease.

But what I hadn't counted on was Caelan's agility. In one graceful movement, the Shifter Lord leapt into the air, reaching out a claw tipped hand to grasp me. I nosedived to dodge and swept away, warbling at him in annoyance.

Just as I was flying away, I heard the large man remark. "That's Evie? Does she know only the male fairy wrens have that coloring?"

I almost fell out of the air. Not a single person had ever successfully identified me. Curious, I swept around and got a closer look at the big man.

He noticed. "Hello, pretty birdie. Clever work on that flytrap of yours."

Caelan lunged for me again.

"You won't get her," Ben observed as I darted away. "She's far too small."

"Again, Ben. Shut the fuck up."

I warbled at Caelan, dipped my head to the big man, and shot back into the air, before nosediving so low I brushed the Shifter Lord's hair.

"She has no idea what she's started, does she?" the big man asked.

Caelan's wicked laugh sent a shiver down my spine. "That's what makes this so much fun."

I was back in my car in less than ten minutes and back home in less than twenty, feeling a little unsettled about the night's events. What had Caelan meant by that last remark, and why had it sent a shiver of foreboding down my spine?

Shaking my head, I poured myself a glass of wine and was about to collapse onto the couch when the doorbell rang. Groaning, I padded barefoot to the door and peered out the peephole.

Moira stood there, a thunderous expression on her face.

I opened the door, and she stalked in, tossing her purse on the floor. Moira headed straight to the kitchen without a word, poured herself an enormous glass of wine, took a long sip, then closed her eyes.

"I love you, but what the hell were you thinking?"

This could only be about one thing. I opened my mouth to respond, but Moira held a hand up. "No. Don't say a word. The answer is you weren't thinking!" She stomped over to the couch and sat down, not spilling a single drop of her wine.

"How did you know? I just got back."

Moira rolled her eyes. "There's a mutant Jacaranda tree growing in the Shifter Lord's front yard! I wouldn't be surprised if you can see that purple fucker from the moon!"

I blinked. "Those trees don't grow here."

Moira scoffed in disbelief. "They do when your idiot Floromancer BFF gets a hold of your yard and sends so much magic through the ground the entire Keep is lit up like an amusement park!"

"Oh." I cringed. "Um. I might have over corrected."

"Ya think?" Moira screeched.

"I gave him a check for the repairs to the shop and the replacement equipment."

"And a massive hard-on. Idiot."

I snorted. "Hardly. He was so pissed off he tried to eat me."

Moira leaned forward. "Evie, you beautiful, brilliant moron. There's only one thing on your body he wants to eat."

A crimson blush stained my cheeks. "Moira!"

She set her wine glass down and reached for my hands. "Promise me you will leave the Shifter Lord alone. No matter what he asks or requests. Treat him like a customer, nothing more. If he tries to antagonize you, and he will because it's in his nature, promise me you will not react. Every time you do, he discovers how powerful you are. It won't be long before he discovers far more about you than you want him to."

"I want him to stop messing with us."

Moira nodded. "And you know how to do that?"

"I'm going to guess the answer is not growing a hundred-foot Jacaranda tree in his front yard?"

"Gray rock him."

I frowned. "What?"

"Become as interesting as a rock. Have zero sense of humor. Respond only to the questions he asks with short, limited conversation. Reveal nothing about yourself. You need to become the most uninteresting person on the planet. Normal Floromancer magic. Nothing flashy. No more of those fancy automatons that got our shop destroyed. No more fairy-tale gardens."

I watched my friend, saw the tremble in her pale, slim fingers, and heard the quiver in her words, realizing for the first time she was truly afraid for me.

"Shifter Lords exist to keep the peace between our people. You never want to gain their interest, Evie, and you are failing terribly. If you don't do it for me, do it for you. Chimera blood is a death sentence, and if Caelan discovers it, he will put you to death. No discussion. No trial. No nothing."

I opened my mouth to plead my case, but the look in her eyes stopped me. So I nodded. "Okay." Clearing my throat, I spoke again, my voice thick with emotion. "I promise. Gray rock from now on. Interesting as a bag of dried beans."

"Good. But nothing interesting like heirloom beans or those Adzuki beans. Be a regular old pinto."

"Got it. Pinto it is."

"Or even a Lima bean. Most people hate those and avoid them like the plague."

"Sure. Of course. Want me to stop brushing my hair or maybe disappear for a while and come back with an internet addiction or something?"

Moira grinned. "Pinto bean is fine. If you go too far with it, you run the risk of becoming interesting again."

"Heaven forbid."

We grinned at each other. Moira let go and grabbed her wine. "You're allowed to be as interesting as you'd like around us."

"And if I ever get a boyfriend?"

Moira's eyebrows rose to her hairline. "Are you looking for one?"

I scoffed. "Not even a little. But I might have to be interesting to land one."

The vampire laughed. "My dear, all you have to do is flutter those pretty eyes at a man, and they'll trip at your feet like an obsessed puppy."

"What you're saying is don't speak, just be pretty?"

"That's all I've ever had to do."

I laughed and tossed a throw pillow at her. We sat and chatted for a while before Moira rose and stretched. "I'm heading home. Be careful tonight and stay incognito tomorrow. It may take some time for Caelan's interest to wear off."

"Interesting as a bean. Got it."

I walked Moira to the door, and she grabbed me, pulling me in for a tight hug. "Come over next week. I've been neglectful of my house plants, and I think they hate me. They could use a friend."

"How about Monday?"

"I'll tell them. They always perk up when Aunt Evie visits."

I laughed and waved her away, watching as she jogged down the steps to her car. Once her tail lights disappeared, I went back inside and locked the door.

My magic slumbered for the first time in a long time, curled up inside me like a contented cat. I'd expended a ton of power on Caelan's property, and I wish there was a way I could do that daily because I felt amazing. Exhausted, but in a good way for once.

After another glass of wine, I showered and headed to bed.

Maybe tomorrow I'd work on restoring the greenhouse. That should expend quite a bit of power.

• • •

THE DREAM SHIMMERED INTO EXISTENCE, revealing Cernunnos sitting on the same rock as the last time I'd seen him. He beckoned me over and held a hand out. Once I was settled beside him, we stared at the heavy moon hanging in the sky.

"You're here because of what I did tonight, I assume."

"Yes. And no. I'm here because the next several days will be a test of your resolve. One you need very much to pass."

I glanced at his handsome profile, noting the tiny blooms curling in his hair, and the way the moonlight shimmered against his perfect skin. "The Shifter Lords?"

He dipped his head. "And others."

A sigh escaped me. Cryptic as always. "Are any of the fae direct in their responses?"

Cernunnos laughed. "We aren't American, Evie."

That one made me laugh. "Can you tell me anything more?"

"Your talent has garnered the interest of powerful people. Most don't know who you are or where the power comes from, but they know it's centered in your town. Your vampire friend is correct in her gray rock assessment. You must become uninteresting. Do not allow anyone to rile you up. They will try. You must possess an iron will. They seek entrance into your life through cunning and charm."

"Like Caelan?"

Cernunnos smiled. "Your Shifter Lord's interest is of a different kind."

My brow furrowed. "Different?"

His smile deepened.

"Oh." My blush was so hot it felt like I had a fever.

"There is a saying humans like to use about poking a bear. Are you familiar with it?"

I knew where he was going with this. "I am. And I know I've done it to Caelan."

"You have. More than once. And now you have his entire keep in upheaval. Some are calling for your execution."

"Damn. What kind of monsters don't like flowers?" I muttered.

"The flowers are fine. Some don't like man eating, dangerously altered flytraps, my dear."

I winced. "Seymour is adorable, though."

"Mmm. The healer is fascinated with the plant." Cernunnos slid a glance my way. "And you."

"I'm not aware of a healer in Caelan's keep."

"You will be."

"Great," I muttered.

"When's the last time you've heard from your mother?"

I froze. "Why?"

"She is near. Your antics have gathered the attention of some divine forces."

I rubbed a hand over my face. "I'm an idiot."

"No. You are what you are, Evangeline. Life flows through your veins. But you did not take my advice."

"The Chimera is dangerous. I am not myself when I become...whatever it is."

"That's because you have not mastered its power."

"How can you master evil?"

He shook his head, a flash of disappointment in his swirling eyes. "Do you think you are evil?"

"Not usually."

"A Chimera is not good, nor is it evil. Neither are humans. Or vampires. Or shifters. There are many facets to everyone and everything. If you are not evil, why do you think your Chimera will be?"

"It hungers," I said softly.

Cernunnos sighed and rose in one graceful motion. He crouched and lay his hand on my shoulder, his face very close to mine. "Then feed it."

He stepped off the edge of the rock and turned into a massive stag. With one last glance, he bounded away into the dark forest.

I awoke in my bed covered in a sheen of sweat, weak sunlight streaming through the windows.

Groaning, I rolled over and covered my head with the pillow.

Twenty-Eight

Every time Cernunnos visited me in my dreams, I woke up feeling like I'd been hit by a truck. What that told me was his visits were not dreams at all. I walked to the coffee pot like a zombie and made twice as much as usual, not doing anything at all until I'd downed two cups. Only then was I ready to check my email and make some notes about inventory for next week. Hattie's order was coming due, so I added as much cheery color as I could to my notes. I'd work on the bouquet when I got back to the shop.

After a couple hours of admin work, I rose and changed into some outdoor clothing. My property was on the outskirts of town, secluded from other neighbors because of the nature of my magic, and surrounded by eight additional acres of uncleared land. The greenhouse was set toward the back side of the house and had seen better days. I'd meant to restore it over the years, but I'd gotten busy with other projects and had neglected to do anything other than bolster the foundation so it wouldn't fall down around my ears when I worked inside.

But it had been quite a while since I'd grown anything inside, and I wasn't sure why other than my own neglect, so I went outside with my sketchbook I used to draw up arrangement ideas and studied the greenhouse from every angle, trying to figure out how I could best utilize the space.

I needed a functional and comfortable space to work in during the summer, and that was easier said than done in Joy Springs. After I'd sketched out the ideal greenhouse with notes about hydroponics and a heating and cooling system, I forced open the creaky doors and went inside.

The greenhouse was empty except for several old pots and some gardening tools that had seen better days. I'd bought the place because of the privacy it offered and this greenhouse, but my magic had grown by leaps and bounds since then, and I needed something more than a simple growing setup.

But I'd just written Caelan a huge check, and it would be awhile before my bank account replenished itself. While I could afford an electrician and a carpenter, I always kept a large chunk of cash just in case I needed to start over. With my behavior over the last couple of weeks, that likelihood was looking more like an inevitability than a slight chance.

Grimacing at my own stupidity, I grabbed the lone shovel sitting against the wall to put in my shed, and stepped back outside, only to see two black SUVs pulling into my driveway. I watched way too much television to be calm about their appearance.

Vehicles like that could mean only a few things.

I was about to be the victim of heavy gunfire.

The mob was about to make me a deal I couldn't refuse.

The cartel was about to make me the same deal, but with a handsome drug lord garnering the deal I couldn't help but fall in love with.

Or the Shifter Lords had arrived at my doorstep.

When Caelan stepped out from the first vehicle wearing a suit and a grim expression, I had a moment of deep regret that it wasn't the cartel. They'd be easier to deal with.

A lean man with silver at the edge of his temples and an air of violence surrounding him slid from the driver's seat of the same vehicle Caelan had just exited.

I began funneling magic up through my feet, spooling it through my veins in anticipation of violence. Caelan gave me a warning look as the second Lord approached me.

Several other males exited the second vehicle and followed behind Caelan and the other one, a Lord, I presumed.

The lean man stopped before me. He was smaller than Caelan, but not weak. Magic snapped around his aura, different from Caelan's. His eyes were dark and flat, and he studied me like I was prey, which pissed me off.

Cernunnos' and Moira's warnings rang in my mind.

Gray rock. Be the most uninteresting thing in the room.

My fingers gripped the shovel I held. "Can I help you?"

The shifter's eyes flickered with displeasure. He wanted to be the one to speak first, and he didn't like that I had usurped him. "Are you Evie Quinn?"

I nodded. Only answer their questions. Never give more information than they ask for.

"My name is Ethan Flint. I control the Rocky Mountain territory. We're here to address some concerns about rogue magic. Unfortunately, your name has come up in our investigation more than once."

I tilted my head and studied him. "Mr. Flint, I'm merely a Floromancer. There's nothing rogue about my magic."

"Be that as it may, we are required to investigate all loose ends, and you are something of an anomaly in town."

"I'm a florist. We're always anomalies when people realize we like plants more than them." I offered him a tight smile.

Ethan's eyes flashed with anger. "Perhaps we could take this conversation inside?"

Not a chance, buddy. "Sorry. I'm right in the middle of an outdoor project. I don't take much time off, and I've neglected my greenhouse for far too long. I'm sure this won't take long, will it?"

Caelan's lips twitched.

Shit. Stop being interesting, Evie.

The other shifters behind Caelan shifted uneasily. Ethan's eyes narrowed. "Fine. We've seen evidence of your work on Caelan's property. Care to explain?"

My gaze flicked to Caelan who stood there still as a statue. No help there, then.

"Sure. The Shifter Lord expressed interest in bringing more color to his property when he hired me to provide floral arrangements for a funeral. I'm always looking to bring in more funds and build my landscaping portfolio, so I offered to provide the work for free."

Caelan's eyes positively sparkled.

"Interesting. The Shifter Lord does not have any paperwork supporting this." A cold smile tipped his lips. "I find it hard to believe a professional business woman performed such a stunning amount of work with no contract."

I laughed. Ethan froze, anger flashing over his face. "Insisting on a contract would assume the Shifter Lord would not make good on his word. He authorized me to enter his property at my leisure and gave me free rein to do what I wished. As an experiment." I shrugged. "I took him up on it, trusting someone as honorable as a Shifter Lord would keep up their end of the bargain."

I could almost hear Ethan's teeth grinding. If he responded in the negative, he would imply Caelan was untrustworthy. But he recovered faster than I expected. "And yet, you had one for the funeral job you did."

I lifted a shoulder in a shrug. "My business partner insisted on one. She is a stickler for paperwork, no matter who you are. The Lord dealt only with me the next time, and we did a handshake deal. It's a small town. They're much more common around here than in northern territories. Southern hospitality and all that, you know."

"And you were happy with the work you did?" Ethan said,

thinking he had me. I'd basically vomited flowers all over the place.

"The first time was a trial run. Floromancy is a complicated magic, Mr. Flint. His soil was in deep need of nurturing and restoration. Planting native grass and wildflowers was only the first step. Once those run their course, I will follow up for the next step."

Tension hung in the air, heavy and thick. Ethan's fury smothered me like a coat. "And the Jacaranda tree?"

"Pretty, but an accident." My gaze flicked to Caelan, who remained silent. "Though I have assurances the Shifter Lord is quite enamored with the purple blossoms."

Caelan's lips twitched.

My eyes slid away and back to Ethan. "But, if he wishes, I'll be happy to take the Jacaranda with me the next time I visit the property. I aim to please all my customers."

"Unnecessary," Caelan said, his voice rumbling with amusement. "It's a real conversation starter."

"I suppose I can see how the state of Caelan's property would contribute to rumors of rogue magic, but I have to stress that most people do not know how to properly care for a native landscape. The amusing but true concept of a lawn care obsessed human has been devastating to our natural ecosystem. No one should have a lawn. We should all be doing our part to nurture the earth and all its wonderful gifts. This means ensuring we plant native grasses and flowers and staying away from chemicals that kill 'pests' and weeds. A weed is a plant, and every weed has its place within our ecosystem. As awful as mosquitoes and wasps are, they are also pollinators. With the way the world has decimated the bee population, we need every pollinator we can get our hands on before our food supply is wiped out. I'm sure you understand."

I was not doing a good job at being a gray rock. Dammit.

Ethan blinked several times. "Uh."

Caelan rubbed a hand over his mouth and looked at his feet.

"I will say that I have also heard the rumors of rogue magic, though I was unaware at the time I was a suspect. The only magic I've done is boost the natural cycle and beautify the land. It's my nature, Mr. Flint. A Floromancer is born to heal the land. If that is a crime, I must insist you lock me up."

Ethan said nothing for a long moment, but he studied me, his dark gaze missing nothing. "Perhaps I will seek out your services one day, Miss Quinn. You seem to have quite the talent for beautifying spaces."

I pushed magic through my veins to keep my heart rate steady. The absolute last thing I wanted was more attention from the Shifter Lords. "Most people hate dandelions, Mr. Flint. If you're willing to put up with the weeds and overabundance of natives for a while, I'll be happy to help you."

"Sans contract," Ethan said.

I lifted a shoulder in a shrug. "I'm sure you and the other Shifter Lords are as honorable and trustworthy as ours is."

Caelan made a choking noise.

Ethan dipped his head in acknowledgment. "I'm sure we will see you around soon, Miss Quinn."

I certainly hoped not, but I slapped a friendly smile on my face. "Follow the dandelions."

Ethan spun on his heel and returned to the SUV. As if on cue, the other shifters, except Caelan, did the same.

Our eyes met. "Be careful, Evie," he said, his voice so low it was almost a whisper. "The other Shifter Lords are not like me."

I wasn't sure if that was good or bad. "Do you like that Jacaranda?" I whispered back.

"I like the woman who gave it to me." Caelan winked and turned to follow the others.

Oof.

That did not go so well.

Shit.

Twenty-Nine

CAELAN

All the Lords had convened at the Keep once more, requiring me to be on constant alert. We sat in the War Room, at a round table reminiscent of days of yore, except with a massive pile of food and drinks in the middle instead of maps to plot our conquering.

There were seven Shifter Lords in total. I controlled Texas and the Borderlands. Halvar, Lord of the Midwest, sat to my right. He was dark-haired and blue-eyed and possessed a melodic accent, European, if I had to guess. Maybe Irish. I'd always been crap at identifying accents.

He was different from how he used to be, and none of us could pinpoint why, though some of us guessed it had to do with his wife leaving him a few years ago. Bringing it up would be a certain death sentence, so we all tiptoed around it and pretended everything was fine.

Rowan was at my left. Lord of the Pacific Northwest. He was a strange shifter, deeply tied to his lands. I suspected he possessed more than a little nature magic. If I had to call any of the Lords a friend, it would be Rowan.

Next to him was Soren, a silver-tongued asshole who ran the Deep South territories. Ethan was beside him. I knew him the least, but knew him to be a paranoid bastard, deeply tied to tradition. He was the most likely to oppose me if tensions in our Council ever got to that point.

Thorvin sat next to Ethan. He was the quiet scholar among us and Lord of the Northeast territories. I respected him and knew to listen when he spoke.

The last Lord was Donovan. I liked him the least. He craved alliances more than power, which made him the most dangerous because our Council relied on votes to pass motions. He was susceptible to flattery and bribery, meaning you could easily win his vote if you had the right amount of money to offer.

"The Floromancer might be a danger," Ethan said once the gavel cracked against the table, announcing the start of our meeting.

Rowan snorted. "You think a plant mage is a danger? Pray tell what makes you draw that conclusion."

Ethan gave him a dark look. "She feels like no other Floromancer I've been around."

"Still not a reason," Rowan said. "Perhaps there is something additional in her blood that makes her magic different. She's committed no crimes."

"I'd say that massive purple eyesore outside is a crime," Soren said dryly.

Evie's display of power still had the Keep in a tizzy, though I'd instructed everyone to keep their mouth shut once the other Lords had arrived. If anyone was going to investigate Evie, it'd be me. Not the others who didn't belong here.

"The reports of rogue magic aren't Floromancy related," Thorvin said quietly. "They are divine in nature. Did you sense any presence of the divine in this Evie woman?"

Ethan gritted his teeth. "No. But that doesn't make her innocent. Divine beings can disguise the truth in their blood."

"It doesn't make her guilty either," Rowan said mildly. He glanced at me. "Care to chime in, Caelan?"

"Evie has not posed a danger to my people." If my people

heard this, they would beg to differ, but she'd hurt none of us. All she'd done was fight for her independence and embarrass the hell out of me. The flytrap wasn't her fault either. Not technically. She did warn the others to keep away from it.

What the fuck was wrong with me? I should be siding with the other Lords. Evie was dangerous. I knew it in my bones, and yet, she'd done nothing violent. I'd been the one to launch through her window and terrify her. I'd been the one to react each time. But I was dangerous, too. We all were.

Every mage was dangerous, and we didn't put them down, did we?

"We have a professional working relationship. She occasionally acts as a florist for Keep events. The eyesore, as Soren so eloquently put it, was merely a misfire of her power." I smirked. "I hardly think an oversized tropical tree is cause enough to merit a meeting of the Shifter Lord Council."

"If she is not the cause of the magic, then we must know where it's coming from before we leave," Ethan said.

Fury slid through me. "You are welcomed into my territory for one week and one week only. You've already been here too much this month."

Ethan's eyes narrowed. "And why is that? Are you hiding something you don't want us to see?"

A bark of laughter escaped me. "Every one of us has secrets no one wants revealed. We are not friends, Ethan. Do not pretend to be. One week and you'll vacate based on the rules of our Accords."

He flicked a dismissive hand at me. My power rumbled through the room at the insult. Rowan stilled and gave me a warning look. Soren chuckled under his breath. Halvar, who'd remained too silent, merely lifted a brow.

"And you, Halvar?" I questioned. "You've been silent both times we've met. What is your opinion?"

Halvar merely stared at me, the deadness in his eyes sending a chill down my spine. "I'd like to meet this Floromancer and make my own determination."

"Then we will visit her shop tomorrow," Soren said, still looking at me, his eyes sparkling in challenge. "I'm sure our Floromancer won't want to turn down business from any of the Lords, would she?"

"Do not terrorize any of my citizens," I growled, the threat in my voice clear.

Halvar smiled, showing too many teeth. "Relax, Caelan. We merely want to gauge what we're dealing with. Your precious Floromancer is safe." He rose, nodded, and headed for the exit.

The other shifters all did the same, except for Rowan who stayed behind, a contemplative look on his face.

The doors opened, revealing Garrett and Simone, both armed to the teeth and guarding the door. Once all the Lords had passed, Garrett poked his head in, spotted Rowan, and gave me a questioning look.

"Close the doors. We will be out shortly."

Garrett nodded and obeyed.

When we were sealed behind the doors again, Rowan spoke. "Is she a threat?"

I gauged how much to say, but Rowan sighed. "Caelan. Cut the shit. You and I have been through too much together not to trust each other now. Tell me about the woman."

I rose and gestured for him to follow. We went out through a secret door in the War Room, bypassing the normal exit. Without a word, Rowan followed until we were in my study.

I didn't have to say a word. Rowan let out an exclamation and headed right for Seymour.

"Careful. He bites," I warned.

The Lord grabbed a chair and placed it a few feet away from the plant. He sat down and studied it. "You've been bitten?"

I shook my head. "It took out one of my shifters, though. He was down for a few hours."

His eyebrows rose. "Down?"

"The damn thing is poisonous. A paralytic."

Rowan let out a delighted laugh. He sent out a touch of bright green magic as he examined the flytrap. "Red Dragon," he murmured. "But not quite. Something else."

"Gelsemium," Ben said as he entered holding a spray bottle and the bag of worms Evie had given us.

Rowan snapped his fingers. "That's it! How in the world did she do that without changing its physical properties?"

Ben shrugged. "She did change them, technically." He crouched and pointed at the flytraps' teeth. "If you look closely, you can see the poison dripping there."

Rowan chuckled. "She is a danger, then." He turned and looked at me. "Tell me how you came to be in possession of this genetically spliced delight?"

Ben grinned and pulled up a chair.

"She sent it as a message, along with a check to repay me."

Rowan tilted his head in curiosity. "Repay you for what?"

I clenched my jaw. Ben let out a guffaw but covered his mouth and pretended to cough when my eyes started glowing. "I destroyed a good portion of her shop and took it upon myself to...repair the damages."

Rowan's eyes went wide. "May I ask why you damaged her shop?" His mouth fell open as he made a realization. "No. No fucking way. Evie was the one responsible for those automatons, wasn't she?" A dark chuckle escaped him. "Those were the talk of the council. I thought for sure the florist you hired had a mage's help with those."

"She was taunting me," I growled.

"Hmm. And what did you do to make her respond like that?" Rowan asked, crossing his arms.

I blew out a breath and sat down. "Victim blaming is beneath you, Rowan."

Ben snorted and fished in the bag for a handful of worms. Seymour perked right up and opened his mouth like a dutiful puppy. At the first toss, Seymour grew four inches in height to snap the worm from the air.

Rowan swore and scooted his chair back.

"He acted like every Shifter Lord," Ben mused. "Like he owned Evie and the entire town, and he strong armed her into working for him when she didn't want to."

Rowan clicked his tongue. "She's a brave girl to stand up to you."

"She's a damn fool," I snapped. "Look where we are now."

The other Lord rubbed his jaw, his face thoughtful. "Do you think she's responsible for the rogue magic?"

"No. I'm having her monitored."

"Ah," said Rowan. "And how do you imagine Miss Evie might respond once she realizes you've added stalking to your list of crimes against her?"

"Goddammit, Rowan. I'm trying to help her." Frustration rose inside me. Seymour sank back down to his regular height and tilted his head. The damn thing was looking at me. I knew it. Even without eyes, I knew I had fallen under its scrutiny.

"A Shifter Lord's help always comes with strings attached, Caelan." He shook his head. "You old fool. You pissed her off, and she responded, only to come under the scrutiny of the Council. Now you've probably screwed her worse than if you'd killed her."

"I would never harm her," I swore savagely.

I realized my mistake when the room fell silent. Rowan's look was contemplative. Ben's was concerned.

"Ah," Rowan breathed. "My friend, you've gotten yourself into quite the pickle, haven't you?"

But Ben, one of my oldest friends, sat back in his chair and studied me, an unreadable expression on his face. "You and I go way back, Caelan," he said before rising and closing the bag of worms, setting it on the windowsill. Seymour reached for the shifter and rubbed the top of its trap against Ben's forearm. The healer chuckled and gently scratched Seymour before returning his attention to me. "I always respected your choices and deferred to your authority, but we may be at an impasse when it comes to the Floromancer."

Rowan's brow furrowed.

"Oh?" Power prickled against my skin. I suspected where this was going, and I was hit with both grief and rage and an insane amount of jealousy all at the same time. "Why do you say that?"

"Because," Ben said as he walked to the door, "if the Council goes after her, you will stand against me."

Rowan sucked in a breath and went still.

"You would stand with a lone Floromancer against your own people?" I asked in a low, deadly tone.

Ben, not even a tenth as scared as he should be, grinned and tapped on the door jamb. "As long as she says yes when I ask her out," he said and began whistling a tune as he shut the door behind him.

I swore and kicked Ben's chair so hard, it shattered into pieces against the wall.

Seymour's pot shook as the plant grew an extra foot in length, its main trap shooting out like a snake to bite me right on the arm.

"Fuck!" I snarled, numbness setting in the second Seymour drew his teeth back and slithered back to normal size.

Rowan's hearty laughter rang throughout the room. "Should I call your healer back or do you just want to deal with it?"

"Get bent," I snarled as I tried to stalk from the room, only for my legs to give out.

Rowan was bent over double with laughter as I fell to the floor with a hard thump.

For the next few hours, I held a massive grudge against all plant life and a beautiful Floromancer who was fast becoming a massive and literal pain in my ass.

CHAPTER

Thirty

The raven sat atop my roof, watchful and quiet. I waved, but didn't bother him. After escaping my mother's clutches, I left the bird to his own devices. He'd come when he needed me or for occasional companionship.

The Shifter Lords' visit had left me shaken, so I stayed outside the rest of the day, working on new landscaping. I had several trees I needed to boost, and I needed to do a walk-through of the property to make sure nothing was amiss, again something I'd neglected to do over the last several months. I had a four-wheeler, but I preferred walking so I wouldn't miss anything that required attention.

Part of me wanted to call Moira, but I didn't want to drag her into this mess. If I pretended to be only a Floromancer of middling power, maybe the Council would leave me alone. As long as Caelan kept my secret. And why the hell would he do that?

I sighed and peppered magic at some pesky thorns that were beginning to choke my marigolds. They retreated, but not far enough away for my taste, so I popped them again.

"Stay away from the front yard and the paths I walk, you hear me?" I scolded.

Someone stepped onto my land. I stilled, straining to hear.

"I know you sense me," a deep voice said.

I rose and turned, only to see the same shifter who'd been with Caelan last night. He was massive, a bear of a man, and handsome as sin. Magic curled from the ground, rising up through the soles of my bare feet.

"I come in peace and promise no harm," he said, holding his hands up. "My name is Ben Walker."

"Are you here to deliver a message?" I asked, still wary.

"Not quite. I'm here…" His voice trailed off, and he huffed a laugh. "Well, I suppose I'm here because I want to meet the woman who managed to so handily infuriate a handful of Shifter Lords."

I rolled my eyes. "They're overly reactive."

Ben laughed. "I agree. May I approach?"

I tilted my head and studied him. He was well over six and a half feet tall and must have weighed two hundred and fifty pounds. If he got his hands around me, I'd have a real fight on my hands.

Ben's brows drew together. "Do not study me like a predator," he said quietly. "I would never put my hands on a woman without their permission."

I swallowed hard. "Every woman studies every man like he's a predator. Most men aren't emotionally intelligent enough to notice."

Ben made no move to come closer. "Look your fill, Evie. Use your magic to know me."

My eyes narrowed. No man had ever offered to allow me to look that closely. I took a few steps closer, his unusual, fresh and clean scent washing over me. "You aren't a wolf."

"No."

He did not elaborate.

I sent out a thread of tourmaline colored magic through the ground. "Are you sure you want to allow this?"

Ben smiled. My heart did a little skip bump at the sight. "Know me," he said again.

His breath caught when my magic touched him.

"Last chance," I whispered.

Ben's eyes glowed a startling blue. "I wish to know you, Evie. That means I want you to know me, too."

My magic swept around his ankles, seeking entrance inside the massive shifter's body. He made no move toward me, but when my power entered his body, his head tipped back, exposing his throat. It was a submissive gesture, and the sexiest thing I'd ever seen.

My breath caught as I moved close enough to touch him. The power always worked better when I was in close proximity, and while I didn't have to touch him, I realized I wanted to.

I pressed my hand gently against his upper chest, my magic touching his heart. Closing my eyes, I lay my head against him and took a deep breath.

Pain. Ben had known so much pain in his life. So much tragedy. The magic showed me no pictures, and if it tried, I would deny them. I didn't need to share his private thoughts. I only wanted to know he was safe. This was the part of my magic I showed no one. Plants felt things. Every living thing felt emotions, pain, joy, hope, heartache. Ben was no different. Except most of his life had been painful, only small moments of joy brushing against my senses.

He wasn't a violent man, though violence had found him many times.

A small sigh of sadness escaped me. Ben's massive arms wrapped around my waist.

"Every trial in my life brought me to this moment," he said quietly.

The only darkness I found was external, things that had happened to him. Ben was guarded, deep, secretive, and had a well of power almost as large as mine. And to his credit, he made no move to examine me the same way.

I withdrew my power and wrapped my arms around him, tears streaming down my face. "Why?" I croaked.

We stood together wrapped in each other, and I can't remember a time when I'd felt so safe. The last time someone had held me this close—

I sucked in a breath and pushed Ben away, my heart thundering in my chest.

His eyes opened, a fierce glow shining from them, a terrible look forming on his face. "Who?" he snarled.

I shook my head.

Ben inhaled a deep breath and closed his eyes. When he opened them, the glow was gone, and his face was a neutral mask. "Did you find what you were looking for?"

"Why are you here?" I asked quietly. "No one wants to know me without an ulterior motive."

A sad smile curved his lips up. "I'm sorry that has been the case." His eyes swept my land. "Were you about to walk your property?"

My brow furrowed. "How did you know?"

He pointed at my bare feet. "You have boots and socks right by the edge of the uncleared land. Mind if I join you?"

I believed he wouldn't harm me, but it didn't mean he was here without an ulterior motive, especially with Caelan as his Lord. "You can, but I won't tell you anything."

Ben laughed. "The Lord is my friend, but he is not happy I am here. You might say we are in a bit of a disagreement."

"I can only imagine he disagrees a lot," I grumbled.

He grinned and gestured for me to go ahead. "I'll wait at the edge for you."

I hurried over to put my socks and boots on, tucking my overalls into my socks when I was finished. When I rose, Ben was watching me. Not in a predatory way, but in a soft way. Color touched my cheeks. I found the shifter unnerving. Not in a threatening way. In a...dangerous for my heart kind of way.

But I'd found Caelan the same, even as I feared for my life. I didn't fear Ben, though. He had a gentle energy about him, and I hadn't recognized his magic, though it felt peaceful.

"I'm a healer," he said, answering my unasked question.

I snapped my attention to his face. "Was I that obvious?"

He lifted a powerful shoulder in a shrug. "You are the first person I've allowed to examine me like that. Thank you for not taking advantage."

"You're the first person who's allowed it."

We smiled at each other, and I felt an odd magical tug, drawing me toward him. I shook it off and stepped into the woods, the big shifter behind me, silent as a mountain cat.

As we walked, I realized how nice it was to have someone with me. Allowing Ben to get too close would be a deadly mistake, but I could enjoy this onetime outing. As we walked, the shifter asked questions about the flora and fauna, and to my surprise, seemed interested in the answers.

I asked him about his healing abilities and limitations, divulging a little of my own skill without giving away too much. He told me how long he'd been with Caelan and how he worked as the Keep's main healer.

I boosted the nutrients in the soil where I found it lacking and healed some spots on my apple trees that looked to be diseased. There were several areas where seeds had gone too far to ground, so I gently tilled the soil to move them closer to the surface. In a few weeks, several parts of my land would be blanketed with native wildflowers.

I trimmed areas that needed to be trimmed to encourage more growth and buried plants and animals too far gone for my help. In the earth we began and to earth we returned. Life was a cycle and to disrupt it meant disrupting life itself, the very balance of nature.

Ben stayed quiet but watchful, and I realized I liked having someone watching over me while I communed with the earth. Every time I stood, he held a hand out to help me up, and by the time we made it to the back of the property, he stopped letting go of my hand.

I'd known the man for less than two hours, but I knew in my

soul Ben had a gentle spirit saddled with lifelong trauma. As sad as it was, like recognized like.

At the edge of the uncleared land, I stopped abruptly, sensing the tingle of familiar and very unwelcome magic. "Stay here," I warned.

Ben's wicked chuckle tightened long unused things inside me. "If you think I'll let a woman walk into danger alone, you've sorely misjudged me."

"I don't have time for macho nonsense," I hissed. "Have you ever dealt with the gods, Ben?"

The shifter stilled, his brows drawing together. "Apparently you have."

"I have, and you do not want to be on their radar. I will be fine. You may not."

Ben's upper lip curled, but he relented. "I'll stay here for now. If there's a hint of danger, I will not hesitate to come to you."

Today felt like I'd stepped into a paranormal romance. A beautiful man built like a brick shithouse randomly showed up in my yard, said beautiful things to me, allowed me to inspect his inner spirit, then walked with me for hours, didn't make a single thing about him, then wanted to protect me when danger showed up at my doorstep. Who the hell was this guy?

I felt like I was being punked by the universe.

Ben slipped back into the tree cover as I stepped into the yard, squaring my shoulders as I prepared to face my mother.

Thirty~One

My mother was stunning. Considered one of, if not *the* most beautiful goddesses of the fae, Cliona or Cliodhna, sat on my porch, her skirts gathered around her feet. Shining dark hair flowed down her back and gently shimmered in a phantom wind. Her eyes were the same color as mine, but her features had always been more delicate. I had a stubborn chin and higher cheekbones, and my skin had always held a faint golden sheen. Cliona's skin was pale as pure Irish cream, her face unmarred by freckles or age.

She straightened when she saw me coming, a slight wrinkle of her forehead breaking up the perfection of her features. "Cavorting through the woods again?" she said by way of greeting.

I ignored the insult. "Hello, mother."

Cliona rolled her eyes and rose, graceful as a swan. "Come. Invite me in for tea and let me catch up with my daughter."

I made no move and stood there like a statue. "We both know you only visit when you need something. What is it this time?"

Displeasure flickered in her eyes, her staggering magic loosened for a second before she brought it back under control. Lightning cracked atop our heads, and thunderclouds rolled in, there and gone in an instant.

I hoped Ben stayed hidden. The last thing anyone needed was my mother's interest.

"We are not peasants, Evangeline. That is not how you speak to a queen."

"It is if that queen is my mother," I muttered.

One of her dark eyebrows rose.

"Mom. Come on. What do you want?"

She huffed. "I want a cup of tea and to see how my daughter is."

Sensing she wouldn't give up, I sighed and opened the door. Mom sailed in before I could swing it all the way open, her eyes cataloging everything and missing nothing. I kept all my treasures hidden in a below ground room and spelled to avoid detection. My mother had been to my house a few times and had yet to sense it, though it wasn't for lack of trying.

She tried to inhale discreetly, scenting out magic.

"Searching for anything in particular?" I asked, my voice dry as the Sahara.

Mom clicked her tongue. "You honestly think the worst of me, don't you?"

If the shoe fits. I stilled my tongue and busied myself putting the tea kettle on. Mom walked around the living room investigating everything before she pulled a chair from the island and settled onto it, crossing one slim leg over the other.

"Tell me how you are settling in, Evangeline."

"I've been here for five years."

Five years was nothing but a blink of an eye to the Fae, and I sometimes forget how ancient my mother truly was. Understanding her felt like someone dumping Scrabble tiles onto the floor and asking me to assemble a ten-letter word in five seconds. Overwhelming and futile.

I pushed over a cup of Earl Grey tea and took out a small jar of sugar and the small silver container of cream I kept fresh just for her random visits.

"None for you?"

"No. I've been outside all day. Summer in this town is rough."

Mom paused in the act of stirring. "You don't enjoy it here?"

What I didn't enjoy was the sudden gleam in her eye. "I enjoy this place very much."

"Hmm. You can always come home, you know."

"Home?" My mother put me out at eighteen with a small amount of cash and a pat on the back with strict instructions to make my way in the world and never come home again. Now I was even more suspicious.

Mom's delicate snort put me on edge. "Yes, home."

"As in the Otherworld?"

Mom gave me an annoyed look. "Where else could I be speaking of, darling?"

I stared at her for a long moment, wondering if she was gaslighting me. "I've never lived in the Otherworld. Why would I want to go back there?"

She scoffed. "Nonsense, Evangeline. You lived there for years!"

I one hundred percent had never stepped foot into the Otherworld. My mother had left me with human parents until I was fifteen, though she'd paid them handsomely to ensure I stayed alive, I guess. She visited me twice a year, and it felt like the sun had come out every time I saw her. After that, she purchased a house in Seattle, and we lived there until my eighteenth birthday.

"Mom," I said firmly. "You left me with humans, remember? Then we lived in Seattle?"

Mom's brow furrowed. Her eyes clouded for a moment before she smiled. "Oh. Silly me. Yes, of course. It doesn't mean you can't visit now."

Mom always swore I wouldn't be welcomed into Underhill because of my "filthy human blood." What the hell was going on?

"I'll keep that in mind," I said slowly. Mom's moods were

capricious on a good day, and with Ben in the woods, I didn't want to set her off.

Speaking of Ben, I sent a small wisp of magic through the ground and had the vines close to him curl around themselves until they spelled out:

Everything is fine. Thank you for a nice afternoon. I'll see you around.

An abrupt dismissal, yes, but Mom showed no signs of this being a short visit.

"Evie, have you had any visits lately?"

Ah. Here it was. "Visits? I own a shop in town, so lots of people come and go."

Mom rolled her eyes. "I know you have a flower shop. I'm talking about dream visits or day walking from any...fae or other creatures."

Danger, my senses screamed. I kept my heartbeat perfectly steady. "Um. No. That's an odd question. Why do you ask?" Telling her about Cernunnos seemed like a bad idea.

"Odd magical pulses here and there," Mom said, her azure eyes pinning me to the chair.

"Who would visit me? No one knows I'm here."

"Your attack brought many questions," Mom hedged. "There are some who are interested in knowing about your abilities and how they might have changed."

"No one knows about my attack, Mother." Or they shouldn't.

Mom waved a delicate hand. "They have no idea what attacked you. Only that you were seriously wounded." Her lips pursed in a perfect pout. "Everyone was asking about you, and it seemed like a natural time to bring it up."

My hands tightened around the edge of the countertop. "And you thought the worst night of my life was a great conversation starter?"

Anger flickered in the azure depths of her eyes. "You are my daughter, Evangeline. Naturally, I worry about you."

"Naturally," I said, unable to keep the deep sarcasm from my voice. "We both know no one ever asks about me. I'm not sure why you're here, but I think it's time we get to the point."

Mom set her mug down with a sharp click. "No one has visited you?"

This must be it. "No one ever comes to the property unless it's for work, Mother. And my dreams are just that. Dreams."

Worry flashed over her face, there and gone so fast I almost missed it. "Who would you think would be visiting me?"

"No one," she said far too quickly.

Cernunnos' words from his first visit came back to me in a flash of memory.

Do you know who your father is?

And me answering that he was human, only for Cernunnos to ask me if I was sure.

Mom hated when I brought up my father. The subject could send her into a blinding rage, but I tried to broach the subject once more. In a roundabout way, of course.

Fae hated direct conversation and confrontation, very reminiscent of a southern mother-in-law. "Is there something I should know?"

Mom's stillness betrayed her. "Of course not."

I waited, but she didn't elaborate. "I've heard reports of rogue pockets of magic. Could it have something to do with that?"

Mom shrugged. "I'm worried about you."

No, she wasn't. "Why? Everything is normal here." No sexy Shifter Lords on my tail. No hot, gentle shifters walking my land, and certainly no Council sniffing around me.

"Have you discovered any...new abilities?"

I kept my face uninterested. Mom was under the impression I'd developed zero new abilities after the Chimera mauling. She knew what attacked me because she showed up right at the tail end, but she had no idea of the aftereffects or that the tattoos I wore protected me from others sensing what I was. Hazel had watched from the woods until my mother disappeared, leaving me to die brutalized and alone, then hurried to gather me from my almost grave and helped me save myself.

Even I didn't know what abilities a Chimera had other than being able to shift into almost anything.

Cliona asked no questions unless she had an ulterior motive.

"Nothing," I said with a rueful smile. "Looks like my half fae blood purged most of the virus. Every once in a while, I get a red tinge to my eyes, but other than that, I'm the same old Evie."

I had to give her something. She was far too smart to believe I'd walked away from that attack completely unscathed.

"My kind are gathering around this place. They sense anomalies in the magic." Her eyes narrowed. "Are you sure you're not experiencing anything new?"

I held both hands up and shrugged. "Not that I know of."

Mom rose, gathering her bright shawl around her shoulders. "Our kind flocks to power, Evangeline. Something dwells in this town that's drawing the wrong kind of curiosity. If you receive any visitors in your dreams, you must let me know at once."

"I still don't know who'd visit me. I'm sure I can take on a demi-fae with no help from my mother." I smiled to soften my words.

Cliona left her mug on the counter. "The Fae King is sniffing around this place, Evangeline."

I laughed. "There's no way he'll pay me a visit." It took years of practice for me to lie successfully to my mother. "I work with plants and flowers. I'm far under Cernunnos' radar."

Mom flinched when I said his name. "Never let his name pass your lips," she hissed. "You'll draw unwanted attention."

"Could it be my father?" I asked quietly.

Mom froze, her eyes turning from the color of a Mediterranean Sea to a frozen over lake. "Your father is dead."

I pushed my luck. "Is he?"

For a moment, my mother disappeared, and the Banshee Queen stood before me, pale and terrible, unholy magic crackling around her like a lightning storm. Ghosts screamed through her body, and my house turned into the land of the dead.

A second later, we were back in the kitchen, and my mother wore a rueful smile, the only sign of her horrific magic the puff of steam my breath made in the still freezing room.

"Oh, Evie," Mom said with a click of her tongue. "I would never lie to you."

She bent down and pressed a cool kiss against my skin before disappearing in a puff of mist.

It took a long time for my hands to stop shaking.

Thirty~Two

The next day proved just as weird as the day before. I peeked in at the egg March had given me, but Poe was there, faithfully pulling dad duty. After a scratch on the back of his head, I nudged him out of the way just to take a peek, but nothing had changed.

"Soon?" I asked the raven.

"Soon," Poe agreed.

"Come get me if you need me. I'd like to be there when the egg hatches, so the baby feels safe."

Poe gave me a disapproving look, and I laughed. "I know you can keep it safe, but I need to know the breed so I can know what kind of food to buy. You know I trust you implicitly."

My flattery soothed the raven's ruffled feathers, and he settled back atop the egg and fell silent.

It was a slow day at the shop. Mondays usually were, so we spent those days doing inventory and placing our orders for the next week. We ordered more than normal. With the Shifter Lord's patronage, curious and nosy customers started coming in, but when they were confronted with the shop's charm and Moira's pretty face, they usually didn't leave empty-handed.

I'd grown complacent with the lazy day and found myself

unprepared for my next visitors. The bell over the door rang, and before the first person stepped in, a blast of incredible power washed over the store.

Moira and Tess, joking around about their prowess in the kitchen, fell silent. Ash came out from the back, a look of concern on his handsome face.

I knew who it was before he stepped in, but what I didn't expect were the two others behind him.

"Lord Ethan," I greeted without my usual smile. Moira reached under the desk and gripped my hand in warning. Tess went still. Her form shimmered as she fought to control her fear, but I could smell it. Just like the Lords could.

"Miss Quinn." He held the door for two others. Both were tall, but not as massive as Ben. Well-muscled and fit, the first had shaggy brown hair and light hazel eyes. He had a friendly face and winked at me as he brushed past Ethan.

The last Lord made my palms go slick with sweat. Power sluiced through the air when he stepped inside my shop, his pale gaze sweeping through the main area, stopping on me. He didn't drop his gaze, and I knew I should drop mine as proper deference to the Shifter Lord, but there was something about him so unnerving I couldn't look away if I tried. My stomach dropped to my toes, and fear, unlike any I'd ever known, cut through my veins like a hot knife.

Moira squeezed my hand tighter.

"How can I help you today?" I tugged my hand from Moira's and stepped around the desk. "Are you shopping for you or a loved one?"

"Neither I'm afraid." Ethan's' tone wasn't friendly, but it wasn't cold, either. Neutral was the best way to describe it.

"Oh? Then I'm at a loss." I offered a polite smile and waited.

"Rowan," the friendlier Lord said. He offered his hand, and I took it. His palm was rough in mine, but he didn't squeeze too hard. A nice firm, professional handshake and a smile with a hint of something. Did he have a little bit of plant mage blood? When some of my pothos shivered and moved their vines closer, I decided I liked him.

I hitched a thumb over my shoulder. "Tess is on the right. Moira is on the left. Ash is by the door, there. I couldn't run the shop without them."

Rowan nodded. "This is a great place you have here." He walked over to the pothos and touched a few of their leaves. "It's nice to see a florist have more life in her shop than just cut flowers." He inhaled deeply. "It smells of green things and fresh life here. I could live in here, I think."

Color touched my cheeks. I put a hand over my chest. "Extremely kind words, Lord Rowan."

"Just Rowan, please."

"Thank you. Rowan," I added.

The last Shifter Lord let the door close behind him. "My name is Halvar Aster. I rule the Midwestern territory."

His voice scratched against my brain. Although his tone was melodic with an accent I couldn't quite place, the sound of it made me itchy. I didn't like him here and wanted him to leave as soon as possible. I tilted my head in acknowledgment. "Lord Aster. Welcome."

All three Lords sucked all the air from the shop. Their combined power sizzled over my skin, making me itch to release some of my own. "Would you like to browse for a little while?" I asked.

Rowan spoke before anyone else. "We would. Thank you, Evie."

I nodded and went back behind the desk, grabbing my notepad and a pen while the Lords investigated or "browsed." I wasn't dumb enough to believe they were actually browsing. Well, maybe for Rowan I could believe it, but the other two looked like they were searching for something. I scrawled a note across a blank piece of paper and pushed it to Moira.

Say nothing. Their hearing is far sharper than a normal shifter's.

Moira scrawled a note back. *Do we need to worry?*

I'm not sure yet.

Tess floated away from the register toward the Shifter Lords.

"Tess!" I hissed.

She sent me a reassuring smile back, but it was anything but reassuring.

"How long will you be here?" Tess asked Ethan.

The Lord flicked a glance at her. "As long as we need to be."

"That's a cryptic answer," Tess mused. "Did you know one of the first signs of declining cognitive ability is giving people answers that don't make sense?"

Moira let out a horrified gasp.

Rowan's eyebrows went up, and he shot Tess a darkly amused look. "Is that true, banshee?"

"I read it on the internet, so it must be."

Ethan's brow furrowed. Halvar stared at Tess. "Don't you have somewhere to be?"

I hated Halvar's voice.

"No," Tess said cheerily. "The only place I have to go is to the grave, but I have quite a while before that happens."

I closed my eyes and whispered a prayer.

"Perhaps not, girl," Halvar snapped. "Be gone with you."

"I'm a banshee," Tess said. "I know exactly when I'm going to die, but I don't think you know your date of death." A terrifying smile curled her lips. "Would you like me to tell you?"

The shop grew so quiet, we could hear the clock above the door ticking.

Even the terrifying Halvar looked unnerved. Rowan broke into a cheerful laugh. "You're the first banshee I've ever met. I didn't know your kind could do that."

Tess shrugged. "It's one of many gifts our queen has bestowed upon us." She tilted her head and studied him. "Would you like to know?"

Rowan blinked. "Absolutely not." He leaned closer. "I'm quite the cad, you see. If I knew when I was going to die, I'd spend the rest of my days chasing women and drinking the finest whiskey so I could die a happy man."

"Happiness is only a construct. Nothing matters once you cross the waters into the mist."

Rowan winked. "Right. But thank you for the offer, dear banshee."

Tess nodded. "You are welcome." She leaned forward and stage whispered into Rowan's ear. "Rest assured, you have far more time than your counterparts. Especially the one who keeps staring at Evie like he wants to eat her." Her gaze flicked to Halvar, and her form flickered in and out of existence. "Your time draws near. Perhaps you have affairs you need to settle?"

Halvar's snarl echoed off the walls. I hurried over to Tess and took her by the arm, firmly leading her away from the stunned Lords. Once I had her back behind the register and in Moira's firm grip, I smiled apologetically.

"Sorry about that. Tess normally doesn't offer to show that particular gift to strangers."

Rowan laughed. "No worries, Miss Quinn."

"Evie, please."

"Evie, then. I find your banshee delightful." His gaze slid to Halvar. "Though I admit to some concern about Halvar's fate. Perhaps I should take a taxi back to the Keep."

Even Ethan was having trouble keeping a straight face.

A hysterical laugh bubbled from my throat. "I'm sure that won't be necessary."

Rowan glanced over to the desk. "Tess? What say you?"

Tess pinned Halvar with her silvery stare. "He will live through the night."

Jesus, Mary, and Joseph. My smile froze. "Well. Then it's settled," I said in a strained voice. "Your transportation home is safe."

"That's not as comforting as you might think," Rowan said, giving Halvar an odd look. "We're sharing a rental car."

"Umm. Well, please look around. We won't interrupt again." I headed back to the desk, giving Tess a wide-eyed WTF look. She looked mighty pleased with herself.

Rowan pulled a few plants and brought them over to the register. "These are for sale, right?"

"Yes. I can send you home with a bag of special fertilizer as a welcome to town gift if you like."

His eyebrows rose. "It's what you've been using?"

I nodded.

"Are you willing to part with the recipe?"

I studied him. "Do you have the gift, Rowan?"

"Not quite like you do, my dear, but I do have nature magic. I'd love to talk shop one day."

His energy was calm and friendly. I felt confident he wasn't here to kill me. Just wasn't sure about the other two. "I'd like that too."

"Good." Rowan walked away to continue browsing.

Halvar and Ethan's heads were together, whispering in hushed voices. Ethan shook his head and stepped away.

"Not here, Halvar." The command in his voice was absolute, but none of the Lords ruled over each other. They ruled over us.

Power rumbled in the room. I steeled myself and slowly spooled magic, preparing for a strike if I had to make one. I had to ensure Moira, Tess, and Ash got out of here alive if things went sideways.

I glanced over at the dryad. He stood stock still, but he felt the same thing I did. Ash's eyes glowed amber. He was not built for extended battle, but he could defend himself if need be. If Tess was forced to fight, her scream would destroy every piece of merchandise in the store, so I had to keep her from engaging.

Moira's eyes flashed the bright green of her vampiric and witch nature. Claws slid from the edges of her fingers.

Halvar turned to face me. "Attack me at your own peril." Violence shivered through his body as he watched us.

"No one is going to attack unless you do, Lord." It shocked me that my voice was so steady.

"You are not what you seem, Evie Quinn." His eyes pinned me in place. There was something about him that sent fear bleating through my veins. Every one of the Lords was terrifying, but none of them attacked with impunity. They were leaders first and enforced justice. But Halvar...he had violence etched on his bones.

I inclined my head. "No one is ever what another assumes they are, though I venture to guess I am not the only one, Lord. Joy Springs is full of magical talent and mixed blood."

Halvar's eyes flashed, a thin sheen of crimson rolling across his iris. The sight made me freeze. My eyes narrowed. A second later, his eyes were back to their normal icy pale color. Had I imagined it?

Chimera power rose within me, and I squashed it down so tight I had trouble breathing. Halvar was a threat to me. All the Shifter Lords were threats, but this one had chosen to antagonize me.

He's trying to get you to react, I told myself. *If you do, it will be a death sentence.*

"Halvar," Rowan snapped. "Tone it down."

One side of the Lord's lips tipped into a cruel smile. "One day, Evie Quinn, you and I will meet alone."

My heart stopped. "Oh?" I smiled. "Is this your weird way of asking me out on a date?"

"Evie," Rowan warned.

Fury snapped in Halvar's eyes. He lifted his hand, and the bell over the door rang, announcing the presence of another Lord. This time, a familiar one.

Halvar dropped his hand and turned to greet the new arrival.

Caelan was a sight for sore eyes. Dressed in grey athletic pants and a fitted t-shirt that emphasized every muscle in his chest, he looked like sex on a stick. His eyes swept over me first, then the shop, before turning to the other Lords. "I came to see how it was going." He frowned. "From the magic saturating the air, I don't think we're all going to be friends."

Rowan snorted, the look on his face knowing. "Halvar and

Evie are a little at odds for some reason, but Ethan and I are just fine." The Lord looked down at his full hands. "Though my wallet won't be by the time we get out of here."

"Shop all you want," I said, relief making my shoulders drop as Halvar stalked out of the shop.

No one spoke until the door closed behind him.

"Don't take it personally. He hasn't had a girlfriend in years." Rowan winked and made one more trip to the register to set his next round of goods down.

But Caelan had turned and watched Halvar as he walked to the vehicle. "What happened?"

Rowan sighed. "Not sure."

Ethan spoke. "Your Floromancer's banshee scared the shit out of everyone, and Halvar was just being himself."

I almost laughed. Ethan sounded so over it.

"She's not my banshee. Tess is her own person."

The banshee gave us a cheery wave.

"Is she always like that?" Ethan muttered.

"Depends. I've never seen her quite that feisty, but Halvar wasn't exactly friendly to any of us."

"Lords don't need to be friendly," Ethan said, his eyes resting on my face.

"Ah," I said lightly. "There you are. For a moment, you seemed to be somewhat human."

Moira snorted.

Ethan bared his teeth at me and turned away.

Caelan's stormy gray eyes held a touch of worry. "Did anything else happen?"

The question was directed at me.

"No. Halvar isn't a fan of Floromancers or maybe just me," I said tightly. I wanted to tell him how relieved I was to see him, but that would make it weird. Caelan had saved me. From what, I didn't know, but I'd come within inches of battling a Shifter Lord in my shop, I could feel it in my bones.

And that tinge of red ...

I had to be imagining it.

Rowan plunked two more plants and a massive bouquet of seasonal flowers next to the register. "This is it. I swear."

Moira's eyes went a little wide, but she rang him up. Before she gave him the total, I went over and added a twenty percent discount. Rowan grinned when I told him the total.

"Nice! I got the friends and family discount?"

Caelan growled. "I've never received a discount."

I shrugged. "Rowan didn't come in here demanding anything nor has he thrown his weight around."

Rowan's eyes sparkled. "Yes, Caelan. I am a polite and demur customer. Not an oaf. You should try it sometime."

Caelan smacked the back of Rowan's head, which only served to make the other Lord laugh.

He leaned over the register desk. "Do you want me to be nice to you, Evie? Is that what you like? A kind and gentle man?" His eyes flashed with impotent rage, and I knew he wasn't speaking in generic terms.

I handed Rowan his receipt and smiled. "Being kind and gentle isn't a weakness, Caelan. Women always respond more to inner strength than outer physicality, no matter how good that outer shell looks."

His lips pulled back in a savage smile. "So you're saying you think I'm pretty."

I laughed. "I'm saying Ben is kind and gentle and pretty."

Rowan's brows hitched up, and he took a step back.

Moira and Tess edged from behind the register. "We're going to grab a box to pack up Rowan's stuff," the vampire murmured quietly.

"I should kill him for that," Caelan whispered, his eyes flaring gold.

I blinked. "For what? Ben has the right to pursue whomever he wishes."

"Not you," Caelan snarled.

I leaned forward, so close our noses were almost touching. "I am allowed to do the same. We've done nothing but antagonize each other, and you piss me off even when I think you're trying to be nice."

"I'm never nice."

"I know that now!"

"Go out with me."

I scoffed even as my heart thudded like a drum inside my chest. "No."

"You like Ben better?" Muscle corded through his arms as he leaned forward. His eyes glowed with magic, and power limned his entire frame.

"Ben is certainly nicer than you are," I snapped.

"Nice will not protect you!" Caelan roared.

"You think Ben is weak?"

"I think you don't want nice. You seek safety. Protection. Peace. I can give all of that to you."

I threw my hands up in the air. "Where in the world is this coming from? A week ago, you tried to kill me!"

Rowan huffed a laugh. At Caelan's snarl, the other Lord winced and slipped to the back where Moira and Tess were. When we were alone, I took a couple steps back. "This is getting awkward. You aren't interested in me. All you are is curious." I offered him a tight smile. "And you know what they say about curiosity."

His eyes gleamed. "Curiosity killed the cat. But do you know what brought him back, flower girl?"

My blood heated.

A slow smile curved his generous lips. "Satisfaction."

An annoyed huff burst from me. "Regardless, this—" I pointed between me and him, "is not happening."

"And neither are you and Ben."

"I never said anything was happening there either." I started to turn away, but Caelan reached over and grabbed my arm.

"Then why did he come home smelling like you, Evie?" He leapt over the desk and took two steps. My back bumped into the wall. Caelan boxed me in with both his arms on either side of my head.

My heartbeat leapt in my throat.

Caelan buried his nose in my neck and inhaled. "You smell like deep magic and mysteries." He nipped my throat, a burst of pain before pleasure flooded my veins. "Like a gift I have yet to unwrap."

I pushed against his chest. "Stop."

His wicked chuckle against my skin did terrible things to my willpower. "Admit you don't want nice, flower girl."

"I don't want anything," I whispered. His proximity scrambled my thoughts. I wanted to pull him to me, but I also wanted to push him away. Caelan smelled like wild forests and the full moon, a hint of something not wolf sparkling in his blood. My fingers itched to run through his thick hair and bring him against me.

"Everyone wants something." He dipped his head and pressed a searing kiss to the top of my collarbone.

A GASP ESCAPED MY THROAT, and the overwhelming urge to surrender to him flooded my brain.

The bell rang, announcing a new visitor. My eyes fluttered closed with relief.

"Go away, Garrett," Caelan growled. Gold light flared over our bodies.

The shifter cleared his throat. "Lord, I...apologize for the interruption, but there's been a disturbance at the Keep." Disapproval echoed with every word Garrett spoke.

Caelan inhaled and closed his eyes. "I'll be there in a minute. Wait for me outside."

The door closed.

"This isn't over, Evie." The Shifter Lord straightened and adjusted his shirt, then ran a hand through his dark hair.

"It never started," I said, my voice hoarse with desire.

One side of his mouth quirked up. "I'm going to find out what you are."

Fear made my throat click. "You'll be sorely disappointed to know I'm merely a Floromancer."

"We both know that is a lie, flower girl."

He still stood far too close. Caelan leaned in, his breath warm against my mouth. "Stay away from my healer, Evie. You are far too dangerous for his heart."

Without another word, Caelen leaped over the desk and headed outside, the bell jingling against the oppressive silence of the room.

Rowan, Moira, and Tess came back out a minute later, silent and with their heads down. The Lord carried a large box. Moira took it from him and carefully wrapped and packed his plants up.

When it was finished, Rowan picked up the box and gave me a sympathetic look before walking to the door where he stopped and turned toward me.

"Evie, for what it's worth, and you may not want to hear this right now…" He trailed off for a moment. "Caelan is a good man. Quick to anger, slow to love, slow to trust, and even slower to commit. He sees something in you he wants, and if you don't want it too, I suggest you run. Go now, go far, and never seek him out again." He shook his head. "Caelan always gets what he wants, and I'm afraid he has his eyes on you." The Lord pushed the door open. "He's right, you know."

"Oh?" My heartbeat sounded like an ocean in my ears.

"There is something off about you. We all sense it." He gave me a sad smile. "But he's also right about you not wanting someone nice. You're a deadly thing wrapped in an innocent package. Take care you don't endanger everyone around you when that package finally unwraps and exposes your secrets." He stepped outside and let the door close behind him.

No one said anything for a long time.

"Fuck," I whispered when I could catch my breath again.

Thirty~Three

Someone or something was watching me. I couldn't see anything, but the hair on the back of my neck stood straight, and I sensed eyes on me all the way home. Once I was in my driveway, I sat in my vehicle for a few minutes waiting for whatever or whoever it was to show themselves.

But when there was nothing, I slid out of the car, keys in hand, and hurried to my door. Once I was inside, I slumped against the door and let out a shaky breath. Regrets had been playing inside my head for hours after the Shifter Lords, including Caelan, had left the shop.

I should have played ball with Caelan at the very beginning. Kept my head down, performed my duty as a florist, and gray rocked it all the way to easy town. Except I really hated bullies, and I felt like that's what Caelan was when I first met him.

And now look at me. Jumping at imaginary shadows and under investigation by the Council. Way to go, Evie.

I poured myself an obscene amount of wine, kicked my shoes off, and curled onto the couch. Ever since that moment with Halvar, my magic had felt off. Not my Floromancy. That only went wonky when I wasn't siphoning properly. The Chimera magic I kept shoved down had been coming in small flares, and I was having trouble keeping my human form. The others noticed it, and Moira finally forced me out the door, telling me not to come back in until I had eight full hours of sleep.

She was probably right. Restless nights and stressful days often contributed to magical fluctuations, and Hazel had warned me to do my best to keep my emotions steady. Speaking of her, I dug through my pocket for my cell phone and scrolled through my contacts until I found her.

She answered on the second ring. "Evie?"

"Hi Hazel." It was good to hear her smoky, accented voice.

"What's wrong?"

I laughed. "Nothing is wrong. It's been a while since we talked, and I wanted to catch up."

"You never wanna catch up." The doubt in her voice was clear.

"I promise. Everything is fine. We've had some interesting developments, but my tattoo is still stable."

"What about fluctuations?"

"Some here and there."

"Mmm. I feel like there's much you aren't telling me."

"How about a visit?" I asked, ignoring her statement.

"To the U.S.?" She barked a laugh. "It's a little crazy pants over there right now, ain't it?"

Hard to deny that. "Not for the magical community. We're the same, and Joy Springs is full of us. I'd love to see you."

"You can always come to Scotland."

Fear skittered up my back. "I'm not ready."

"There hasn't been a Chimera sighting since your attack. Everyone thinks they're gone."

"I'm still not ready," I said quietly.

Hazel sighed. "Fine. But you're missing out on an entire country because of one bad man."

"He wasn't a man." My fingers tightened around the phone. "He was so much worse."

"Maybe I'll come," Hazel said, relenting. "How about a month or so? I have things to clean up around here."

"A month is good." If I were still alive by then.

"Done." Her voice softened. "Whatever's going on, hang on until then. I'll bring some of my special magic." Hazel cackled and disconnected.

That was the thing about her. I never got the chance to say goodbye, and I felt like I should have this time.

After mindlessly bingeing shows for a couple of hours, I headed to bed, hoping I could get some sleep tonight.

Unfortunately, my brain had other ideas and replayed the image of Caelan nipping my neck on a loop for hours.

I woke before the sun came up and immediately felt something off. Quiet as a whisper, I slid my feet into my slippers and crept out of my bedroom, my eyes sweeping the living room for intruders. I sensed no one in the house and couldn't scent anything unusual. After checking every room and cursing my paranoia, I made a pot of coffee and downed the first cup before refilling my mug and heading outside to grab the mail I'd forgotten to grab last night.

But when I opened the door and glanced down, there was a basket wrapped in cellophane and pretty ribbon and an envelope attached to the top addressed to me.

It smelled like shifters.

I was pissed beyond words. Three weeks had passed since the incident in my store, and now here I was, inside Caelan's Keep decorating the ballroom for a Council sponsored full moon event. Supposedly the dinner was to support local businesses and raise money for town events and to beautify Joy Springs, but something about this event felt off.

For one, everyone was staring at me. I'd been here since the morning, and every shifter who'd passed by had stared at me so intently I felt like I had a booger up my nose or something. Moira and Tess noticed, too. Ash had stayed back to man the shop, but he was also invited to attend the dinner and would be here at seven tonight.

I'd seen only one of the Shifter Lords since my arrival, and thankfully it was Rowan. He gave us a somber nod and passed by to murmur I should be on my best behavior because everyone was on edge.

Considering this was supposed to be a happy event celebrating the town, his words made my spine stiffen. If the Lords were antsy, that meant I should be antsy, right?

I cursed as the pin I was using to fasten one of the blooms onto the ribbon poked me in the pad of my thumb. The scent of blood rose in the air, and several pairs of shifter eyes snapped to me.

"Shit," Moira said. She dug in her pocket for a liquid bandage and hurriedly applied it to my finger. Within seconds, the smell of blood dissipated, but it was still on the ribbon. Moira cut that part away and handed it to me for disposal. I climbed off the ladder, shoved the ribbon into a potted plant, and instructed the bacteria in the soil to do its thing. Within seconds, the ribbon was completely gone, my blood absorbed into the soil. I'd have to ask Caelan if I could have the plant, but I'm sure he wouldn't mind.

He'd been disturbingly nice over the last few weeks, and that was more unnerving than anything else. I'd caught him looking at me a few times with pity, and that had disturbed me to my core.

Tess floated around the ballroom, commenting on the lack of ghosts. "I wonder if shifters eat everything when they kill people, including their souls?" she mused aloud.

Moira shook her head. "We shouldn't ask questions we don't want the answers to," she muttered.

"But I do want the answer," Tess insisted. "If they do devour their spirits, maybe we should create a shifter only assassination squad and have them target all the bad paranormal criminals so they won't come back as poltergeists?"

Moira and I gave each other a look before the vampire shrugged. "That's actually not a bad idea," she muttered, making me laugh.

"We could call it Spirit Dogs," I said.

Moira let out a cackle.

The sound of an amused throat clearing made me wince. I turned to see Simone in the doorway. She hadn't been around much lately, so I waved happily when I spotted her.

"Ladies," she said as she walked in. "How's everything going?"

"Almost finished." I pointed up at the ceiling. "We have a few more garlands to stream, and then I need to activate them."

Simone grimaced. "No funny business this time, Evie."

I crossed my heart. "No funny business. Scout's honor."

Simone rolled her eyes. "Were you actually a Scout?"

"Nope, but I'm using the spirit of the word and not the actual Scout oath."

"Is there an oath?" Moira wondered aloud.

I shrugged. "I'm sure there is. Something inspiring about fidelity and tree trunks, probably."

"Focus, ladies," Simone warned. "We only have a few hours before catering has to come in and set up. Will you be finished by then?"

I nodded. "Yes, but I can't be interrupted when I start activating spells, otherwise you might get a man-eating vine in place of a friendly, thornless climbing rose."

Simone blanched. "Ah, yes. We can't have that, can we?"

Moira huffed a laugh. "Is this a formal dinner?" she asked.

The Omega gave her a horrified stare. "You don't have a dress yet?"

Moira jerked like she'd been shot. "A dress? No. I wouldn't wear a dress to a funeral even if it was my mother in that box and it was her last wish."

Simone blinked. "I—I'm not sure how to respond to that."

"Focus." I grinned at her. "Moira always looks fantastic. She has that vampire flair for fashion. It's me you should worry about."

Moira grimaced. "She is not wrong. Evie's fashion tastes skew more Sunday hobo than sexy chic."

The Omega cleared her throat. "About that..."

Foreboding skittered up my spine. My smile dropped. "Spit it out, Simone."

To her credit, Simone looked uncomfortable. "The Lord left something for you. I'm to take you to it."

"Does it bite?" I said flatly.

Simone sighed. "Honestly, Evie. Can you give him at least a little credit?"

At my flat look, she shook her head. "Follow me, then."

Moira and I exchanged glances before I got up and dusted the clinging leaves from my hands. Simone led me down several hallways until we reached a room with two large double doors. She pushed one open and gestured me inside. I balked the second I stepped into the room.

A massive four-poster bed sat pushed against the back wall, covered in a satin bedspread the color of midnight. A large white box with the same color ribbon sat in the middle of the bed.

"It's there," Simone said, pointing at the box. "He's instructed you to wear this to the event."

One of my eyebrows rose. "Instructed?" I echoed, rage spiraling through my veins.

Simone shut the door behind us. "Evie."

I turned at the urgency in her voice.

She came closer and took both of my hands in hers. "Listen carefully," she whispered. "Something is going to happen tonight, and I believe you're involved."

"What is it?"

She shook her head. "Not even Caelan knows. Please wear this dress. I know you and the Lord have issues, but he has your best interests at heart. It is primed and may help you if there is an attack this evening."

"Primed?" I questioned.

She lifted a shoulder in a helpless shrug. "I do not know. Caelan said you would know once you unpacked the dress."

Curious, despite myself, I tugged the ribbon, watching it unspiral and fall away from the box. The lid lifted easily, exposing a mass of tissue paper. I folded the paper away, exposing a stunning ebony dress with hundreds, possibly thousands of multicolored, hand embroidered flowers.

I let out a soft gasp and pulled the dress from the box. It unfolded in a mass of satin. The dress' neckline was straight across and strapless with a tightly cinched waist and voluminous skirt. And though it would look spectacular on, that wasn't what made me catch my breath. My fingers trailed over the embroidery only to feel the faint hum of life in each meticulously crafted pistil inside the center of the flower.

"What in the world?" I breathed. Setting the dress carefully on the edge of the bed, I sent a tiny pulse of magic through one of the embroidered pistils only to feel an answering hum. Concentrating, I sent my senses through the dress and felt thousands of answering pulses. A brilliant smile broke onto my face even as tears filled my eyes.

Caelan had succeeded in finding the perfect gift and the perfect weapon for a Floromancer. Each pistil possessed either a seed or a cutting of a dangerous plant, carefully preserved with a spell. I sensed Water Hemlock, Belladonna, Oleander, flytraps, mundane thorned vines, Poison Ivy and oak, Castor beans, White Snakeroot, Rosary Peas, and others. This dress, if worn by the right person, would be the deadliest thing in the room, even if said room was occupied by seven Shifter Lords.

Caelan was placing an insane amount of trust in me with this gift.

"Does it meet your approval?" Simone asked.

"I will wear the dress," I said hoarsely.

"Good," the Omega breathed. "I will leave you to it, Evie. Please be careful tonight."

"Thank you," I said, unable to take my eyes off the gown.

The door clicked shut behind me.

With more care than I showed most things, I carefully stowed the dress away, carrying the box from the room and into the ballroom. After I placed it next to my purse, I took a more detailed look at the place we were decorating and realized someone had deliberately placed numerous heavy potted plants around the room.

Caelan expected tonight would go wrong and had given me a hefty advantage.

"Are you alright?" Moira asked quietly.

"Not here," I whispered. "I'll tell you when we head back to the shop."

Moira nodded. "Then let's hurry up and get out of here. I need to scrounge something together to wear for the dinner."

I got back to work, even though my thoughts lingered on Caelan and his generosity, marveling at his clever gift.

Thirty~Five

Moira whistled low when she saw me a couple hours later. "Holy shit."

Ash's eyebrows rose to his hairline. "That dress..." He shook his head and swallowed hard. "I sense the life pulsing inside." But Ash frowned. "Will Rowan sense it as well?"

"More than likely, but I believe he's Caelan's ally. I don't think we will need to worry about him tonight."

"Let's hope," Ash murmured.

Tess floated over, her pale eyes studying me. "You look like a deadly princess."

She was right. The dress fit me like a glove. The train fell to the floor so I could get away with wearing slippers instead of heels. Easier to run in if I had to make a mad dash outside the Keep.

I'd styled my hair but left it loose, and it fell in thick curls all the way to the middle of my back. I wore a silver pendant in the shape of a poppy and simple diamond studs shaped like daisies.

Ash wore a brown suit with a forest green tie and matching shoes. Tess wore a simple silver gown with matching shoes. Moira wore a pair of high-waisted, black satin pants, four-inch silver heels, a silver sequined camisole, and a matching satin blazer.

She'd scooped her dark hair into a slicked back high ponytail and wore only mascara, a touch of blush, and crimson lipstick.

"We all look devastating," I said with a grin.

Moira held a finger up. "Oh! Before I forget." She dug through her purse and pulled out a small box. "Marnie and Twila made this for you, just in case things go wrong this evening."

I opened the box and pulled out a tiny silver pin shaped like a rose. Moira plucked it from my fingers and pinned it to my skirt, disguising it between the embroidered flowers.

Faint magic beat from the pin. "What is it?"

"Healing spell," Moira answered. "Designed to trigger automatically if you lose fifty percent of your energy."

"Like an RPG!" Ash said.

Tess gave him a quizzical look. "How is a healing spell like a rocket-propelled grenade?"

All of us gaped at the banshee. Maybe one of us needed to step in and police her television habits.

Ash blinked in confusion before his expression cleared. "No, Tess." His voice was gentle, and it warmed my heart that he didn't laugh at her. "It can also mean role playing game. That's the context I was using."

The banshee tilted her head in curiosity. "What's a role-playing game?"

Ash's face lit up. "You've never played before?"

Tess shook her head. Ash draped an arm around her and led her off, babbling about clerics, warriors, and mages, as a bemused Moira and I watched.

"She's in her twenties, right?" Moira whispered.

I nodded. "Sheltered, but yes."

"Poor girl." Moira laughed. "Ash is going to talk her ear off."

But the banshee was watching Ash with rapt interest. "Somehow I don't think she's going to mind," I said.

.   .   .

Moira dropped the keys into a shifter's waiting palm as we exited the car. I struggled not to laugh as we walked up the steps to the front door. Caelan hadn't changed a single thing about my "landscaping" services. Dandelions still swayed in the gentle night wind, and the columns in the front of his house were still covered in blooming flowers. I inhaled the heady floral scent surrounding the property and listened as hummingbird moths and other night creatures buzzed through the new and stunning native landscape.

The front doors opened, and we were escorted inside. Fairy lights hung throughout the main hall, giving the place a warm, cheery glow. A smile tipped my lips as I explored further, noting with some delight just how many plants Caelan actually had.

There'd been no sign of the healer since he'd disappeared during my mother's visit. While I was disappointed, it was best for his continued health if he stayed away from me. Hundreds of shifters and local business owners mingled in the ballroom, the sound of soft, classical music playing through the speakers. In the middle of the room sat a large basket of flowers and greenery next to a wooden structure. I'd been told this was a symbolic gesture as well as a test of my abilities, basically a way of Lord Caelan welcoming me to town and for the town to see I was no threat.

It didn't make a lick of sense to me because I'd been here for five years, but Rowan had lowered his voice and told me the Council had insisted because they were still sure I had something to do with the rogue magic pockets, and this was their way to see I was nothing more than a Floromancer. Still didn't make sense, but whatever. So, I agreed to put the full moon centerpiece together after dinner. Once it was finished, the ceremony would begin.

Simone appeared before me. "Evie," she said with a nod. "Caelan would like to speak with you before everything begins. May I escort you?"

My heart fluttered, but I nodded.

Neither of us spoke as Simone led me to an office away from the ballroom. She knocked once and opened the door.

I gasped when I saw Seymour. The flytrap perked up immediately once he sensed my energy and tried to scoot his pot closer.

"I'll come to you," I murmured happily.

"Nice to see you're more excited about the plant than the Lord," Caelan murmured.

I spun because I hadn't even noticed him and smiled sheepishly.

His eyes widened and skimmed down my body, leaving a trail of heat everywhere he looked. "Stunning," he murmured.

Color touched my cheeks.

Simone excused herself and shut the door. The sound of ceramic hitting wood made me laugh. I held up a finger. "Sorry. Let me take care of this first."

Caelan's eyebrows rose as I turned to the flytrap to murmur sweet nothings to him. Seymour made a happy little noise and butted my finger with his trap.

"That is quite disturbing," Caelan said.

"Did you bite him?" I whispered to Seymour.

The carnivorous plant cooed happily.

"Good." I gave him an extra scratch and turned to Caelan. "Thank you for the dress. It's spectacular."

He nodded. "I am a cautious man, which is the reason I called you in tonight." Caelan gestured for me to sit, but I grimaced.

"It's hard to sit down in this thing. I'd rather stand until dinner if possible."

"Of course." He leaned against his desk. "Rowan has professed his support for you. Ethan is still on the fence. Halvar is against you. Thorvin has made no move either way. Soren will support me, and Donovan wishes to meet you before he makes up his mind."

I blinked. "Why does any of this matter?"

"Any threat to my territory is a threat to them."

I sighed. "I'm not a threat to anyone."

He grinned. "You're such a lovely little liar, Evie Quinn."

I threw my hands up. "I don't even know why I try."

"The ball will end outside once the centerpiece is complete, but you will be required to stay."

My heart skipped a beat. "Why?"

"The Shifter Lords wish to test your magic." Caelan's jaw tightened.

"Do you test everyone's magic? Or am I just special?"

He sighed. "There's no need. Everyone in this town has a straightforward gift. Their lineage is easily traceable, but you've been secretive about yours. We can find no records of your birth parents."

Ben hadn't told Caelan about Cliona's visit. My heart warmed. "That's because it's none of your business."

His eyes darkened. "You know this could go much easier for everyone if you were a little more forthcoming about yourself."

I snorted. "Like you are?"

"I am a Lord."

"Yes," I said bitterly, "thus allowing you to get away with anything you want."

Caelan rose. "Evie."

I held my hand up and turned to leave. "Don't bother. Test me, don't test me, I don't care anymore. Just don't expect me to fall at your feet when this is over." If I survived, a negative voice inside my head said.

I hurried back to the ballroom, schooling my expression into mild neutrality. If the Shifter Lords were going to test me, so be it.

Gray rock, Evie. Be an uninteresting stone.

But even the blandest stones had interesting properties. I had to be gravel.

My life depended on it.

CHAPTER
Thirty-Six

We made it through dinner with no drama, though I felt Halvar's icy pale gaze on my skin the entire evening. Once the last dish was over, several lower-level shifters came in to move the structure and flowers, and everyone was instructed to attend Caelan and the other Lords in his garden. The moon hung full and heavy in the sky, casting precious silver light across the blooming flowers.

A night garden. I breathed in the heady scent of tobacco flowers and moonflowers, also catching the surprising scent of Mirabilis. Most people didn't plant those because they were invasive, so I was curious if Caelan's were cultivated or growing wild. Once this was over, I planned to go find them to check.

I'd primed every seed and cutting in the dress, spelling them to act in a certain way when I commanded them. Destroying the dress would be regrettable, but if it saved my life, it was worth it.

A massive bonfire crackled cheerfully outside the garden gates, surrounded by stone seats. Caelan's Pack gathered behind those seats and stood there, an anticipatory gleam in their eyes. Ben was nowhere to be found.

This was the first time I'd been around shifters during the full moon. The threat of violence laced the air, and the shifters' magic gleamed in their eyes and over their skin. They obviously couldn't wait to shed their human forms and run, and now that we were outside, it was much more obvious.

Caelan stood before the fire as the rest of the guests assembled. When the noise died down, he began to speak.

"Thank you for attending tonight's festivities. As a gesture of peace and cooperation, each Lord is delighted to present a monetary donation to our town's fund to be split equally between each downtown business."

Cue polite applause.

"Tonight, we have a special guest, one of the newer members in town, though she's been here for a while. I've been remiss in welcoming her and wanted to take a moment to introduce her to everyone because I know she hasn't met all of you yet." He turned to me. "Please welcome Evie Quinn, owner of Little Shop of Florals, and a talented Floromancer."

More polite applause. I wished I was in my pajamas.

Moira and Ash gently nudged me. I waved politely and stepped up beside Caelan. His heat and tightly leashed magic pulsed against me. My nerves were shot. I didn't want to perform like a circus elephant, and if I could punch Caelan in the kidney and get away with it, I would.

"Evie will offer a brief demonstration of her unique magic this evening as she sets up our centerpiece for tonight's full moon run." He gestured, and I stepped up to the wooden structure.

"Do you have two shifters who might assist me?"

Caelan nodded and gestured for two of his shifters. "Do what she asks," he commanded. Both shifters nodded.

"Please step up on either side of the structure." I gave them a tight smile. "All I need you to do is anchor the container so it doesn't tip."

"Easy enough," one of the shifters murmured. They crouched and gripped the sides.

Caelan stepped up beside me, dipped his head, and whispered in my ear. "Be on guard."

I didn't respond. Caelan stepped away and walked over to stand by the other Lords.

Anticipation hummed in the air. Hundreds of pairs of eyes rested on my back. My skin itched, and a single trickle of sweat rolled down my back. The bonfire crackled, heat searing my front.

I closed my eyes and called my magic.

The first flower rose from the basket as delighted gasps sounded from the audience. I picked up four more flowers and a garland of thorned greens, wrapping the vine around the bottom of the structure, weaving it up the wood. Flowers danced in the air, an easy command keeping them moving while I focused on the first layer.

When the initial layer was finished, I wove the white roses through, then picked up pink peonies, baby's breath, purple clematis, moonflowers, and red roses. I wove morning glory vines through, coaxing their sleepy blooms to open for me for just a little while, then honeysuckle and jasmine, sending each flower dancing through the air before I wove it into the display.

Someone struck up music, and gentle classic tunes melded with the crackling fire. To amuse myself, I changed the cadence of the dancing flowers, now keeping them in time to the music's beat, much to the delight of the audience.

While I loved my magic and I loved communing with the natural world, I didn't like this. Performing wasn't me. Nature answered to no one. I kept a faint amused smile on my lips, but inside I was steaming, pissed off at what the Lords were making me do. This proved nothing. I was giving them what they wanted, not what I was.

Until everything changed.

Sweat poured down my face, dripping down my back in a steady trickle. It felt too hot. I was close, but not close enough to feel like I was standing in the inferno.

A quick glance revealed the fire was burning too hot, the bottom of it glowing a faint blue. Since everyone's eyes were on me, no one noticed. I glanced back and caught Halvar staring. Not at the flowers or the display, but directly at me, a faint, cruel smile over his lips. The crackling fire sent an orange flame glowing in his iris, but then his smile widened, and that same strange crimson sheen rolled over his eyes.

He flicked his fingers toward the fire, a dart of blood red magic shooting from the tips. Fire shot up through the air, far higher than normal. The base rumbled, magical pressure building toward a massive explosion that if allowed to go off would kill us all.

"Caelan," I croaked.

The Lord stepped up.

"Something's wrong," I whispered, my voice hoarse with barely kept in check power.

His eyes narrowed. "What is it? Your magic?"

"The fire," I breathed. If I told Caelan what I suspected, I would give myself away, and Halvar knew it.

"Should we evacuate?"

My gaze went to the still grinning Halvar. He sent another dart of magic out, but not at the fire.

Right at me.

Terrible memories rose when that familiar magic struck. Pain and claws and terror and grief. I closed my eyes against that pain, Halvar's terrible laughter echoing in my ears.

"Evie." Caelan touched my back.

"Get back," I croaked. "I'm dangerous."

"What's wrong?" His voice was low and urgent.

"Get back," I pleaded.

Caelan stepped away. I looked back at Moira and mouthed, "I'm sorry."

Her eyes went wide.

Magic exploded from my body.

CHAPTER

Thirty-Seven

CAELAN

She was glorious. Evie exploded in a riot of color, her dark hair glowing like a star. She was crimson and gold and all the colors of the rainbow. My breath caught as her back bowed, her arms spread out like a sacrifice.

Moira lurched to her feet. "Caelan."

"What is she?" I whispered.

"Snap out of it," Moira barked. "Get everyone out of here. Now."

I turned to her, ready to bite her head off for ordering me around, but when I saw the look on her face, I paused.

"Tonight's festivities are now over," I said, my voice tight. "Anyone who is not a Lord or Pack will be escorted out." I gestured toward the right. "Please follow my Omega, Simone."

Simone's eyes burned with concern, but she put on a polite, unworried smile and began ushering people out of the Keep, all while Evie burned like a supernova.

"What's wrong with her?" I said in a low voice.

Moira's jaw tightened. "Someone sabotaged her, Caelan. Was it you?" Her eyes flashed the vivid green of her kind.

"You know the answer to that," I snapped.

"Someone did."

When I started to approach her, Moira reached out and stopped me. "Don't."

A golden orb shimmered around Evie, covering most of her features. I squinted to see inside, but seeing past the bright glare of her magic was almost impossible.

I glanced toward the Lords. Rowan's eyes were wide with stunned awe. Thorvin studied her like a new specimen. Soren wore a slight smile, and Donovan looked like he'd seen a ghost. Ethan looked like he wanted to say I told you so, but Halvar...Halvar was laughing, his eyes on Evie's glowing form as if she wasn't doing anything unexpected.

But then...she did.

Strands of red and gold magic mixed with the calming watermelon tourmaline she normally had flowed from her feet and wrapped around the base of the bonfire.

Then her dress came alive. A vine snaked out from the side of her dress and wrapped around Halvar's leg, jerking him off his feet with a satisfying yelp. Other vines reached out and wrapped around every other Lord, but those vines gently picked those Lords up and deposited them at the edge of the property, far away from the chaos.

Then she picked up Halvar with her vine and slammed him onto the earth repeatedly.

I heard Rowan's bark of laughter all the way across the yard.

"How dare you!" something that didn't sound like Evie said from her voice. The orb disappeared, revealing Evie's glowing golden skin and generous lips. But her eyes...those stunning azure eyes were not the same.

They glowed the color of cut rubies.

Halvar laughed through a mouth filled with blood. "There you are. I knew I'd find you."

I stilled. They knew each other.

Every single embroidered flower on that dress came alive,

building a cage of flora around them, shutting me and Moira, and everyone else out.

"Don't interfere," Moira warned. "This was a long time coming."

I glanced at her in disbelief. "How does she know Halvar?"

The vampire's smile was filled with grief. "That's not Halvar."

CHAPTER

Thirty~Eight

The Chimera had found me. After all these years, I'd finally found a home and people who loved me, and I relaxed, thinking I was finally safe.

The Lord, who was not a Lord, sliced through my vines with a razor tipped claw and came to his feet, his features melting to a face I would never forget. It was his face that attracted me first, dark hair and brilliant blue eyes, lips that could charm a nun, and a smile that made my knees weak.

I was devastated and grieving the end of my marriage, and I'd come to Scotland for some relaxation, a way to get out of my head. We met at a crowded bar on the third night, and I was a moth attracted to his flame. Within hours, we were dancing, our hands everywhere, our mouths entangled. I'd fallen in love that night, or at least what passed for love when you were so entangled in grief all you could do was stop moving and wait to drown.

But then he asked me to meet him for a moonlight walk, and stupidly, I did.

And it had changed me forever.

"You cannot deny what you are, Evangeline."

My lips pulled away from my teeth. "Don't call me that," I hissed. "You have no right. I am not yours. I was never yours."

"You were mine the moment I tasted your skin. The moment you melted so sweetly against me."

"No. I was lonely and desperate, and you were a distraction, Finn." Not Halvar. Never Halvar.

"I didn't know what you were until you stepped into the moonlight, and your scent overwhelmed me." He inhaled, magic flaring in his eyes. "And then I had to have you."

"You almost killed me!"

He inclined his head. "A regrettable loss of control."

A hysterical laugh bubbled from my lips. Finn had stopped paying attention to the bonfire, but I hadn't. I'd banked the fire just enough to keep it from blowing immediately.

"A being of great power showed up, and I had to abandon you. When I came back you were gone."

Finn didn't know Cliona was my mother.

"I've been trying to find you for years. There is much you need to know about your power."

I stared at him in disbelief. "You can't believe I'd ever work with you. Are you fucking insane?"

That heart-stopping grin formed on his lips. "I am one of the last living Chimeras. If not me, who?"

"No one!" I screeched.

His eyes sparkled as he lifted his palm, a crimson ball of magic spooling in his palm. "I am your Maker, Evie. You cannot deny me."

"I don't give a shit if you're Jesus, you arrogant asshat!"

He tossed that magic at me, and I couldn't avoid it because I'd trapped us in a cage of flora. Finn's power hit me square in the middle of my chest and spread, not painful, but staggering in its intensity.

"A gift," he said.

I dropped to my knees, my mouth opening and closing like a fish as magic burned through my veins.

"If you would have stayed and waited, you would have received it all those years ago. You walked away incomplete." His face sobered. "Now you will be exactly what you are meant to be."

"I'd rather die than be anything you want me to be," I croaked as I struggled to breathe.

Pain flickered over his face, there and gone in a heartbeat. "You won't have a choice, Evie."

I slowly worked an opening through the cage I'd built on the side of the bonfire, silent and methodical.

"I always have a choice." Tears rose in my eyes. "You don't know anything about me."

"I know you are a Chimera. Forever changed." His eyes glittered. "Forever mine."

I lurched to my feet. "I BELONG TO NO ONE!"

A vine snatched Finn off his feet as I loosened the grip on my power, dragging him into the fire. His pained screams shattered the night as the cage of flora exploded outward.

In a burst of light, Finn's body disappeared, too fast for the fire to have consumed him.

Fear flooded my veins, but I couldn't move to follow wherever he might have gone. His power burned through my body, flaying me alive from the inside.

I swayed, barely keeping my eyes open, and I reached for the flames, pulling water from the ground to extinguish the fire, all the magic inside expended. When there wasn't even a flicker left and I saw no sign of Finn, I staggered forward, only to fall to my knees.

"Evie!" Moira called.

A low moan came from somewhere inside me. Wetness soaked the side of my hip as Marnie's healing spell activated.

My friend's face swam into view. I gave her what I hoped was a reassuring smile before I thumped forward, face first into the grass, darkness finally claiming me.

Thirty-Nine

CAELAN

"You fortunate sonofabitch," Rowan growled. "How'd you get so lucky?"

Ethan snorted. "I'm not sure that's luck."

"Yeah," Donovan agreed. "That woman is a godsdamned curse."

I shot him a dark glare, but Donovan shrugged, completely unrepentant.

Thorvin hadn't said a word since Evie's display of staggering power. Soren, usually unable to keep his mouth shut, sat back and watched me, a strange look on his face.

Moira hadn't let me touch Evie when she fell, barking at me to stay away from them if I knew what was good for me. And after seeing everything, I was starting to think the vampire might be right.

Evie might be a Floromancer, but she was something else. Something far more dangerous than anything else in this town. Probably more dangerous than anyone sitting in this room, and that was a problem.

Against my better judgment, I sent Ben to follow them back home. Moira could decide whether to use his services. I was itching to see Evie again, to ensure she was okay, and I knew that to be the height of stupidity.

I should have killed her the second I suspected she wasn't what she seemed.

But how could I kill something so stunning, so powerful...so rare?

Fuck.

"You should kill her while she's still vulnerable," Soren said.

The room fell silent as I mulled Soren's words, the urge to kill him itching at my fingertips. "You keep a museum's worth of unusual, precious treasures, and you, of all people, think I should kill her?"

Soren's lips thinned. "She is a threat to your rule. To all of us. If she wants power, all she has to do is reach out and take it."

"That girl wants to be left alone to talk to her plants, Soren." Rowan sighed and looked away. "She has no use for politics and certainly not with our nonsense."

"And you know her so well, Rowan?" Ethan drawled. "Or are you just as fascinated by the temptress as Caelan is?"

Rowan rolled his eyes. "None of us can sit here and claim she isn't stunning. Perhaps she can become an ally." His eyes glittered. "Or something more."

"More?" Soren asked a second before his eyes widened. "Ah. Always thinking ahead, aren't you?" His eyes slid to me. "Though I believe you'll end up in a dominance fight if you try to take her."

My chest rumbled with an involuntary snarl.

Soren laughed. "See?"

"And what of Halvar?" Rowan asked.

"The real Halvar?" Soren asked. "Probably dead, cast away by whatever that intruder was for his skin."

Ethan's face turned grim. "You think we're dealing with a Skinwalker?"

The last Skinwalker on U.S. soil disappeared hundreds of years ago. I shook my head. "No. It has to be glamour magic. We should send a party out to search for him. If he's dead, we'll hold a quorum to appoint a new Lord."

"And if that thing knows our secrets?" Donovan asked.

"If we don't find him, Evie will," I drawled. It was unclear what happened under the cover of Evie's magic, but something had changed her. When the magic fell and Evie lay there, I sensed a difference in her. More powerful, if that were possible.

"That's exactly what we should be worried about," Ethan snapped.

Rowan sighed. "Enough about Halvar. We will find him and make the appropriate decisions when we do. Let's return our focus to Evie."

"Yes," Soren said, amusement coloring his tone. "Let's talk about Rowan's new bride."

The possessive snarl clawed its way out of my throat, silencing the table for a long moment.

"We should ask Evie what she wants," Donovan said, giving me a wary glance.

"No. She does not have a choice. Evie must ally with us through marriage or contract. There is no other way." Ethan rubbed a hand over his jaw. "It's the only way to ensure she fights for our side and not against us." He glanced over at me. "I have a solution that will strengthen your territory dominance, Caelan."

I growled. "My dominance is just fine."

"Rival packs intrude on your territory. We are not trying to encroach and strike while you are vulnerable, but with Halvar's disappearance and now Evie, I think you should consider our proposal."

I sighed. "And what proposal is that?"

The doors opened. A tall, lean woman with piercing green eyes strode in. She was stunning and savage and mean as a gods-damned snake. Her lips pulled away in a wicked smile.

"Hello, darling," she said to me.

Epilogue

Four weeks had passed since Finn had revealed himself, and two weeks since I'd fully recovered, changed but healed. My Chimera magic was more powerful than ever, and my tattoo was acting up, no longer fully suppressing the power.

Hazel would be here in a week to restore it and help me with my next steps. She knew about Finn showing up, and we both agreed he was not dead, only biding his time.

Until then, it was business as usual. We had several weddings on the books, and there were never enough hours in the day to get everything done.

The Shifter Lords had stayed away. Everyone except for Rowan. He'd come by a week ago to say goodbye and leave his number.

He'd also left me with a small silver sculpture of a wolf that doubled as a planter. I gifted him with a special hybrid vine I'd created—a mix of night-blooming jasmine and passion flower that bloomed every quarter and produced seedless passionfruit. He was delighted by the gift, and I promised to go visit him in a few months to juice up the soil and roots.

Ben had made himself scarce after the events at the Keep, once he'd helped Moira to stabilize me and ensured I was going to live. Perhaps seeing me in that state was too much for the gentle healer. I couldn't blame him. Moira, Ash, and Tess stayed around because they were my family.

Ben was kind, but he was still a stranger.

As was Caelan, though he wasn't kind, not exactly. I hadn't seen him in a month, but there were odd rumors surrounding a new presence at the keep. No one knew if the new arrival was a threat or a boon to his rule, and I'd started tuning those rumors out. It hurt to think about him.

The bell rang, announcing a new customer. I glanced up, stunned to see Simone standing there. A smile broke over my face.

"Hi!" I waved her in with the bouquet I was arranging, a mix of lilies and roses. "Need some flowers?"

Simone's smile was tight. "We do." She looked me up and down. "You look much better."

I squashed down the hurt at not seeing her until now. The shifters owed me nothing. "I'm feeling much better."

"Good." She handed me a slip of paper. "This is everything we need. The event is in three months."

I opened the paper and skimmed down the contents. "Wow," I breathed. "This must be some event." But as I continued skimming, a sick feeling began in my stomach. "What kind of event is this?"

Simone's eyes flickered with regret. She shifted nervously on her feet. "Lord Caelan is getting married."

Moira and Tess gasped.

The bouquet I held went up in a puff of crimson flames, there one moment and black ash the next. A vase behind me shattered. Simone went very still and took a step back.

I calmed my rage and pasted a smile on my face. "Tell your Shifter Lord I will do everything in my power to make this event *unforgettable.*"

Also by S.E. Babin

Shifter Lords

Shift of Heart

Shift of Morals

Power Shift

Shifting Winds

Shifting Resolve

Shift of Rule

Shift of the Wild

OTHER SERIES

A Shelf Indulgence Cozy Mystery Series

Book of the Virago

Trailer Park Transylvania

Psychic Cleaner

The Magical Soapmaker Mysteries

The Goddess Chronicles

Cocktails in Hell

About the Author

Sheryl likes cake too much and can be found hoarding it while hiding from her children in the pantry closet.

Follow her on Amazon at: https://www.amazon.com/S-E-Babin/e/B00J1J236A